D1423862

THE
PATTERN
UNDER THE
PLOUGH

Also by
GEORGE EWART EVANS

Ask the Fellows Who Cut the Hay
The Days We Have Seen
The Farm and the Village
The Horse in the Furrow
Let Dogs Delight : and other stories
Welsh Short Stories (edited by)

The Pattern under the Plough

Aspects of the Folk-Life
of East Anglia

GEORGE EWART EVANS

illustrated by
David Gentleman

FABER & FABER
3 Queen Square, London

First published in 1966 by
Faber & Faber Limited
First Published in this edition 1971
Reprinted 1974 and 1977
Printed in Great Britain by
Whitstable Litho Ltd Whitstable Kent

ISBN 0 571 08977 1 (Faber Paperbacks)
ISBN 0 571 06886 3 (hard bound edition)

To my Mother

To tellen al wold passen eny bible
That o where is . . .
        CHAUCER

How can a literature of notations have any value?
        PROUST

Acknowledgments

I wish to acknowledge my debt to those groups – chiefly Men's Fellowships, Women's Institutes, W.E.A., and Cambridge University Board of Extra Mural Studies – who have discussed with me a great deal of the material of the present book and have occasionally given me new light on some of the topics. More than this, their enthusiasm for the subject has greatly helped me during the labour of collecting and checking. In addition to those mentioned in the text I wish to thank Norman Halkett who gave me so much information and enlightenment, and without whose help one chapter, at least, would not have been written; also H. Audrey Beecham, Christina Hole, Francis Cutting, Anthony Dent, Frederick H. Foster, and George Ordish. I am particularly grateful to Lionel Reynolds for his valuable suggestions and for his reading of the proofs; and I owe a debt to David Thomson for his encouragement. I also thank the editors of *The Builder*, and *New Society*, Matthew Evans and all those correspondents who have suggested source material. I wish to make grateful acknowledgment to Professor E. Estyn Evans and Dr R. H. Golde for permission to quote from their writings. Lastly, I am grateful to those – mainly country people of the older generation – who have answered my innumerable questions so readily and have identified themselves with a work to which they have contributed no small part.

Contents

CONTENTS

Abbreviations

Introduction

In TWO previous books I attempted to record aspects of the old rural community in a part of East Anglia. The present book is essentially a continuation of these two works with reference here to the whole region. It was suggested in the first two books that since the beginning of this century there has been a revolution in the countryside, due chiefly to the new farming methods and the development of the motor engine both as a means of power on the farm and as a link between the towns and the villages. But this revolution is not confined to a region or country or even to a continent: it is world-wide, and has occurred over precisely the same period—the first sixty or so years of this century. The First World War was the watershed in Britain. The old society, quickly changing even before 1914, emerged radically transformed after the Peace: the former rigid social caste system had been loosened; women had proved their ability to enter into industry, commerce, and the professions on equal footing to men; and the Corn Production Act of 1917 had at least recognized the need for defining a system of fair relations between the farmers and workers in the rural areas. It was not simply that a mode of life had greatly changed but a whole culture that had preserved its continuity from earliest times had now received its quietus, and was swept aside in less than a couple of generations.

A similar revolution has occurred in the rural areas of North America; and an American writer and sociologist, Andrew Lytle, has narrowed it to about the same period as in Britain and he has named the same precipitating cause:[1] 'The last active expression of

[1] Henry A. Murray (Editor), *Myth and Mythmaking*, New York, 1960, p. 141.

17

this Society seemed to fall somewhere between 1880 and 1910. The mechanics of change are obvious to all. The most effective was the automobile since it uprooted the family by destroying its attachment to place.' The same process has been observed in Africa where the revolution is going on at a tremendous pace.[1] Villages or settlements that received their first sight of Europeans in 1905 have already been brought, for good or ill, into the orbit of western civilization; and already their old culture has been almost inundated. The same is happening in the East.

The study, therefore, of a local community at this time has more than local relevance: it should inform and extend the consciousness of the people who live in the district or region, pointing to the richness, variety and depth of their heritage; it should record as far as possible the true lineaments of the old culture that has been so lately swept aside; and it should above all extend their awareness of similar changes and stresses occurring all over the world wherever the traditional and immemorial cultures confront the twentieth century; a century to which science has given those innumerable skills and techniques that make the control of large sectors of our physical environment a reality; and—perhaps most important of all —has given us a confidence that falls short only of the awareness that now for the first time we are called not merely to suffer our own history but to make it. But make it on what? This question immediately points to a sense in which the study of the old, traditional culture is not simply a praiseworthy academic exercise but an essential preliminary to the building of a new order. For in spite of the quick break-up of the old framework, now dismantled almost entirely in most areas of Britain, it did house something permanent: the values, the communal responses that were the flower of its long growth. And without an appreciation of these no attempt to make a new community here in Britain or elsewhere is likely to survive the present century.

But before going on to write further about the old rural community in East Anglia it would be as well to define it more precisely. The last generation of people who came to maturity under the old

[1] Dilim Okafor-Omali, *A Nigerian Villager in Two Worlds*, London, 1965.

culture were those who were born about 1885, and not much later than 1895. It is true that people born after this date remember well the old pre-war society; but there is an important difference between these and the preceding generation: they lived their early years in this old society but they were too young to be formed by it. Their adolescence coincided with the Great War; and in many ways they were the first generation of the new age, the generation that escaped taking active part in the War but whose outlook it largely fashioned. The difference between these two generations is nowhere more sharply defined than in their attitudes to the traditional lore which is the main subject of the present study. The older generation had the lore in abundance; it was part of their existence and they had rarely paused to consider it as something separate from themselves. To a large extent it was not a question of believing in it but of living it. The next generation held a much attenuated version of the old culture and its lore. During the last fifteen years I have talked to hundreds of people of both generations about the old society, and I have found this difference emphasized over and over again. But even more striking than the difference in the amount of lore they held was their attitude towards it: the older generation accepted the old lore as part of the air they breathed; the later generation had already grown away from it. They knew much of the lore but they were sceptical, evaluative, and sometimes plainly dismissive; tending to adopt a similar stance to the African who considered that his new bicycle and bowler hat—badges of a specious emancipation—gave him licence to scoff at his own native culture.

The area of study also needs defining. East Anglia is a term loosely used since few people, it appears, agree where its boundaries lie; and while local and county authorities on the fringe of Norfolk and Suffolk vie with one another in opting out of the concept of East Anglia as an administrative region, many in these two counties would exclude everybody else as not qualifying for the *Folk* of which they are the north and south divisions. But the region is demonstrably a natural unit which was once almost divided from the rest of England and more accessible to the Continent—by way of the North Sea—than to most parts of Britain. The northern and eastern boundaries are the sea; the western boundary was the Fens which were an impassable barrier on that side from the beginning of the historical period, and—except for islands of occupation such as Ely —a sparsely inhabited waste. In the south lies the west–east flowing river, the Stour, and its marshy estuary—the present boundary between Suffolk and Essex; but the historic barrier was further south than the Stour—the heavily forested clay belt which was the natural march between the kingdom of the East Saxons (southern Essex) and the kingdom of East Anglia to the north. And even if the kingdom of East Anglia is one of those historical fictions in which the dark, pre-Norman period seems to abound, there is still evidence that this natural division just outlined was at one time a tight, well defended political or administrative unit. For the only access to the region from the rest of England was along the downlands of drift-covered chalk lying in the south-west. It was along here that a comparatively easy route-way could be made; and it was here that the Icknield Way, travelling north-east from Royston into Norfolk, penetrated the region. Here, too, if East Anglia was to be a self-sufficient unit would we expect it to be defended. The ancient dykes running across these downlands undoubtedly served this purpose; and although no one knows exactly who constructed them we can be certain that it was for this reason they were built; to defend this gateway to the region and to exclude invaders from the south-west. Indeed, one need not be an archaeologist to observe that the defence ditches of both the Fleam Dyke and Devil's Dyke near Newmarket are on the south-west side of the earthworks. This close definition of East Anglia as a unit is emphasized here because it is important as a basis for the claim that at one period of history the region was allowed to develop on its own and to acquire its own characteristic culture.

But it is likely, however, that two other natural factors have played even a greater part than this isolation in bringing about the distinctive culture of the region. These are the soil and the climate. The whole region has been more than once covered by the sea, and it was during this period that its chalk 'bed-rock' was formed. But it has also been submerged during the Ice Age by extensive ice-sheets. On melting, these left a rich mantle of drift material, notably boulder clay interspersed with fragments of chalk; and this chalk gave the clay an excellent texture and composition, ideally suited for the growing of corn. This naturally limed soil together with the comparatively dry summers and hard, winter frosts that helped to break up the heavier soils and give them a good spring tilth have made the region one of the natural corn-growing areas of Britain. The effect of these natural advantages on the history of the region would be a subject in itself: they have made it the cradle of most of the improvements in arable farming during the last two hundred years, and they have been indirectly responsible for the siting here of two of the region's most profitable industries: farm fertilizers and the making of farm machinery. For it was here in East Anglia that firms like Packard, and Fison; Garrett (of Leiston) and Ransome, Sims and Jefferies received their first impetus.

But more important, though less spectacular than the founding of great modern industries, is the effect of these natural factors on the folk-life of the region. Arable farming, the growing of corn, has given it its distinctive character, and part of the present study will be concerned in bringing out this fact. But here again, one more definition is needed. What is meant by the folk-life of a region? The concept of folk-life is a Scandinavian one.[1] *Folk* here does not carry the derogatory sense it has acquired in Britain, especially in the universities. It is used in a purely referential sense, and means the people of a country or region irrespective of class or creed; and the study of folk-life implies not only a systematic examination of the material culture of a region, but the relating to it of the region's beliefs, customs, language, myth, and social organization. It is, too –particularly at this time–an examination of how much of the old recently displaced culture is still alive and accessible within the present society. Folk-life implies a holistic approach whose main definition is not in method but in the field of study; and it is for this reason that it is a most fruitful approach to an area such as East Anglia. For what obtains here is a transient folk-life situation. It is no use the investigator–if he is working alone–standing on

[1] Iorwerth C. Peate, *The Study of Folk Life*, *Gwerin*, Vol. II, No. 3.

the dignity of one method or discipline whether it is sociology, history, social anthropology, archaeology or dialect study; nor can he afford to pay too much respect to the convention that each discipline has its local specialist who has the *ipsissima verba* on his subject. To a worker in the field the dangers of specialization are very much more apparent than its advantages. He has to get what he can and as quickly as he can.

But the proper study of the folk-life of even a small region implies a lifetime's work. In the present book I have, therefore, selected for study what I consider to be the main foci of the life of the old community: the house and home, and the farm. I am well aware of the omissions. The town in East Anglia, as in other regions, has also been transformed by the revolution of the last sixty years; and its crafts and industries have experienced an equal degree of change as the country ones; so too has its social life. The rich and ancient connection of East Anglia with the sea has also been omitted. Ideally, both these aspects should have been given equal prominence with the others. Yet the selection of the house and the farm was not an arbitrary one. Experience here and elsewhere has shown that for many people the concept of history or even the *past* is an abstraction with little or no meaning for them. But the history of the development of their own *work* has absorbing interest: it speaks to their own condition, appeals to them in a segment of life where they can respond. Similarly the evolution of the kind of house they knew as their home, and an account of the home life of their ancestors is the sort of history with which they have no trouble in identifying. The *work* in East Anglia has been historically arable farming: it has been carried on in this region for well over two thousand years; and it is a tradition that is in the bones of the indigenous population. And *work* here has a wider significance than is perhaps realized. For one has only to scratch a townsman in East Anglia to find that he is a farmer or a farm-worker under his skin, almost as knowledgeable and interested in the farming of the land as the cousins he has left in the country.

The folk-life approach, apart from its value in itself, is also able to supplement and illuminate information gained in the more specialized disciplines. Professor Grahame Clarke has given an out-standing example of this.[1] An object found in prehistoric sites was variously misinterpreted by archaeologists as a musical instrument, a machine for making peat-bricks, a model of a boat, and a device for catching pike. Its true function was established only when a Scandinavian, Holger Rasmussen, found similar objects still in use among people of the old culture in eastern and central Europe. The objects were *tread-traps*—wooden devices for entrapping the foot of wild animals. It is worth noting, too, that the leister or fish-spear which the same author illustrates[2] in his book and identifies as of mesolithic origin—first made in bone, then in bronze, and later in iron—is almost identical in form with the fish-dart used until recently in the Cambridgeshire Fens; and probably still used although this form of fishing has now been made illegal. The leister, too, is very similar in design to the eel-pritch, glave, or pilger, which was in common use in East Anglia before the First World War.

As the designs of these material objects—and of many more like the corn-sickle—have lasted since prehistoric times it should not surprise us that some of the ideas and beliefs of this period should have survived also. For beliefs, ideas, and customs are at least as tenacious of their identity as the design of physical objects. This is another aspect of the old culture which I have attempted to bring out in the present book. Moreover, the collecting and recording of many beliefs and customs associated with the old rural community have also been useful in throwing light on various literary references as widely spaced as Virgil, Shakespeare, and Gibbon. This, too, should not surprise us since the culture of which the survivors of the old community are the last carriers, embraces a span of time from the recent past to a period well before the coming of the Romans to Britain; and its continuity up to the present century is so apparent now at this time because it is only now that it is in danger of being broken. But this danger will have its uses if it persuades us to look without delay at the old rural society to which change has given a highlight, and the imminence of its passing a new perspective.

[1] *Prehistoric Europe*, London, 1952, pp. 52–3.
[2] *Ibid.*, p. 58.

I have written much about the material background of the house and farm in the two books already mentioned; and they form a necessary adjunct to most of the following chapters. Many authors have written about the physical shape of the typical East Anglian house and some of their books are here recommended. In the first few chapters I have attempted to supplement this information with material from my own experience. I have given the book the title it has because its subject bears an analogy to the crop marks seen in the aerial photographs of some of our fields. Just as the pattern of the ancient settlements is still to be seen in spite of years of repeated ploughings, so the beliefs and customs linked with the old rural way of life in Britain have survived the pressures and changes of many centuries. They are so old that they cannot be dated; and on this count alone they are historical evidence, as valuable as the archaeological remains that are dug from those sites so dramatically revealed since the development of the aeroplane.

Helmingham, Suffolk
November, 1965.

Part One

THE HOUSE AND THE HOME

I

The House

OWING to the shortage of native building stone, the timbered or half-timbered house is historically the typical house of East Anglia. There are thousands of these buildings in the eastern counties, and they can be easily recognized as such. But hundreds more have been so altered by eighteenth- and nineteenth-century building that they are not always identified as timbered houses. Whole streets in some of the small towns of Suffolk—Needham Market or Hadleigh, for instance—show at first glance few examples of timber construction. Yet the steep pitch of many of the house-roofs gives a clue; and behind the brick or plastered fronts the old timber core will be found intact and durable in the majority of dwellings. In the countryside, in isolated cottage or farmhouse, the timber-work is to be found in its most characteristic and unspoiled form.

Most of these houses were constructed during the period of the great rebuilding,[1] the time of intense social ferment and upsurge which fell roughly between the years 1570 and 1640. The majority of parishes in the region can show at least a few good examples, and some also have an occasional example of an earlier house. The Suffolk village of Framsden, for instance, has a fifteenth-century open hall type of house that was 'ceiled' a century or so later; and it illustrates how hard it is to determine the age of some of these houses without a fairly detailed examination of the interior. Few people standing outside Framsden Hall would suspect that at one time its interior had more in common with the nave of a local church or one of the more solidly constructed barns, so common in

[1] W. G. Hoskins, *Provincial England*, The Rebuilding of Rural England, London, 1963.

this district, than with the ordinary, storied dwelling house its exterior now presents.

The main framework of these houses, then, has lasted between four and six hundred years; and in most houses it is likely to last a few hundred more, in spite of the fact that they were constructed of what some modern building bye-laws would describe as short-lived materials. These houses have also been much studied, though the local variations of the different types within the separate counties—and even districts of counties—often fall between the meshes of the architect's or historian's generalizations. Moreover, anyone who has lived for a fair length of time in an old timbered house will testify

near Hoo

what an amount of hitherto unnoticed detail he is continually discovering about the building—particular and often minute detail that not only illuminates the structure of the house but often the mode of life of its former occupants. Most of the present chapter is concerned with the writer's own experience in finding constructional and other detail in a half-timbered house[1] during a period of six years' occupation.

[1] 111 High Street, Needham Market, Suffolk. A town-house built probably by a substantial wool-merchant during the early sixteenth century.

One such detail is the carpenter's or construction marks found in many timbered houses. These were first noticed on an old stairs leading to a loft at the back of the house. The stairs, really no more than a solid oaken ladder, were undoubtedly the original Tudor stairs demoted to the back of the house when the house was reconstructed later. As well as the oaken ladder, the trap door above it is still in position; and it is an excellent example of the means of access from the ground floor to the bedrooms in Tudor houses of this type. The trap door and ladder remained the only access in houses built during the sixteenth century, and in earlier ones that had been ceiled; and stairs as we know them today did not become common in farmers' and merchants' houses until well into the seventeenth century,[1] so we are told; and this generalization is supported by the date of the stairs in the Needham house—late seventeenth century with a typically Jacobean balustrade. But the steps of the Tudor ladder bear the marks the carpenter made to ensure that each tenon fitted into the mortice cut for it. The marks, made in this instance with a chisel, are usually stylized Roman numerals, and they are most common where a tie-beam or a joist is tenoned into a wall-plate or vertical member. The examples given here are from houses of similar age, and some from a house in the same street.[2] They were made by an implement called a timber-scribe.

timber scribe

The longest arm gouged out the straight marks on the timber; one of the two short arms was a point around which the other rotated to cut a circular groove, as in the merchant's mark on page 39. A similar tool was used by coopers up to recent years.

[1] W. G. Hoskins, 'The Englishman's House', The Listener, p. 996, 20th June, 1957.
[2] 60 High Street, Needham Market, Suffolk.

The carpenter's marks on the timbers indicate that the main framework of the house was pre-fabricated. Each tenon on any member of the framework was made and marked to fit into a particular mortice; and the trusses, the floor joists, the main rafters, the studs and the wall-plates were all constructed and fitted together in sections, to try them out, in the wright's or carpenter's yard before he transported them for erection on the actual house-site. This had to be the method when most of the sawing was done in a sawpit, a permanent structure close to the carpenter's workshop.[1] After finding out the owner's requirements the chief carpenter designed and was responsible for the construction of the house. He was in fact the architect[2] as well as being the wright or chief crafts-

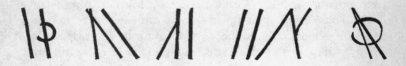

man; and the prevalence of the surname *Wright* in East Anglia (there are about two hundred Wright's in the telephone book of one area—north Essex and south Suffolk) is perhaps an indication of the importance of the carpenter in this region during medieval times and later.[3]

But the house framework, once constructed and dismantled and carried piecemeal to the site, then had to be fitted together again, and this time *raised*. The huge frames had to be lifted off the ground and held upright long enough for them to be fixed temporarily together. This task was usually beyond the resources of the wright and the future owners of the house. They sought help, therefore, for the heavy task of lifting and pushing the frames of heavy oak into

[1] *v. A.F.C.H.*, photograph facing p. 142.
[2] *Pensaer* (literally head–carpenter) the Welsh word for architect preserves to this day the former identity of functions.
[3] Suffolk wrights made the roof of the Royal Exchange at Battisford Tye to the order of Sir Thomas Gresham. (Norman Scarfe, *Suffolk*, London, 1960, p. 25.)

position. They went to their neighbours. This house raising or *rearing* (*levatio* in medieval Latin), sometimes referred to also as 'the setting of the house upon ground', was in fact a real communal occasion, a working together; and after the work was done a time for cakes and ale and merry-making. This was also so in Kent,[1] and in Ireland[2] where the 'house raiser' took the precaution of hiring a fiddler to ensure that the work went with a swing. The North American colonists of the seventeenth and eighteenth centuries built their houses to the same plan using exactly the same method as they had used or seen used in the home country. An extract from a book published in 1913 at the bi-centenary of the township of Needham, Massachusetts illustrates what happened:

'It was a morning in August 1774. The scene was the great social function of the olden time, called "a raising". The solid frame of the new meeting house had been hewn and put together, and now it was to be raised and placed on the massive sills, tenon fitting mortise and the whole jointed together very much as the Apostle Paul describes the Living Church in one of his epistles. To lift one of these huge structures was no easy work. The entire male population of the town was summoned.'[3]

This custom has endured in the United States up to the present day. The old American barns—just as their counter-parts in East Anglia—are essentially the same in structure as their timbered houses. 'A barn-raising' was one of the occasions in the American countryside when neighbours came in to help; and this occasion was afterwards sealed with a frolic or jollification in which the wives and the children also took part. American photographs[4] show that the house raisers pushed up the frame with long poles, as well as pulling it with ropes. To prevent the poles from slipping they first cut notches in the vertical members of the frame; and when they had raised it into position they next secured it by nailing the pole into the notch, for the time being, removing the pole when they had fixed the other timbers which joined the frame to the one at the

[1] George Ordish, *The Living House*, London, 1960, pp. 20-1.
[2] *I.F.W.*, p. 57.
[3] *cf.* C. F. Innocent, *English Building Construction*, p. 86.
[4] Holbrook and Rugoff, *Down on the Farm*, New York, 1954, p. 41.

a house-raising

other end of the bay. These notches are still visible in many East Anglian buildings notably in Lavenham,[1] and in a timber-and-thatch cart-shed at Hemingstone Old Hall, Suffolk. Here, the nails which temporarily held the timbers at the raising, are still in position in the sunken notches.

The raising ceremony survives to a certain extent in the modern custom of placing a flag on the roof of a house when it is ready for slating; also in the 'topping out' ceremony which has enjoyed a revival in recent years. In this there is a ceremonial drink[2] taken by the workmen who have been engaged on the building and by its promoters. In a recent[3] 'topping out' ceremony at the new halls of residence at Nottingham University the purpose was reported to have an added significance: 'to ward off evil spirits'; and it is true that this purpose was also in the mind of some of the early builders who took precautions to safeguard the house. There is, for example, a tradition in the Suffolk village of Gazeley that on completion of the house-raising a bone was placed on the roof, later to be incorporated into the thatch. The bone, discovered in one house[4]

[1] 89 High Street, and a house in the centre of the square.
[2] This ceremony was called Closing-hale in parts of England. The flying of a flag from the chimney top of the nearly completed house was a signal for drinks.
[3] *The Times*, 4th June, 1964.
[4] The Hutch, a fifteenth-century house in Gazeley.

during recent years while it was being re-thatched, is the shin-bone of an ox; and there seems little doubt that it was placed there as an amulet;[1] a custom that will be discussed more fully in a later chapter.

But a house that had been pre-fabricated could also be taken down and constructed elsewhere without too much trouble, if its main structure was already appropriately marked by the carpenters at its original raising. The Paston correspondence contains a letter from Sir John Wingfield of Letheringham in Suffolk about the removal of a house a distance of about twenty miles. The letter concerns Thomas Ratcliff, the owner of Framsden Hall just mentioned:[2]

'Brother Paston, I recommend me unto you praying that ye take the labour to speak with Thomas Ratcliff for the deliverance of part of a house which lyeth in the wood at Framsden; which house the owner hath carried part thereof to Orford, which, so departed, the remanent that remaineth there in the wood shall do him little good and it shall hurt greatly the workmen and owner thereof also, which is my tenant; and the house should be set upon ground.'

But occasionally some of the old timbered houses were moved bodily without dismantling, so securely were their timbers jointed together. One such building was the alms-houses at Stonham Aspal, Suffolk. These were originally built in the churchyard, but were removed bodily to a site further down the street. The workmen used wooden rollers and teams of horses to drag the heavy structure along the road. At one stage the horse-traces broke, but the change of site was successfully carried out.

From the same Suffolk village also comes an account of a comparatively modern form of truss raising:[3] 'We used to take a big old wagon-wheel off its axle. If you could get a wheel from a "timber-jim"—you know, they're about seven feet in diameter—so much the

---

[1] It is well to define this here: an amulet wards off evil; a talisman brings luck.
[2] Paston Letters, Letter XLV. Vol. I. p. 47 (*Everyman* Edit.). See also *Ipswich Journal* 31st March 1759: 'To be SOLD at Badley Hall (near Needham and Stowmarket in Suffolk).

The Frame of a Building, about fifty Foot long and eighteen Foot wide; the whole is of good sound Oak Timber, and fit to be fixt up in any other Place with very little Alteration.'
[3] A. W. Wythe of Stonham Aspal.

better. You got your wheel near your building and then you fitted a straight-boled fir-tree into the nave of the wheel. If the fir pole was the same diameter as the axle, so much the better fit. We first of all fixed a pulley-block and rope to the top of the pole; and then we up-ended it, using the pulley to hoist up the truss to roof level. People I've told this to always ask: "How did the wheel keep steady?" There was no trouble at all about this, because—as you know—all those old wheels had a right good *dish* on 'em; and the *dish* gave the structure stability.'

new thatch at Gosbeck

Marks, very like the construction marks and again in Roman numerals, are to be found on the only piece of considerable stone-work in many of these old timbered houses. This is the shallow stone sink, the original installation rarely found now even in East Anglian farmhouses. There was a typical one in the backhouse of the Needham Market house until it was removed into the garden. This appears to be the typical manner of exodus; and many of these old Tudor sinks are to be seen forming the centre-piece of a rockery in cottage or farm gardens. The sink was used for ordinary domestic purposes and was placed near to the indoor pump; but it was very shallow, not more than five or six inches in depth. Many farming families gave this type of sink a greater capacity by building a wooden framework on its wide rim, and making the framework secure and water-tight with cement. It was used in this form for many years by at least one farmer's wife from north Suffolk.

2

Surface Detail

THE lintel-beam or chimney-breast over the open fire-places of the East Anglian timbered houses often shows a wealth of the 'skin' or surface detail that helps us to fill in some of the house's history. The Needham house is no exception. The beam in one of the largest rooms is covered by a flock of 'face-marks', haphazard cuts made purposefully in the wood with a chisel. The face-marks represent a stage which is common to the development of the timbered house in this region. This was the time when neo-classicism had filtered down to the yeoman's or merchant's house and it became fashionable to give a decent covering to any part of the house's anatomy that was exposed. In this particular dwelling the remodelling seems to have taken place comparatively late—about the middle of the nineteenth century. The Tudor front of the house was given a severe façade of Woolpit brick; and in one of the front rooms the exposed timbers —notably the lintel-beam—were plastered over. But the plasterers first of all pitted the comparatively smooth surface of the wood with these face-marks to ensure that the plaster adhered to the beam and did not flake off when it was exposed to the heat rising from the fire beneath it.

On the right of the beam there is a large circular hole, over an inch in diameter. This was made with an auger, and its purpose was to take the rod which held the spit engine, the spring device that was connected by an endless band to the spit hook in front of the open fire. On the side of the beam opposite to the hole there is a vertical scar that had obviously been burned into the wood. It is about three inches in length, and tapers towards its top, giving it the appearance of a candle flame. Similar scars occur on the lintel-beams of many houses of this period, and they are sometimes explained as taper-burns made by the flame of a wax taper that was fixed in brackets attached to the beam. But the scar looks exactly as if a younger member of a former household had been experimenting with a red-hot poker. And in fact this is what these burns possibly are: scars made by hot pokers, not wielded though by irresponsible youngsters but by a sober paterfamilias who mulled his beer by heating a poker in the fire and plunging it into the copper beer-muller, but not before he had first either tested or partially cooled the poker on the lintel-beam.

But the most interesting mark on this beam is barely visible in the flurry of face-marks that surrounds it. It is small and casual-looking but it is undoubtedly a merchant's mark whose design is echoed in the bigger and firmer marks found on an old door in one of the attics of the same house. The practice of inscribing merchants' marks on beams is not unusual in East Anglia, and they have also been carved on stone fire-places.[1] The marks in the Needham building, how-ever, link it with the richest period of the timbered house in this region—the period from the fourteenth to the seventeenth century;

[1] F. W. Kuhlicke, *East Anglian Magazine*, Vol. II, 1951, pp. 427, 568.

and they also identify it with the rising merchant or yeoman class who were largely responsible for building this type of house in the sixteenth and early seventeenth centuries, and who adopted the marks first as a trading device and then as a symbol of their emergence from the collective anonymity of the Middle Ages.

It has not been possible to identify with any certainty the owner or owners of the marks found in the Needham house. But it is not unusual for the owners of these marks to remain unnamed; yet it would be safe to assume that they were connected with the wool trade since weaving, and especially wool-combing, were well established in this town during the period above mentioned. Merchants' marks were used much as trade-marks are today: to ensure quick recognition of a trader's goods. But at a time when comparatively few people were literate there was a greater need for a man's goods to be identified by a mark rather than by his name. F. A. Girling[1] has pointed out, though, that merchants' marks is rather too exclusive a term: for the marks were adopted by people other than merchants and used as a means of personal identification. They were engraved on signet rings and used for witnessing documents; and they were sometimes used by their owners to mark their swans. They are, of course, closely related to masons' marks to which they have an obvious resemblance.

Some of the 'new men' of this period, the wool staplers and the clothiers who were getting rich and establishing themselves and their familes as new social groups to be reckoned with, attempted to make good their lack of status by elevating their marks into their own peculiar form of heraldry. Thus they had the marks engraved on their tombs either on brass or in stone. If, as often happened in East Anglia, a wool merchant contributed large sums towards the building of a church—either out of piety or a politic attempt to buy off spiritual retribution in the next world for getting rich so quickly in this—he was commemorated by having his mark carved in the fabric of the church, or incorporated in a stained glass window. Occasionally, when a merchant eventually attained a grant-of-arms, his mark was included in the blazon. The Springs of Lavenham, one

<hr>

[1] *English Merchants' Marks*, London, 1964, *passim*.

of the richest English clothier families of the fifteenth and sixteenth
centuries, are a good example. Thomas Spring III, with the Earl of
Oxford the lord of the manor, made himself responsible for building
the great tower of Lavenham Church; and on the plinth of the
tower the masons carved, in addition to the coat-of-arms of the
de Veres, the merchant mark of Thomas Spring as a memorial of his
part in the enterprise. But Spring's fortune rose with his tower. He
acquired a grant-of-arms just before his death in 1533; and with the
141 feet structure almost completed he was able to instruct the
masons to carve a new emblem at the tower's top. They were
determined, it seems, that his new honour should not go unrecorded;
and in carving the new Spring coat-of-arms no less than thirty-three
times on the parapet of the tower they could not have carried out his
wishes more thoroughly.[1]

i   ii

Some writers have read a fairly elaborate symbolism into these
merchant marks. It has been suggested that the upright line around
which most of them are constructed, represents the mast of a ship;
and with the horizontal arm forms the shape of a cross whose purpose was to invoke the blessing of God on the merchant's ventures
overseas. The symbol at the top of the mast resembling a figure 4
stands—it is said—for the four corners of the world where the

[1] Nicholas Pevsner, *Suffolk*, London, 1961, pp. 296–7.

School House

merchant seeks his trade. There seems to be little solid support for these theories, and it would be as well to be cautious about a subject which has not been much studied. Yet we do know that the symbol at the top of the upright was used in merchant marks long before the figure 4 was known in this form in the West. Arabic numerals did not appear in Britain until Elizabeth I's reign; and it is for this reason that the carpenters made their crude markings in unmistakable Roman numerals.

It is possible that this figure is a transliteration of a runic mark; for scholars agree that the linear type of mark (such as the bigger ones in the Needham house) are often similar to the old pagan runes or combinations of like runes. The writer already quoted gives an example of a sixteenth-century Aldeburgh merchant whose mark is built on the rune 'E' reversed. He also suggests that the addition of a horizontal line to the upright stem of the mark was a device to Christianize what was essentially a pagan symbol.[1] And it came as a surprise to the present writer, after long familiarity with the Needham merchant's marks to see the same basic line[2] repeated in a tenth-century runic cross in the Dick Collection at Thurso near

[1] F. A. Girling, *ibid.*, espec. pp. 9–17.
[2] Especially the oblique cross-stroke at the base of the mark No. iv on p. 41.

John o' Groats. The fish-hook, or gladiate quality of the wedge-shaped engravings in the comparatively soft red sandstone of the Thurso cross was also identical with the carving of the sixteenth-century merchant's marks on the hard oak of a Suffolk door.

The runes, however, in addition to their function as letters were also magical symbols; and there is a theory that a runic mark was carved on the ridge-pole of a house as an apotropaic, or evil averting, sign. Undoubtedly the early masons took over a number of these pagan signs which had a ritual significance in their craft organization; and these still exist and are used in the derived society of the Freemasons. And it would well accord with a Tudor merchant's temper that his marks should have a dual purpose: to identify his goods and to protect them on his pioneer ventures overseas.

Before leaving this subject it is worth pointing out that the base of one of the Needham marks (ii) is like that of another mark[1] on

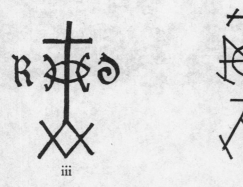

iii   iv

the brass shield of a grave in Nayland Church in Suffolk. The splaying of the central line makes a shape like an inverted 'V'—the rune for the letter 'A'—and this is complicated by a 'V' superimposed on this. The Nayland mark (iii) is note-worthy because it belonged to a wool craftsman or merchant—Richard Davy. Joined to the ring that threads the upright of the mark are two havettes or harbicks, twin

[1] No. iii

hooks that were used in the finishing process of wool cloth. After the cloth had been fulled and stretched it was then treated with teazles to bring up the loose fibres of wool. The cloth then went to the shearman; he fixed it securely to a cropping board by means of these hooks or havettes, and trimmed it with his huge scissors to give it a final, smooth finish.

Framsden

3

More Detail

THROUGH getting to know the structure of the Needham house fairly thoroughly the writer also noticed one way in which the Tudor builders of timbered houses effected a kind of primitive insulation. The spaces between the floor joists on the first and second floor had been packed tight with oat husks, presumably for both sound and heat insulation; but chiefly–one imagines–for the former. The practice of insulating floors with reeds, straw, or other material was once widespread.[1] A house of a similar age in Suffolk–Rookery Farm, South Elham St Margaret–also has the same kind of packing between the floor-joists; and there are a number of houses so insulated at Bildeston, a wool town not far from Needham Market and of a like age and like size in its hey-day. One housewife there said that she well knew that the first floor of her house was insulated with corn husks; she was reminded of it every time there was a high wind. Then, the whole house interior was covered with a fine dust that sprinkled down from the decaying husks as the timber frame moved imperceptibly. Specimens taken from the Needham house show that there is a large concentration of fine dust in the husks, which is to be expected after the husks had lain nearly four hundred years under the dry floorboards.

But as well as oat husks walnut shells were found in the Needham house, mixed with the husks, as packing between the joists. The owner of an early seventeenth-century Ipswich house[2] has also found walnut shells and oat husks under the floorboards; and there can be little doubt that this insulating mixture was used in many

[1] C. F. Innocent, *op. cit.*, p. 160.
[2] L. H. Brown, 134 Fore Street.

more houses in East Anglia. But sea-shells were used for a similar purpose in houses built as recently as the nineteenth century. At Theobalds House, Cheshunt—a house erected during the last century, a little to the west of the site of the Tudor Theobalds Palace —sea-shells were used as insulating material between the joists of the first floor at the front of the house; and an old house in Whitehall, now part of the Ministry of Labour, shows the same device: 'This was the Duke of Buccleuch's town house . . . every ceiling triple-layered and insulated with sea-shells, all the doors rosewood'.[1] Yet the present writer has no need for further examples to convince him of the need for insulation of the old timbered houses. While living in the Needham house he and his wife often had occasion to discuss his youngest daughter who slept above the living-room. The parents were completely unaware of the room's limitations until one morning the daughter came down and reported verbatim their conversation of the previous evening. It turned out that this part of the house had been reconstructed at some time, and the old insulating material had then been removed and nothing put back to replace it.

But wherever sea or walnut shells are discovered in connection with the building of an old house it is arguable that their 'magical' or traditional significance must also be taken into account. The myth of Aphrodite's birth from or, more accurately, arrival in a marine conch is too well known to need elaboration; and in fact the sea-shell, the snail figure, and the pearl were widespread emblems of love and marriage. The walnut, too, has a similar connection. The walnut tree is believed to have been introduced into the British Isles by the Romans: it was greatly valued by them, and they scattered the nuts at their weddings. The elder Pliny says[2] that the walnut was used along with the fescennine songs at nuptials because it was a symbol consecrated to marriage, and a protector of the resulting offspring. It should not, therefore, surprise us to find in the chamber, the sleeping place of a Tudor dwelling, walnut shells performing a dual function in the house structure. Walnut trees, too, appear to have had a kind of special treatment in East Anglia, as well as being

---

[1] Richard Church, *Memories of my Double Life*, London, 1965.
[2] *Nat. Hist.*, IV, Book XV (Loeb ed.), p. 349.

very highly valued for their wood, as indeed they are today. A Suffolk farmer[1] has said that in his area the men who travel round felling walnut trees that have been sold often find a gold coin buried near the tree's roots.

A detailed examination of the walls of the same house revealed horse-hair used as binding for the plaster round an old doorway. The colour of the hair was unmistakably that of a chestnut horse—Suffolk Punch; and it was a reminder of how important hair—cattle-hair as well as horse-hair—was in the building and maintenance of timbered houses in eastern England. An eighteenth-century receipted bill shows how the cost of hair, along with other items, was set against the rent charge for £30 for a Suffolk farmhouse;[2] Park Farm, Bacton:

Account: George Pretyman of Bury St Edmunds

		£	s.	d.
Allowed	Thatching Bill	1	7	4
Do.	Bill for Straw	3	3	0
Do.	Brick Bill	1	18	0
Do.	Lump Bill	1	10	0

[1] F. R. Penistan, Moat Farm, Earl Stonham.
[2] *Morley Papers* 562/2 Ipswich and East Suffolk Record Office.

		£	s.	d.
Allowed	Bricklayer's Bill	1	2	9
Do.	Blacksmith's Bill		10	5½
Do.	*Hair Bill*		4	3
Do.	Carpenter & Lime (?) Bill	13	5	6

The item *Lump Bill* refers to clay lump: puddled clay that was cut into rectangular blocks, dried in the sun and used as building material. Clay-lump cottages or farm buildings are still to be found in East Anglian villages: the clay walls, treated with salt to prevent damage by frost and covered with successive layers of lime-wash, were very durable as long as they had been provided with good *footings* and covered with a well-kept thatch. This clay-puddling was another instance of the Suffolk horse being brought directly into the building operation. But on this occasion it was for his shortage of hair and not its abundance that he was preferred. The Suffolk was led round and round over the clay which had been softened with water and lightly covered with straw, thus working in the straw and puddling the material to the required consistency. He was better equipped for this job than the Shire horse, for instance, because the absence of *feather* (hair) on his legs made him much easier to clean and much less liable to develop 'grease' on his heels after the muddy exercise. A Suffolk builder[1] described how he had seen the above process used in the last thirty years; and he pointed out that in the building of many of the timbered houses in the countryside the builders dug out the clay from the site. The digging served two purposes: as the clay was won, a pond was also made for the family's water-supply. Observation has shown that many of these sixteenth- and seventeenth-century thatched 'cottages' (built it should be emphasized as yeoman's houses) have ponds adjacent to them. These were in many areas the sole source of water; and some of the ponds had the rather ambiguous historical distinction of remaining so right up to nine or ten years ago in many Suffolk rural districts.

The same builder also described how unbaked clay bricks were

[1] A. W. Wythe.

often used in the chimneys of timbered houses. In more than one cottage he found that baked bricks had been used for the base of the chimney and up to a point a couple of feet above the lintel-beam over the hearth. Above this, and up to a position just below the thatch, the chimney was made of bricks of unbaked clay. The Tudor builder probably did this to save cost—perhaps an early example of sub-standard material going into a house—but he assumed that the bricks would be baked *in situ*. The lower ones

pond house - near Monewden

probably were. But most of the upper ones remained exactly as they were when laid. Yet there was not much harm in this provided that the thatch adjoining the chimney was kept in good repair; for, as already suggested, clay is no use as building material unless it has an adequate covering. Once the thatch leaked the unbaked clay bricks deteriorated. The Suffolk builder illustrated what happened then: the leaking thatch softened up the clay bricks; and in more than one house he knew the water had eventually caused a hole to develop in the chimney. It was only a matter of time and the occasion of a rather bigger fire than usual in the hearth for the heat to penetrate through the hole, to dry out the straw and set fire to the whole thatch.

One more surface mark of historical interest was found in a loft at the rear of the Needham house. It is a rough circle engraved in the plaster of the wall: inside the circle are the initials S.A.M., and the date 1750. The monogram belonged to Samuel and Mary Alexander who lived here, and it is repeated on the front of the adjoining house. The Alexanders were Quakers and like many of their fellows had taken to trade because of what was, in the eyes of the State, their religious disability. This prevented them from entering a university and taking up a profession, and commerce was their only outlet. The Alexanders were originally ironmongers, but like other Quaker families, the Barclays, the Lloyds, and the Gurneys, they became engaged in banking, making loans and transmitting payments to many parts of the country by means of bills of exchange. In 1774 the Alexanders opened the first bank in Suffolk at this house which at that time included the present adjoining house. The Maws, another Quaker family who lived in this house in the nineteenth century were also bankers. Alexander's Bank later became Barclays; and at its present branch a few doors away, banking has been carried on in this Suffolk town for over two centuries.

The crown glass window-panes in the Needham house, though by no means rare in East Anglia, come under the heading of surface features of a house that are worthy of notice. They replaced the small leaded panes of the original Tudor lights. Some of the Tudor glass has been relegated to windows in the stables at the back of the house; some of it remains in a dusty corner of one of the attics where it was cast aside after one of the occasions when the house was brought 'up to date'. One of the crown glass panes has been scratched with a man's name in what looks like a nineteenth-century hand, and it is probable that the glass was fitted at the time when it received its new façade. The 'bull's eye' effect of crown glass is considered by some to give the true atmosphere to an old timbered house; but originally the thick boss of glass was a very second best: indeed, it was a kind of reject. The glass-blower used to make crown glass by taking the molten glass from the pot with his pontil or ponty, the iron rod he used to support the glass while working it. It was then blown and whirled until it became globular. The craftsman next applied a pontil tipped with molten glass to the bulb, at the same time taking away the blowing tube, which left a hole. He then whirled the globe of molten glass on a flat surface until it *flashed* into a circular disc which still adhered to the pontil by a boss at its centre. The last step was to cut the panes from the clear glass at the periphery. The pane which contained the boss left after the pontil was snapped off was, as already stated, the least prized. Today, however, this type of pane has acquired a scarcity value; and is difficult to replace if it is broken. When it is replaced the new pane is often found to be of imitation crown glass—glass that has been cast in a mould and not blown in the traditional way. The difference can be detected by examining the boss at the centre; if the glass there has a sharp edge, indicating where it snapped when the craftsman removed the pontil, it is likely to be true crown glass. The boss in the replacement variety usually has a smooth, even surface.

There is one structural feature of the house that helps to illustrate the way of life of the early occupants. This is a series of wall-cupboards—seven in all—in line along the south, brick wall; and continuing through adjoining rooms. Each is of the same size, and each has the same shape; a miniature gabled house with a sixteen-inch base, and a like measurement from the base to the gable's ridge. Each is let into the brick wall for a depth of nine inches. A wall-cupboard, or keeping hole as it is called in Ireland, is a very ancient device; and its prototype is to be seen in the Stone Age settlement at Skara Brae in the Orkneys. These niches are not unusual in East Anglia for they were an essential feature of the medieval and early Tudor house, chiefly because it was very scantily furnished; and space to keep ordinary domestic articles which would be available close at hand was very limited. The church aumbrie is a development of the keeping hole and served roughly the same purpose.

It is worth observing that this particular shape and size of cupboard must have been common in medieval Britain. There is one in the dairy of a Welsh farmhouse[1] which is identical with the Suffolk cupboards except that it is in a stone wall not a brick one.

[1] Penywaun, Nelson, Glamorgan.

But there is one niche in the Needham house with a shape and size that is apparently rare. Its form is something like an early English, lancet-type window. It has a base of seventeen inches and a measurement of thirty-two from the base to the blunt point of the lancet. There is a narrow wooden shelf dividing the cupboard into approximately equal sections.

Finally, there is one surface detail which, though not occurring in the Needham house, is to be seen on houses of a later date in the same town; and it is mentioned here because it is sometimes assumed—perhaps wrongly—to be associated with old timbered houses. This detail appears to be a decoration on the sides or *cheeks* of gablets or dormer windows. From the ground they look like white 'bull's eyes' surrounded by black circles; and anyone could be excused for thinking that they are a house-painter's grace notes, a few flourishes to show his skill, or possibly a remnant of some ancient practice or belief long since forgotten.

In fact the 'bull's-eye' or dot is austerely functional. They are known as *soldered dots* and they are made in this way. The carpenter first makes the wooden framework of the dormer and covers the

Helmingham

cheeks with boarding which is then covered with lead sheets. But before the lead is fitted on to the boarding, the wood is first hollowed out at the places where it is to be screwed. Then the lead is placed against the boarding and dressed into the hollows. In the centre of the hollows brass screws fix the lead to the boarding; and to prevent water from seeping down the screw, the hollow—which is a couple of inches across—is filled with plumber's solder. Before this is done, however, a circle of plumber's black is painted round the outside of the hollow, partly to confine the soldered dot, and partly to give the whole a neat decorative finish. The black circle often disappears in time because the material it is made with is not a durable exterior paint; but house-owners sometimes have the circle renewed at a later period in the life of the house purposely to preserve its decorative effect.

4

The Protection of the House

THE timber-framed houses of East Anglia were erected for the same reasons as houses at all places and periods: for protection against wind and weather; for comfort and security; for ease and—later with the increasing wealth of the merchant and yeoman class—even for the grace of living. But to these new men, the merchants and yeomen who had arrived and wished to build a house in the pattern of a medieval manor, no longer though with open hall but with separate rooms and brick hearth and chimney, the house was more than a necessary physical object, an essential adjunct of living: it was an affirmation of their position. To a man who had emerged out of the ruck and turbulence of the wars that saw the break-up of the political structure of the medieval system, who was as yet uncertain of his social identity, a house was both an extension of his new self and an assurance that he and his family had real status. 'This is what I built,' he could say; 'and this is what I am.' And the temper of the new age, especially the reaction of the individual against the remnants of the rigid communal ideal of the Middle Ages[1] showed itself in the development of the house with private rooms that were not only formally separate but had the true privacy of sound insulation, as we have already seen.

The house was also something more: it was as much a hostage to fortune as a man's own child; and when the wool merchant or farmer built his house he did not neglect to take the traditional steps to propitiate fortune and to avert evil from the spot where he hoped to spend the rest of his days. He did not do this in the manner of the

[1] Jacob Burckhardt, *The Civilization of the Renaissance in Italy*, London, 1944, pp. 81–2.

Moat Farm –
Birds Lane

revived 'topping out' ceremony today—in a kind of antiquarian wistfulness—but in severe earnest, believing that the devices he followed would have the effect that men had always hoped for them. The ways in which he did this are still to be found in these fifteenth- and sixteenth-century houses, small and usually obscure evidences of a ceremony, implied or perhaps actually carried out by the owner or his surrogates the carpenters, to ensure that his house would stand as long as it deserved; and that its occupiers would prosper and escape the many misfortunes that had been too evident in their time: plague, sword, fire and all the evils that attend on a weak or un-settled government.

A foundation sacrifice was the most ancient method of ensuring that a house would not only stand but be blessed, and the victim was buried in the 'footings'. Later it was considered sufficient for his shadow to be 'bricked in' to the foundations; and later still an animal became a substitute victim. By the late Middle Ages the bones of an animal were the usual apotropaic device, or just the animal's image carved on the building. Bones, either buried in the foundations, built into the flint wall or concealed in the wattle and daub or somewhere about the structure of the house, are com-monly found in East Anglian houses. There is the Gazeley example, and the number of bones collected from buildings in the Cambridgeshire Fens by Enid Porter.[1] An ox-bone, part of the spinal vertebrae, was found in the Needham house, packed between the joists in one of the attics. Many of these bones are, however, horse-bones; and their significance will be discussed in a later chapter.

But at this point it would be as well to look at the premises that underlie the treating of such obscure, tenuous and neglected detail as this with all the seriousness that is usually reserved for examining so-called *hard* historical evidence: the physical features of the house itself, the deeds or inventories or any other document concerning it. It is suggested that although much of the structure of medievalism had been dismantled by this time, men themselves still thought in the same traditional or primitive way: there were forces outside their control that had to be placated; their hold on life was uncertain; they lived closer to nature[2] and they knew what nature's dominance could mean: fair crops and plenty one year, poor harvests and subsequent famine the next. Murrain and pestilence fell upon them as though out of a clear sky and compelled them to use the small resources of knowledge, however misconceived, that they had at their disposal.

The Black Death, for instance, was known to have come into Britain from the south. It started in the port of Melcombe Regis in Dorset and spread from there all over England.[3] Evidently—so was the reasoning—the plague had been carried on a south wind; therefore it was sensible to expose the house as little as possible to the south wind—perhaps only a gable or a blank wall in that direction. They built houses on a north–south axis; and the man who built in a street would, if his house faced south, eschew a front door by which the plague might enter and be satisfied with a more modest but perhaps safer entrance at the side.[4] Measures like this, though

---

[1] Curator of the Cambridge Folk Museum.

[2] Marc Bloch, *Feudal Society*, p. 72.

[3] Hugh Braun, *Old English Houses*, p. 89: v. Thomas Tusser, *Five Points of Good Husbandry*, 'The South (wind) as unkind draweth sickness too near'. H. C. Wolton, a Bury St Edmunds estate agent, has noticed that most of the larger Tudor houses in East Anglia forgo a southern aspect. The builders believed that the south was 'too enervating'.

[4] The side entrance was also preferred for privacy's sake, as it almost certainly was in the original structure of the Needham house.

ineffective, could not be proved to be so, and at the time they did a great deal to ease a man's anxiety and give him that hope which is the necessary mortar of any new endeavour. He took the usual precautions according to his best knowledge; and if he was still anxious his anxiety could best be attacked directly by using the old traditional magic.

For magic, whatever its pretensions, is ultimately addressed to the mind of the person or persons concerned, its exterior object being no more than an extrapolation of his own desires or fears; and although—like prayer or ritual—its direct effect on external reality is almost certainly nil, its influence on the mind of the participant might be considerable. The rationale of the old magic might be obscure and lost in time but that did not make it any the less effective in this respect. Luck, like misfortune, need not be given a specific name; but if securing good fortune involved merely having a small animal image carved on the ridge tiles or the chimney, throwing a horse-bone into the foundation or secreting an ox-bone in the structure it was better to be on the side of luck. When this had been done, whatever eventually happened, the house would at least *feel* a more secure place to live in. It is, therefore, claimed that these small and obscure details about a house, although negligible in themselves, tell us a great deal about the mentality of the people who built the house and serve as a corrective to the tendency to read our own enlightenment (dare we say it?) into the minds of people who had been conditioned by an entirely different, less tamed and less predictable, environment.

To the people of the Middle Ages and of a much later time than is imagined, ill-luck took the more immediate and aggressive form of evil spirits and witches. Witches, although conceived as human beings, were nevertheless not subject to the ordinary physical laws: therefore, it was necessary that the chimney as well as the door should be protected against a witch's entry. The hearth and the threshold consequently got special attention to exclude the evil influences that threatened the spiritual security of the occupants.

The main device for keeping the house spiritually sound was iron. To discuss the reasons why iron has been used as an apotropaic device by peoples all over the world and at all times of history would need much more space than we have here. But it is possible to put forward briefly an explanation of the supposed potency of iron against evil. First of all, the earliest iron worked by man was meteorite iron;[1] and a substance that came from the sky was by its nature numinous and taboo. Its widespread use, moreover, for making tools and weapons came comparatively late in man's history, and its spectacular superiority over stone and bronze both as a tool and a weapon caused it to be regarded with superstitious dread by the people who were still using the old materials. It is likely, too, that the users of the new metal played on this fear and claimed that they wielded magic. It is certain that the people themselves regarded the man who worked iron with some of the awe and suspicion reserved for the sorcerer. The first smiths were endowed by the people they served with supernatural powers; and it is understandable why the smith was deified in many cultures.

Yet long after it had become common in certain parts of the world, this awe still clung to iron owing to the *numen* that had traditionally inhered in the metal, and also to another more rational cause. For a primitive tribe at the lowest level of culture would have good reason to view iron with alarm; and this has been clearly shown in recent years when the introduction of a single steel machete to a tribe of Amazon Indians had a spectacular effect on tribal organiza-

---

[1] It is likely that iron pyrites was also mistaken for this.

tion. Undoubtedly, to the earliest peoples iron appeared in the same ambivalent light as atomic energy does to us. It was taboo; something to be viewed with alarm because of the dreadful power inherent in it.

Sir James Frazer has listed[1] many examples from all over the world of this long-standing taboo. No iron was allowed in the sacred grove of the Arval Brothers in Rome, and if a stone inscription had to be cut with iron they sacrificed a lamb or a pig to cleanse the pollution; the Roman and Sabine priests would not shave with iron only with bronze razors. In the Celtic countries, especially, iron has been taboo for certain functions up to recent times. In Wales iron was used as an amulet against *Y Tylwyth Teg*, the fairies, within this century; and there is a theory that the fairies in Wales were a pre-Celtic race, shy and small of stature. They were driven into the fastnesses by a race of conquerors who used iron; and for them iron was not only a substance to be feared, but something to be hated as a symbol of their subservience to an alien race. Some of the legends, notably *The Lady of the Lake*, are built round this taboo on iron; and for the conquerors an insurance against an attack or a visit from the original people was to place iron about the house to prevent their entry. In Wales within the last few generations a poker was placed across a baby's cradle to prevent the child being taken and a changeling put in its place. In Suffolk, in the Eye district, it was a recent custom to place a poker upright against the bars of the grate thus forming a cross 'to keep old Lob from the hearth'. This practice still continues today in some parts of Suffolk because it is alleged to make the fire burn more brightly; and it has even been rationalized in detail by those who say that the upright poker divides the draught and causes the chimney to draw more efficiently.

In many religious ceremonies or rituals whose origins ante-dated the use of iron this metal has remained taboo, as already suggested. The mistletoe, the Golden Bough,[2] was gathered without the use of iron, as was the dwarf elder and St John's wort, plants that were believed to be effective against witches; and in Scotland the *need-fire*

[1] *G.B.*, III, p. 226.
[2] *G.B.*, Part VII, Vol. 2, p. 75.

was never re-kindled with steel and flint but by the old method of rubbing wood against wood. The taboo on iron remains fixed in the ritual and is therefore an indication of its age; and though we should hesitate to call the modern Freemasons superstitious we can point to a part of their initiation ceremony which contains at least one of the elements of an ancient ritual which in other circumstances would be recognized for what it is, and promptly be labelled as something that *stands over* from a former culture. An initiate to the order of Freemasons has, it appears, to divest himself of all metal before undergoing the ceremony. The Masons themselves give three reasons for this; the initiate should bring nothing lethal or offensive into the Lodge; again, if he is received in a state of poverty—without *brass*—his lack of metal is a tacit form of sympathy with those of the brethren (if there are any) who are permanently in that condition; and lastly, the divesting of metal celebrates the building of the Temple of Solomon at which no metal tool was supposed to have been used. To the Masons themselves these reasons may have sufficient weight to explain the injunction against metal, but considered from the outside along with other elements in the Masonic ritual—the All-Seeing Eye, the ritual circumambulation of the Lodge according to the direction of the sun, the broken column—it points to an origin which is pre-Christian and in some aspects even pre-historic.

But to return to the 'vulnerable' parts of the house. The use of iron in the form of a horse-shoe above the threshold is common, especially in the rural areas. The threshold was also protected in another way which will be described later. But in some Suffolk farmhouses horse-trappings were built into the chimney for the same purpose; and it is likely that iron connected with the horse was considered to have an extra potency, as did the horse-shoe particularly.

Another substance used to keep away evil from the house was salt. Chimneys of some of the older houses in East Anglia were lined with salt-glazed bricks because salt had a powerful evil-averting quality.[1] It was considered sacred in pagan times, and even

---

[1] Enid Porter, *v. Some Folk Beliefs of the Fens, Folklore*, Vol. 69, p. 115.

today it is apparently used in the baptismal chrism. It had special significance for the Semites and Moslems, and Egyptian priests carefully observed the taboo on its use.[1] 'The spilling of salt is still considered unlucky, and the sowing of salt on the site of a sacked town probably meant that the place was taboo and ought not to be cultivated.' The scarcity of salt in many countries gave it a special value, and it was in addition a symbol of immortality: not decaying itself it also prevents decay in other things. It was also a synonym for wit or wisdom, and was one of the essential ingredients of the primitive ceremonial meals which established blood brotherhood between individuals.

In Suffolk salt was placed on a corpse up to recent years 'to make sure that it doesn't start rising'; and in the Cambridgeshire Fens,[2] as in Wales,[3] salt was associated with *sin-eating*, a ceremony in which a person undertook for payment to eat a small piece of bread

[1] M. A. Murray, *The God of the Witches*, p. 123.
[2] E. M. Porter, *op. cit.*, p. 15.
[3] Trefor M. Owen, *Welsh Folk Customs*, p. 173.

and a little pile of salt that had been placed on a dead person. By this action he took upon himself the sins of the deceased, having previously received permanent absolution for his own. The custom of placing salt on a corpse underlies this story from Cheshire: at a hiring-fair in that county a farmer approached a worker with the object of engaging him for the coming year. He first asked:

'Why did you leave your last farm?'

'I didn't like the food.'

'What was wrong with the food?'

'Well, while I was there a cow slinked a calf, and we had veal for very nigh on a month. Then the old sow died, and we had hog's meat till we looked like it. One day the Missus died; and when I saw the Master going upstairs with a bowl of salt I thought it were right time for me to leave.'

5
Trees, Plants and Principles

MANY of the older houses in this area were also protected on the outside against evil influences by the planting of small trees and shrubs near the door or in the hedge surrounding the garden. The elder was the most common tree used for this purpose in East Anglia; and the belief that it is in some way useful to have an elder growing near the door or in the garden is still met among the older generation in East Anglia; and the writer has come across two or three instances in different districts here in recent years. In one village not far from Ipswich a wife asked her husband to trim back

Helmingham

an old elder bush that was 'making the garden look untidy'. He obstinately refused, maintaining it was unlucky to cut the elder. But this is one of the old beliefs that are dying out as the conditions which nourished them in the isolated country communities with unbroken links with the past are quickly disappearing.

In Scotland the elder is the ancient bourtree of the ballads; and it was wood that was never burned. This taboo on burning elder obtains in East Anglia, too; but some country people here say that it is common sense not to burn elder as it is a wood that *spits* when it is placed on the fire and therefore likely to be dangerous. Elderberries gathered on St John's Eve—the old pagan, Beltane or Midsummer festival—were believed to prevent the possessor suffering from witchcraft; and elderberries and elder pith were sometimes given in the food of those thought to be bewitched. Like St John's wort it was a kind of *fuga daemonum*, putting evil spirits to flight. The old Prussians[1] venerated the elder; and Robert Graves suggests[2] that the tree was associated with death and the after-life because of the elder-leaf shape of the funerary flints in megalithic long-barrows; and he links the tree with Midsummer because at that time the elder flowers are at their whitest and a true symbol of the White Goddess—or the various names in which she was known: Diana, Hecate, Demeter and so on—whose sacred plant it was.[3]

There is convincing evidence that this pagan Mother Goddess, in her various guises, was the centre of a widespread cult in Britain, and remained so for centuries after Christianity had been 'officially' introduced into these islands. The horse was sacred to her, chiefly in her form of Diana or Epona; and just as the taboo on eating horse-flesh is almost as effective in Britain today as it must have been when the cult was the dominant one, so many of the trees and plants which were also associated with the goddess still preserve some of their ancient favour in the country districts of Britain. Here the importance of fertility and the eclectic attitude of country people to all cults and religions that seem likely to promote abundance

---

[1] *G.B.*, Part I, Vol. 2, p. 43.
[2] *W.G.*, p. 185.
[3] On the other hand, there is a tradition in Suffolk that the elder is a good tree to have growing outside a dairy as its bitter smell keeps flies away.

conspired to keep alive customs and rituals of the old chthonic deities long after their names had been forgotten; and the old Suffolk country people[1] who affirmed that lightning never struck the elder and who believed that a cross made of elder brought into the house secured it against this disaster were invoking protective powers drawn, as often, from entirely different sources.

But there is another theory to explain why country people in Britain regard certain small trees almost with awe. It is summarized by Professor Estyn Evans who stresses the link between long-standing beliefs and the physical conditions in those regions of the world where they evolved:[2]

'In Ireland the trees which the older faiths had endowed with magic qualities were all small trees and shrubs—especially the rowan, holly, elderberry, and whitethorn—and the evidence of archaeology and palaeobotany is that these plants first became common in prehistoric landscape as weeds of cultivation following forest clearance by early cultivators. Thus they would have become symbols of the farming year, their white blossoms a sign of spring and the end of killing frosts, their red berries a token of the fulfilment of harvest and the promise of renewed life.'

The hawthorn or whitethorn still has a place in the mythology of the countryside, and the taboo on bringing the may or hawthorn blossom into the house is well known and still regarded. But in many Suffolk farmhouses there was a custom whereby a servant who first brought a bunch of hawthorn into the house on the first of May was rewarded with a dish of cream for breakfast. The first of May, however, was a special and related occasion, as the name suggests; and it is likely that this can be understood as the ritual breaking of a taboo, the temporary raising of all prohibitions on the holy-day or festival of the goddess. For the hawthorn gets one of its names from the month which in turn celebrates the Greek goddess Maia, the mother of Hermes, and another manifestation of the White Goddess[3]

---

[1] Lady C. Gurdon, *Suffolk Folklore*, p. 4.
[2] *I.F.W.*, p. 297.
[3] It is worth noting that the ancient Chinese had an equivalent figure or daemon (called *P'o*) who was feminine and characterized by the colour white. Richard Wilhelm, *The Secret of the Golden Flower*, p. 114.

to whom the blossom of the may-tree was sacred. Her month was the time of purification in readiness for the Midsummer festival; temples were swept out; houses spring-cleaned; sexual intercourse forbidden; and old clothes were worn until the unlucky month was over. Robert Graves[1] derives two modern superstitions from these last two; the unluckiness of the month of May for brides and their husbands, and the injunction against casting a clout until the month of May is over.

pond — Framsden

Superstition would undoubtedly be a very apt word to denote these perennial beliefs, for the reason that they stand over (*superstant*) from a more ancient religion or culture. But the word has too many overtones; for often the bare mention of these seemingly irrational, mythical, or poetic elements in our own culture provokes a surprisingly violent reaction: many people find it hard to discuss

[1] *W.G.*, p. 175.

them objectively, perhaps assuming that they are being asked to believe in them; and they react strongly against what appears to them as a direct assault on their reason and common sense. The first weapon they catch hold of is the word *superstition*, and by using it as a kind of dismissive sneer, put out of court any rational discussion either of the belief's origin, its place in our own society or its relation to similar beliefs elsewhere. We cannot, therefore, use the word superstition in a referential sense without great risk, and in spite of its aptness it would be best in describing these survivals to use a less suitable but more neutral phrase such as old beliefs and customs. These, at least, suspend the passing of judgment upon them until examination shows that either they have some value or none at all for the historian or anthropologist. For however infantile an old belief's content, there is always a *prima facie* case for looking at it dispassionately and considering, for instance, whether it may be a local variation of an obstinately universal form.

A holly-tree was also considered sacred,[1] and to have one growing near the house was like having an elder, a spiritual assurance against evil. The bay-tree was similarly regarded. A Suffolk woman moving house a few years ago transplanted the bay-tree which had been growing near her door to a similar position near the new dwelling. She said that she wouldn't have been comfortable in the new house without it. The mountain-ash or rowan-tree was looked on as one of the most effective defences against witchcraft, just as potent as iron. In some districts carters kept a rowan-cross in their pockets or wore a sprig of rowan in their hats to safeguard their horses which were supposed to be particularly susceptible to witches.[2] But in East Anglia the rowan was not singled out as much as the elder for this protective purpose and appears to have been held in nothing like the same regard as it was in the Celtic countries and in Yorkshire. In this county[3] witch-posts made of rowan were built into farmhouses specifically to render them safe against witches; and although there are no witch-posts, as far as is known, in East Anglia, the practice has relevance to this region because of the importance

---

[1] *A.F.C.H.*, pp. 201–2.
[2] *E.O.S.*, pp. 289–90.
[3] Mary Nattrass, *Witch Posts, Gwerin*, Vol. 2, No. 5.

attached to the threshold and the chimney or hearth in this connection. It was believed that a witch, to gain power over the house
and its occupants, would try to enter through the door, proceed
past the hearth and then make her exit through the chimney.[1] The
witch-post was, therefore, placed on the appropriate side of the
hearth as one of the supports to the lintel-beam, and as a deterrent
to the witch's passage through the house. The top of the post was
usually moulded and fortified by a carving of a St Andrew's cross.

The rowan like the oak was one of the sacred trees of Thor. A
plant that was also dedicated to him as the thunder- and fire-god
was sengren or house-leek. Culpepper regarded it as a herb of
Jupiter, and mentioned that it preserves whatever it grows on from
fire and lightning. As one of its names suggests, it grows on house-
tops, a small circular plant that is often seen on old tiled roofs in
East Anglia where it was held in special esteem as a folk medicine.
But Culpepper's suggestion that the herb is 'good for all the inward
heats as well as outward' is undoubtedly influenced by its mythical
associations and probably is as much homeopathic magic as empirical
medicine. Though many old country people valued it highly, and
used it for treating skin complaints, burns and scalds. It is a plant
with a long history in this part of England, and as *singrenan* was
recommended as an ingredient of cough-medicine in the old
English *Lacnunga* or Leechdom.[2] Yet the prevalence of sengren on
East Anglian roofs has brought out the suggestion that it was often
deliberately planted there to prevent the tiles from slipping. It is a
fact that when the wooden peg or pin of an old pin-tile rots the tile
slips away; but this theory looks at first glance suspiciously like the
rationalization of a long-standing custom.

Another common insurance against lightning striking an old
East Anglian house was the spiral iron; it is shaped something like
an elongated S, and some examples show the ends pointed like the
conventional representation of lightning or Jove's 'thunderbolts'.

---

[1] Margaret Murray (*The Witch Cult in Western Europe*, p. 10) suggests that this belief
in a witch's course through the house is understandable against the background of
prehistoric mound dwellings, and the taboos connected with the door among those
primitive peoples. (*cf.* the early Latins, one of whose deities was a two-faced door God.)
[2] Gratton and Singer, *Anglo-Saxon Medicine*, p. 197.

The iron forms a lock or tie to the tie-rod which helps to prevent outward thrust in many of these high-pitched, heavy-roofed timber buildings. The tie occasionally takes the form of a cross—a conventional cross or a St Andrew's—but usually it is S-shaped. Sometimes a double-S is found, one arm superimposed at right angles to the other, giving roughly the shape of the swastika, the so-called Hammer of Thor. An old Elizabethan mansion Coldham Hall in Suffolk has an example of this, on the front of the south wing—the swastika design being here enclosed in a circle.

In the eaves near which these irons are found there is often another detail that is supposed to be one of the letters spelling out good fortune to the occupants of these old houses. This is the nest of the swallow or martin. In Suffolk it is interpreted as a good sign if a swallow or martin builds on a house, and it is inviting bad luck to attempt to destroy these nests. This belief may be related to some unidentifiable myth concerning the swallow or martin; on the other hand it may be that the good fortune was directly associated with the happy choice of the house's site; for it has been observed, notably by Shakespeare,[1] that where the martin breeds the air is delicate and pure.

It is clear, however, that we can identify many of the marginal customs and surface details relating to an old house as the remnants

[1] *Macbeth*, Act I, Scene vi.

of old cults or religions; and as such we can claim them as evidence of the many variegated strands that go to make up the rural culture of the British Isles. Often where a belief or custom cannot be referred to a prior culture it has interest as an illustration of some of the principles underlying primitive beliefs all over the world. One of these is the old use of the association of ideas which underlies sympathetic magic. Sir James Frazer has isolated two aspects of this: homeopathic or imitative magic (like produces like); and contagious or *touching* magic (things that have once been in contact will always be linked however distant from one another they become.) Although these two aspects have been isolated to form part of a hypothesis and rarely appear in pure form the distinction is a useful one; and there are sufficient examples in connection with the house and home to show that it has great value in helping to discover how a seemingly irrational even nonsensical belief arose.

Here is an example: A Suffolk farmer's wife was rather annoyed with her young daughter because on a fine day in early spring the child had brought a bunch of primroses into the house. 'If you are going to bring primroses indoors,' the mother said tartly, 'you'll have to bring in more than that. Take them out and pick a bigger bunch!' This incident happened in a Suffolk village since the First World War, but there is a record[1] of a similar belief in Suffolk during the last century. For some time the writer sought out the principle that lay behind this belief but without any success. Then at an old people's gathering at the village of Ringshall one of the members told him: 'Of course, you had to bring in at least thirteen primroses into the house. Do you bring less, it were no use: it didn't serve. Thirteen was the number—or more. It didn't matter if you had more; but you dursn't have less.' The rationale of the custom was then immediately clear as one of the old people very soon pointed out: thirteen is the number traditional to a clutch of eggs placed under a hen during the spring. Each yellow primrose was, therefore, the analogue of a young chick which would eventually emerge from the egg. If one grants that like produces like—an unquestioned assumption of the primitive mind either in Britain or

[1] *East Anglian Notes and Queries* (1864), Vol. 2, p. 202.

in Borneo—it is folly then to bring in fewer primroses than you hope
to have healthy young chicks.

There was again a persistent belief in East Anglia that a child's
first movement after its birth should be upward. This was easily
arranged if the child was born downstairs: the nurse could then
take him in her arms and carry him up to the first floor. But in
most cases the child was born upstairs and his first natural movement would then be downwards. This difficulty was avoided by the
nurse's taking the baby into her arms and stepping up on a chair
before proceeding downstairs. The precaution was not a superstition in the root meaning of the word, simply a logical application
of the principle already stated: start the child on an upward path
right at the beginning of his life and from henceforth he would tend
to continue in that direction. It is not so much the reasoning that is
faulty in these old beliefs as their fantastic premisses.

Helmingham

More beliefs connected with the house illustrate the same
principles, for instance: 'You mustn't sweep the dust out of the
room, do you'll sweep the master out of the house'. Or, 'Don't

sweep the dust out of the house. Sweep it into a pile in the centre of the room and then burn it' (a precaution to stop anyone using for an evil purpose the dust that had touched the occupants' feet). While collecting material the writer came across an example which seems to combine both aspects of sympathetic magic. He was invited inside an old lady's cottage, and on being asked to sit down promptly chose a very comfortable-looking windsor chair. Just as he was about to settle, the old lady exclaimed, half humorously, half seriously: 'Oh, don't set there! Thet's the maaster's chair. Dew you set in the maaster's chair you'll hev to pay the rent!' He got up very quickly. But the inference was clear to him: 'If you infringe the authority of the head of the house by sitting on the chair where it inheres you must also assume his obligations.'

A belief commonly held in East Anglia even today, and not unknown in other parts of Britain, is that in visiting a house 'you must always go out by the same door as you entered'. If one presses for an explanation the nearest one gets to it is: 'If you come out by a different door, you'll never visit that house again.' It is not easy to discover the basis of this belief but here are some attempts: Christina Hole[1] writes:

'It is, of course, very unlucky for a man to pass through carrying a spade on his shoulder. It is a death omen for someone within. It is the spade which does it in this case—omen of a grave to be dug—but only, I think, if the man goes right through.

'The Helston Furry Dancers, when they enter a house, sought to go in at the front door and out at the back in order to bring the true luck of Summer to the indwellers. If they can't then they bow at the householders and go out again the same way. But this is not as powerful a luck-bringing charm as the through journey.

'At Roadwater in Somerset after the apple-trees have been wassailed on January 17th (old Twelfth Night), the wassailers return to the local inn to drink the health of the house and then depart. It is, apparently, essential that they enter by the back door and leave by the front, otherwise bad luck will come to the inn.

[1] Personal Communication.

'In *Bygones*, 17th January, 1900 a writer says that in Montgomery-shire, if a man happened to be the first visitor on New Year's Day (a very unlucky omen) little boys had afterwards to walk through the house "To break the witch".

'All these are, with the exception of the spade case, ceremonial occasions, either luck-bringing or purifying. I don't know the reason for the superstition at ordinary times, but it occurs to me that it may be one of the many notions of what visitors may do or not do to ensure their return, e.g. not putting on forgotten gloves without making a new start; not folding a napkin etc. Could it not be that the finality of passing right through the house meant that the person will never return to that house? Or as the ceremonial passage through adds to the life of the house by bringing luck or purifying evil, could it perhaps draw away life (and bring bad luck) when done without ceremonial excuse?'

It seems clear, as already stated, that the taboo was broken only on ceremonial or ritual occasions; and this points to the custom's link with an older culture–probably Celtic, for although the belief is held all over Britain it seems strongest in the Celtic countries. Here is a relevant custom from the Welsh border:[1] 'As the clock struck twelve it was customary to open the back door first to let the Old Year out; then the front door was opened to let the New Year in'. Probably walking through the house was an analogue of man's passage through life, and for that reason it was a risky and final exercise except on special occasions. A Suffolk clergyman[2] has pointed out that it used to be the custom at funerals for the corpse to be taken through the south porch of the church and then to be brought out through the north porch–wherever a church possessed one. Symbolism has always played a large part in Christian worship; the font, for instance, is the symbol as well as the instrument of entry (through the christening ceremony) into the Church's body; and for that reason it is placed right at the entrance to the church building. It is, therefore, conceivable that the taking of the corpse right through the church was a purposive piece of ritual; and this

---

[1] *F.L.H.*, p. 90.
[2] Philip Barker, Woolpit.

would be sufficient to fix immovably in the minds of country people the taboo against walking right through an ordinary dwelling-house.

But mythical origins apart, there may be a partial explanation of the belief in the actual structure of the Celtic house. In north and west Ireland[1] the traditional house has two opposite doors one in each lateral wall; and it used to have a central hearth without a chimney. Only one door was open at a time. The front door was open normally, but if the wind 'blew contrairy' the back door served instead. Thus, opposite doors, following this explanation, would be necessary to regulate the draught; and it would be impractical for someone to use both doors at a visit; for if he used the door on the windward side he would perhaps smoke out the occupants by opening it even for a few moments. The Welsh long-house[2] with its opposite doors and passage is a type of dwelling where a similar explanation could conceivably apply. And if we hesitate to adduce evidence from the Celtic countries to illuminate East Anglian problems, at least we have the encouragement of the recent excavations at Exning near Newmarket.[3] Here the remains of a second-century house have come to light, a house that was identical in plan with the Welsh long-houses described by Dr Peate, with long sides and opposite doors providing a passage from side to side, and dividing the building roughly in two.

Whatever the origin of the belief, however, it has remained a powerful one; and up to recent years front doors in many farms and country cottages were not opened except for weddings and funerals. Even today many front doors in the country get very little use. Until he became wiser, the writer often used to knock at a front door after approaching rather tentatively along a path aggressively green with moss. And more than once, while waiting for bars and bolts and an occasional chain to be drawn back—reluctantly, so it seemed—and while listening to the protesting creak of the door as it was being slowly opened, he had time to think that even the search for truth

[1] *I.F.W.*, p. 45.
[2] Iorwerth Peate, *The Welsh House*, passim.
[3] S. Applebaum, *Agricultural History Review*, Vol. XI, Part 1, pp. 4–5.

could hardly justify such labour as this, especially as it was someone else's; and it would have been much better for all if he had taken the less interesting but well-worn path and approached the house uneventfully from the side or the rear.

6

The Hearth

THE hearth is the centre of the household and the home, the place
where the family gathers when it is most characteristically a family,
a group united by blood and common interest. The hearth and its
fire were once sacred; and Frazer[1] suggests that the sanctity was
linked with ancestor worship and stems from the ancient custom
among the Romans and other nations of burying their dead in their
houses. The dead's spirits, they believed, hovered round the house
to protect the family; and the *Lares et Penates*, the Roman household
gods, were their symbols. If, therefore, in a climate like Britain's and
particularly during winters like those of East Anglia, additional
reasons are needed to remind us that the hearth is a special place,
here then are some of these reasons. It is probable, moreover, that
the hearth's association with witchcraft stems partly from this
ancient legacy: certainly, under the hearthstone was the spot most
frequently chosen to bury the witch-bottle, a device designed to act
as a repellent against witches, and often found under the hearths of
the timbered houses in East Anglia.

A number of these witch-bottles are known to have been discovered in East Anglia since the last war.[2] Their purpose was to
counteract a curse put on the house and its occupants by an ill-
disposed person; and it is significant that many of the witch-bottles
in this part of England have been discovered in old inns, as if they
needed—as *public* houses—some sort of general insurance against
their high risk of being bewitched. The whole practice and rationale

[1] *G.B.*, Part 1, Vol. 2, p. 216.
[2] *v.* Norwich and Ipswich Museums. The Suffolk finds were on the site of Ipswich
Civic College and at the Duke's Head Inn, at Coddenham. Later finds have been made
at Ixworth, Eyke, Woodbridge and Stradbroke etc.

of the witch-bottle ceremony is a good example of sympathetic magic; but before examining it in detail here is a contemporary account from Joseph Glanvil's *Sadducismus Triumphans* or *A Full and Plain Evidence Concerning Witches and Apparitions*, published in London in 1689:[1]

'. . . which puts me in mind of a very remarkable story of this kind, told by Mr Brearly, once Fellow of Christ's College in Cambridge, who boarded in a house in Suffolk where his landlady had been ill-handled by Witchcraft.

'For an Old Man that travelled up and down the County and had some acquaintance at that house, calling in and asking the Man of the house how he did and his Wife; he told him that he himself was well, but his Wife had been a long time in a languishing condition, and that she was haunted by a thing in the Shape of a Bird that would flurr near her face, and that she could not enjoy her natural rest. The Old Man bid him and Wife be of good courage. It was but a dead Spright, he said, and he would put him in a course to rid his Wife of this languishment and trouble. He therefore advised him to take a Bottle, and put his Wife's Urine into it, together with Pins and Needles and Nails and Cork them up, and set the Bottle to the Fire well cork'd, which when it had felt a little while the heat of the Fire, began to move and joggle a little, but he for sureness took the Fire Shovel and held it hard upon the Cork. And as he thought, he felt something one while on this side, another while on that, shove the Fire Shovel off, which he still quickly put on again; but at last at one shoving the Cork bounced out, and the Urine, Pins, Nails and Needles all flew up, and gave a report like a Pistol, and his Wife continued in the same trouble and languishment still.

'Not long after, the Old Man came to the house again and enquired of the Man of the house how his Wife did. Who answered, as ill as ever, if not worse. He ask'd him if he had followed his direction. Yes, says he, and told him the event as abovesaid. Ha,

---

[1] The date is interesting as it was about this time that the modern scientific movement in Britain was emerging. What had previously been accepted as part of the rural complex of belief was now observed and questioned. Aubrey noted that civil wars 'do not only extinguish religion and laws but also superstition'. Christopher Hill, *Intellectual Origins of the English Revolution*, London, 1965, p. 118.

quoth he, it seems it was too nimble for you. But now I will put you on a way that will make the business sure. Take your Wife's Urine as before, and cork it in a Bottle with Nails, Pins and Needles and bury it in the Earth; and that will do the feat. The Man did accordingly. And his Wife began to mend sensibly and in a competent time was finely well restored. But there came a Woman from a Town some miles off to their house with a lamentable Out-Cry that they had killed her Husband. They ask'd what she meant and thought her distracted, telling her they knew neither her nor her husband. Yes, saith she, you have killed my Husband; he told me so on his Death-Bed. But at last they understood by her that her Husband was a Wizard, and had bewitched this Man's Wife, and that this Counter-Practice prescribed by the Old Man which saved the Man's Wife from languishment, was the death of that Wizard that had bewitched her. This story Mr Brearly heard from the Man and Woman's own Mouth who were concerned, at whose house he for a time Boarded; nor is there any doubt of the truth thereof.'

The main principle here will be recognized as contagious magic; and this is how the contemporary mind reasoned in carrying out this ceremony. The witch had got hold of something that his prospective victim had touched, and by means of this link was able to cast his malevolence over this person and the house she lived in. But in so doing he, by reason of the 'contagious' link, had himself become indissolubly joined with the object of his curse; in fact, the victim had some sort of hold on him and all hope was not lost. A seventeenth-century writer[1] explains the purpose of working on the victim's urine: 'The reason . . . is because there is part of the vital spirit of the witch in it; for such is the subtlety of the Devil that he will not suffer the witch to infuse any poysonous matter into the body of man or beast without some of the witches blood mingled with it.' Herrick, in some lively verses, also gives a prescription:

> *To house the Hag, you must doe this;*
> *Commix with Meale a little Pisse*
> *Of him bewitcht: then forthwith make*

[1] Quoted in Ralph Merrifield's, *The Use of Bellarmines in Witch Bottles*, Guildhall Misc., No. 3, February 1954.

A little Wafer or a Cake.
And this rawly bak't will bring
The old Hag in. No surer thing.

Once the link had been established by the witch she was open to a counter-device through the medium of the urine. Anything that was done to that would instantly be transmitted by sympathetic magic to the person of the witch and would induce in her sympathetic pains that would compel her (or him) to come to the victim's house to ask the victim or his helpers to desist from the counter-measures probably under promise of the removal of the curse.

Most of the East Anglian examples of witch-bottles are the so-called grey-beard, stone-ware jars with well rounded belly and narrow neck, and the distinctive feature of the mask of a bearded man in relief at the neck's top. It has been suggested that the grey-beard jar is an anthropomorphic representation, a symbol of the figure of the witch. But it seems more likely that the jar or bottle was meant to be a simulacrum of the witch's bladder. The fact that it was invariably buried upside down[1] with the corked neck bottom-most points to this, as does the finding of pubic hair in many of the bottles. Glanvil's account implies that the action of the bottle and its contents was pointed directly at a specific bodily function—the nails and pins moving about in the heated urine were meant to transmit intense pains to the witch's bladder. Yet some of the contents of these bottles appear to suggest that a 'shot-gun' effect was often intended: to strike the witch wherever it was possible. In one of the grey-beard jars discovered in Ipswich and now in the Ipswich Museum there was a cloth heart with pins stuck in it among the following objects: sharpened splinters of wood, brass studs, nails, hair, glass-chips, and a much-rusted table fork without a handle. On an occasional jar there is no grey-beard mask but a number of

---

[1] A fairly recent find at Dover House, Ixworth, Suffolk appears to support this. The bottle was discovered in 1950 when a trench was being dug to insert a damp-course in this open-hall type of house. It lay just outside the threshold of a south-west door. A chip off the bottom of the stone-ware bottle probably indicates that the spade struck this part first. (For the house *v*. Sylvia Coleman, *A Wealden House at Ixworth*, Proceedings of Suffolk Institute of Archaeology, Vol. xxix, Part 3.)

imprinted horse-shoes or a kind of horse-shoe motif which no doubt had apotropaic significance.

But witch-bottles were also buried under the threshold as well as under the hearth. They have also been discovered out-of-doors, as suggested in the second part of the remedy in the Glanvil story. These bottles have been dug up in fields and occasionally in hedge-rows. One was found a few years ago in a Norfolk farm, and a recent example came to light in a Yorkshire farm[1] following the ploughing up of a permanent grassland. The purpose of burying the bottle in a field may be, as in the story already quoted, a final gesture of sympathetic magic: first put the bottle underground and the witch will soon follow it; or, more likely, the bottle was placed in the field or in an adjoining hedgerow as a prophylactic charm, either against the bewitching of livestock or the blasting of the fertility of the land itself.

The grey-beard bottles are, however, of interest in themselves. They are usually a very robust stone-ware covered with a brown or grey salt-glaze which is attractively mottled or stippled. The usefulness and appropriateness of their shape for the purpose of witchcraft was enhanced by the salt-glazing which gave them added potency. These jars were made for about two hundred years—1500–1700—first in the Rhineland and later in England, particularly at Fulham in the late seventeenth century. They are sometimes called *Bellarmines*, supposedly after Cardinal Bellarmine, a great chaser of Protestants in the Low Countries during the Counter Reformation period. But they were being manufactured as wine-jars long before Cardinal Bellarmine's appearance, or that of the equally infamous Duke of Alva who has also given his name to them. The misleading name *Bellarmine* has been attributed to a Mr William Chaffers who decided to 'christen them anew' in a paper given to the British Archaeological Association in 1849.[2] But there is another theory that the bearded mask has a much older history, and is the representation of the old pagan, Gallic god,[3] Esus—a name which is probably a variant of Zeus. The oak was connected

[1] Geoffrey Dent, *A Yorkshire Witch-Bottle*, *Gwerin*, Vol. III, No. 4.
[2] *The Times*, 19th July, 1958.
[3] T. C. Lethbridge, *Witches*, p. 102.

with both gods; and an oak-leaf motif often found as a decoration on these jars adds support to this theory. If, too, one of the old gods was depicted on the bottle this would lend them double strength as witch-scarers.

Bellarmine jar

The following account, written about a remote Suffolk parish,[1] shows both the persistence of the old custom and the essentially medieval temper of belief among ordinary villagers up to fairly recent times: 'Will, like many of the old people in the parish, believed in witchcraft—was himself, indeed, a "wise man" of a kind. My father once told him about the woman who had fits. "Ah!" Old Will said, "she've fallen into bad hands." "What do you mean?" asked my father; and then Old Will said that years before in Monk Soham there was a woman took bad just like this one, and "there weren't but me and John Abbott in the place could git her right". "What did you do?" said my father. "We two, John and I,

[1] F. H. Groome, *Two Suffolk Friends*, London, 1895, pp. 27–8.

sat by a clear fire; and we had to bile some of the clippins of the woman's nails and some of her hair; and when ta biled"—he paused. "What happened?" asked my father; "did you hear anything?" "Hear anything! I should think we did. When ta biled, we h'ard a loud shrike a-roarin' up the chimney; and you may depind upon it, she warn't niver bad no more." ' Into such practices as this did a crisis situation and a dim knowledge of the old logic of remote action through sympathy combine to betray its practitioners, causing some of their most bizarre and grotesque performances.

A similar method of boiling a witch-bottle on the fire is recorded by Enid Porter:[1] it comes from the Cambridgeshire Fens. A blacksmith made an iron bottle especially for the operation, and the climax came when the bottle burst. But the most frequent type of bottle discovered in Cambridgeshire is the glass variety—long, thin bottles of greenish glass such as the specimens now in the Cambridge

Cambridgeshire witch bottle

Folk Museum. They are usually discovered concealed in the wattle and daub above the lintel of the door through which the witch was most likely to enter; and their purpose was the same as that of the Bellarmine jar. But the makers of the Cambridgeshire witch-bottles used a different method to draw the witch who had supposedly cast her evil influence on someone in the house. The glass bottle was stuffed with coloured threads, red thread predominating. There are a number of examples of this apotropaic use of coloured thread: mothers once tied threads of different hues around the neck of an infant to prevent it being fascinated by the evil eye (compare the

[1] *Op. cit.*, pp. 121–2.

use of a coral necklace worn in recent years for the same purpose);
and just as horse-brasses were first used as amulets and not prin-
cipally as decorations, so the *hounces*—the coloured worsted braids
worn by farm-horses—originally had this function.

But the use of red thread as an amulet by the old Scottish[1]
farmers demonstrates that although the methods of making the
Cambridgeshire witch-bottle and the Bellarmine were different, the
principle underlying both activities was the same—sympathetic
magic. On farms in Scotland to prevent a cow being bewitched
twigs of rowan-tree were tied to the cow's tail with red thread. As
already stated, the witch was thought to be tied indissolubly to her
victim by a thin but invisible filament of blood or the life-force. The
thread is an analogue of this filament. And what other colour could
the life-force be but red—the colour of blood? It was also believed
at one time in East Anglia[2] that if a witch was suspected of enchant-
ing a person or was known to have expressed an intention of doing
him harm, the best preventative was to draw blood from the witch
herself. The red thread according to this belief would therefore be
a pure instance of sympathetic magic.

But to return to the hearth: a very old custom was the burning of
the Yule log. This is kept up in Essex, so it is reported,[3] even today;
and the kindling of a Yule log by the help of a charred piece of log
from the previous year was reputed to bring prosperity to the house.
The Essex emigrants who formed a large section of the Great
Migration from eastern England to North America during the
seventeenth century, appear to have taken their Christmas custom of
burning the Yule log with them, along with the Essex dialect[4] and
the typical Essex weather-boarded house.[5] Edward Gepp has traced
the connection between the Essex dialect and the speech of the
Southern negroes, and the survival of an Essex custom in that region
is not surprising. It is described by a writer[6] from the Southern

---

[1] Thomas Davidson, *Gwerin*, Vol. II, No. 1 (1958), p. 24.
[2] Robert Forby, *The Vocabulary of East Anglia*, 1830, p. 304.
[3] *Folkways of Essex* (Treasury of County Folklore), Douglas, I.O.M., p. 10.
[4] Edward Gepp, *A Contribution to an Essex Dialect Dictionary* (2nd ed.), Colchester, 1922.
[5] M. W. Barley, *The English Farmhouse and Cottage*, p. 144.
[6] Ellen Tarry, *The Third Door*, London, 1956, p. 158.

States: she mentions that in the slave plantations the Yuletide festival lasted as long as the *backlog* burned in the open-fire-place of the big house. The negro slaves, whose business it was to choose the Yule log, saw to it that it was of the greenest wood with the toughest bark. To ensure that it would burn slowly they soaked it secretly in an out of the way stream, thus hoping to prolong their period of rest to the utmost. Backlog, incidentally, is a seventeenth-century English word which has recently returned from the United States in a derived or figurative meaning.

7

Magic and Disease

IN THE old rural community, even up to this century, where a disease was unknown or its onset was in any way sudden or unfamiliar, the cause was often attributed to an evilly disposed person who had projected his evil thoughts on to the sufferer and reinforced them with magic. The sufferer and his friends did their best to repel this witchcraft, unconsciously using the same principle used by the witch—the primacy of thought. If a man wants a certain effect very strongly he can get the effect simply by imitating it. At no time is a man's desire more strong than in a crisis of disease, especially is this so in a society where the material culture has not developed to the point where a scientific explanation of much disease is possible and a rational cure forthcoming. As Malinowski wrote:[1] '. . . the healthy person suddenly feels his strength failing. What does a man do naturally under such conditions, setting aside all magic, belief and ritual? Forsaken by his knowledge, baffled by his past experience and by his technical skill, he realizes his impotence. Yet his desire grips him the more strongly: his anxiety, his fears and hopes induce a tension in his organism which drive him to substitute activity. Obsessed by the idea of the desired end, he sees it and feels it. His organism reproduces the acts suggested by the anticipations of hope, dictated by the emotion of passion so strongly felt.'

At a critical time in a man's life, in other words, hope and desire are much more powerful than reason; and we have only to remind ourselves of the comparatively recent acceptance of the germ theory of disease and the great advances—only a few years old—made in controlling infections by new drugs to realize that it was not only

[1] *Magic, Science and Religion*, p. 66.

in primitive societies that substitute activities were practised. There was, indeed, adequate room for the exercise of hope even in such a common infection as pneumonia up to thirty years ago. A doctor friend of the writer was in practice in an industrial area of south Wales during the middle 'thirties and was successfully treating a woman for 'double' pneumonia with one of the new drugs. The patient soon responded to the treatment, but the doctor was puzzled by an unusual, fetid smell in the sick-room. At his next visit he discovered that the drug, although effective, had not been strong enough to carry all the hopes of the patient and the desires of her relatives to see her well again. They had, therefore, resorted to a substitute activity and had procured the *lights* or lungs of a healthy sheep and fixed them to the soles of the patient's feet unknown to the doctor. This practice was once fairly widespread and is a good example of the old, pre-scientific fantasy-thought: it was known in Herefordshire[1] where a fish, the tench—called the *doctor-fish* because other fish are supposed to rub themselves against it when they are sick—was tied to the feet to reduce a fever.

Another example of pure sympathetic magic in the cure of disease comes from Suffolk. The disease is jaundice and the cure, practised only a few years ago, was 'Fill a bottle with the sufferer's urine. Place it in a running stream—uncorked, with the neck of the bottle facing upstream, against the current. After the lapse of some time the water in the bottle will become perfectly clear. When this happens the jaundice will disappear from the patient.' The imitative or homeopathic side of magic underlies many other jaundice cures. They all include the use of yellow objects:[2] a gold coin, a yellow rag, or a piece of amber. Yellow flowers were also thought to cure jaundice, particularly the celandine and the flowers of furze or *whin*.

A magical cure from Ringshall in Suffolk was similar to a cure practised in many countries. If a baby had epilepsy a cure was attempted by means of an ash-tree. An ash sapling was split down and the baby was passed through the cleft in the wood. The cleft was

---

[1] *F.L.H.*, p. 80 and *E.O.S.*, p. 339.
[2] Sir J. G. Frazer, *Aftermath*, p. 14, and *E.O.S.*, p. 93.

then tightly bound up, and the sapling as far as possible restored to
its former state. If it lived the baby would then grow up in normal
health: if it died the epilepsy would persist, and nothing more could
be done about it. Another recorded[1] cure from East Anglia gives
more colourful instructions to bring about the cure—this time for
hernia in young children: 'Split a young ash tree and pass the child
(naked) through it at sun rise, each time with the head towards the
rising sun. Then tie up the tree tightly so it may grow together.'
From the same source comes a reference to a man who later in life
showed his friends the tree through which he had been passed when
a baby.

This custom was similar to the well-documented[2] one of 'passing
under the arch'. The sufferer had to crawl under a bramble which
had formed an arch by sending a second shoot down to the ground.
It was a common primitive assumption that trees had a fertilizing
spirit transferable to plants and crops and even to human beings.
But it is likely that the above cures were analogues of re-birth. By
being passed through a living substance the child was being born
again, fortified by the fresh, living substance of the tree or the
bramble, emerging free from all disease or deformity. Another
custom of passing through a cleft stick to avoid the ghost of a dead

[1] *East Anglian Notes and Queries*, Vol. II, p. 215.
[2] *G.B.*, Part VII, Vol. 2, pp. 179 ff. Also, F. T. Elsworthy, *The Evil Eye*, p. 89.

man confirms this symbolism of re-birth: for by this action the living man came out an entirely different person and the pursuing ghost was, naturally, unable to identify him.

A Suffolk cure for ague relied on contagious magic and partly, it seemed, on the potency of iron for its effect. The sufferer had to go at midnight to a cross-roads, turn round three times and then drive a tenpenny nail up to its head in the ground.[1] There were other attendant conditions—the clock had to be striking the hour, and the sufferer had to walk backwards before the last note died away—but the purpose was quite clear. It was to leave the ague behind, embedded, as it were, in the nail; and the next person to walk over it would then take the disease. The driving of the nail into an aspen tree was perhaps a more certain cure, as the trembling of the aspen-leaves more than anything else resembled the symptoms of ague, and thus the two aspects of magic were invoked.

The present writer has not himself come across an instance of the nail-cure, but the idea of transference of a disease is still alive, as he found out when talking to a countrywoman who believed that in 'giving' a cold to someone you were automatically cured yourself.

Iron in the form of a tenpenny nail was often used for charms or cures: to drive into the footprint of a witch; to drive into the bed-post of a woman in childbirth; or into the threshold of a bedroom to prevent the sleeper from having nightmares. A tenpenny nail was recommended so often for this sort of operation that we might suppose that such a nail had some special virtue for the purpose. But what is a tenpenny nail? It appears that *tenpenny* here denoted the size of the nail and that the word is equivalent to ten-pound, *penny* being a reversion to its original association with *pound*. The different sizes of nails used to be known by the weight of metal required to make a thousand of them, and the ten-pound nail was a fairly large one which was appropriated for these unusual services.

Two magical cures for human infertility have come to light recently in East Anglia. A childless couple were recommended to place the dried testicle of a castrated horse under their pillow, and another couple were advised that they had no child because they

[1] *G.B.*, Part VI, pp. 57, 68.

had omitted to sleep with a pearl ring under the pillow. The principle underlying the first cure is obvious and needs no comment; but the pearl has a much more interesting significance. From early times it was the symbol of the generative powers; and like gold and jade, too, it was considered unchangeable and indestructible and, therefore, a symbol for vitality and immortality.[1] This was one of the reasons for the use of pearls and gold in medicine: they imparted their indestructible vitality to those who swallowed them. The pearl also was considered an aphrodisiac and was taken as such; but as a cure for barrenness the pearl, with its implied setting in the oyster, was an analogue of the fertilized egg in the womb.

Many cures are difficult to include under the heading of magic because they are compounded with some other method or substance that gives them some claim to be regarded as rational. Such a one is the curing of thrush or aphtha in a baby. This cure comes from the Hadleigh district of Suffolk and is linked with the blacksmith's shop: water from the smith's quenching trough was given to the baby to drink. The association with iron suggests that this metal's reputation as a counter-force in magic was involved, as well as a possible curative element in the water itself. A similar practice recorded last year on the Suffolk and Norfolk border poses the same question. It used to be a custom here to give a new baby cinder-water with the purpose of 'driving the Devil out of the baby'. In the room where the mother lay the midwife took an ember out of the fire with the tongs and placed it red-hot into a tumbler of water. She then gave some of this water to the baby.

Whooping-cough cures, too, are often a combination of what appears to be nonsense and traditional medicine. Here are some: 'Take a child with whooping-cough into the *nethus*. That'll cure him.' The *nethus* or neat-(cattle) house may contain something in the air, like ammonia fumes from the urine, and this may help to ease the cough: (compare the advice to a town mother to take the child to the gas-works): on the other hand there may be some forgotten reason why the cowshed was singled out, as in some ways it was

[1] L. Levy-Bruhl, *How Natives Think*, p. 22; and Mircea Eliade, *Images and Symbols* pp. 125 ff.

regarded as a very special place. A Norfolk woman told the writer: 'You mustn't enter the *nethus* at midnight on Christmas Eve. The beasts are on their knees at that time and if you disturb them you'll die before the end of the year.'

Another common cure for whooping-cough was by giving the child fried mouse to eat. The cure is not one of those that work by suggestion because of the very necessary practice of introducing a part of the mouse (the liver is recommended) into the child's food without his knowing. But in the Woolpit district of Suffolk the mouse-ear, a hawk-weed (*hieracium pilosella*) is advised as a cure. Possibly the supposed efficacy of the mouse-flesh is a kind of displacement from the properties of the plant itself. Culpepper confirms these: 'There is a syrup made of the juice hereof, and sugar, by the apothecaries of Italy and other places which is of much account with them to be given to those that are troubled with the cough or phthisick.' Since it has yellow flowers Culpepper also recommended the plant for jaundice. On the same principle owl-broth was once advised for whooping-cough.

A common cure for a persistent cough in a child used to be: 'Cut out a heart-shaped piece of brown paper. Cover it with Russian tallow or grease from the Michaelmas goose, and then sew it under the child's shirt next to his skin. Leave it there till it drops off.' This cure can be placed against the practice, here in East Anglia and elsewhere, of sewing up the front of a boy's shirt 'for the winter'.

The following seventeenth-century recipe for a cough-cure, taken from the Blois family papers,[1] is included as an illustration of the use of gold as a medicine:

'A Resight how to make Lozenges for a Cofe or Consumption or any weeke body or for Rume

Take half a pounde of double refined sugar, half a pinte of damaske rose water, two spoon fulls of sourupe of Gilyflowers, two drames of allaumes [allum?], two leaves of best Gold, three penny-worth of powder of pearle [?], as much Elecompany roote (ye powder) as will lie upon a Groate. Beat all this between two dishes upon a Chaffindish of CharkeCoale being always stirred, and when it is well boyled drop it upon a pewter plate and if they look of a dull Colour they bee anough.'

Under the third heading came those cures which can be confidently related to the tradition of folk medicine rather than to magic. But to list all the traditional cures still remembered if not practised would be tedious, as most of them are orthodox medicine now outdated but still used in rural East Anglia long after they had been forgotten in towns and the districts near them. There are, for instance, few cures in the old traditional medicine of the countryside that are not included in the seventeenth-century herbals. Yet there are some that have a much older provenance, as already indicated, and some that have escaped recording in the herbals themselves.

[1] Ipswich and East Suffolk Record Office.

One of these is the cure by moulds which has special interest for present-day medicine. The mould from a hot-cross bun used as a cure for a festering wound would, not so long ago, have been placed without question under the heading of a magical cure. Now, since the discovery of penicillin, it is in a more ambiguous position; though this instance seems to contradict the once widely held belief that bread baked on Good Friday would never go mouldy. Here are other examples, collected by the writer, of the traditional use of moulds in this region. A teacher recalls that she once rated a child who on her mother's advice treated a septic cut with the mould from the top of an old pot of jam. A horseman from the Bilderston area of Suffolk used to put an old piece of boot-leather at the back of the shelf in an out-house until it had acquired a fine mould. He used this to put on a cut or wound. Another man from the same district applied the mould from a piece of old cheese for the same purpose. And a horseman from south Cambridgeshire hung up sliced pieces of apple in an old spare bedroom and used the resulting mould on the apples to give to his horses 'when they had a bit of a cold or something'. 'After the apples are all *clung*[1] a mould will come on them.'

Rather similar to the use of mould is the use of the spores of a puff-ball called *bullfice*[2] in East Anglian dialect. Smiths sometimes kept a ball in their *travus* or forge and sprinkled the brown powder on burns and cuts. The fumes or spores of this large puff-ball are said to produce the effect of chloroform, and this seems to have been confirmed by a practice on the Norfolk border of Suffolk: spores of the bullfice were *puffed* round a hive to calm the bees. Like club-moss spores these are inflammable and were once used in the theatre to produce stage-lightning. Both varieties also did service as absorbents in surgery.[3]

---

[1] *Cling* to wither or shrivel up. *cf. Macbeth*, V, 5, 40: 'If thou speak'st false, Upon the next tree shalt thou hang alive, Till Famine cling thee.'
[2] A rendering of the seventeenth-century word, *bull-fist: lycoperdon giganteum*.
[3] *Lloyd's Encyclopaedic Dictionary*, London, 1895.

8

Cures

As ALREADY indicated in the previous chapter most of the traditional remedies have gone out of use; but there is one sector where they still flourish in spite of scientific medicine and free prescription. This is the curing of warts. During the last twelve years the writer has visited dozens of villages in East Anglia, talking to groups about old country beliefs and practices, and also gleaning a great deal of information from them. With very few exceptions all the villages had a wart-charmer. He might be known to only a few members of the group; and, indeed, the others were often surprised to discover that Mr Smith could cure warts. This is probably due to his not accepting payment or advertising his gift.

But in most villages, too, there were certain known and open remedies for curing warts. These were the physical—mostly herbal—remedies as opposed to the cures by charming or 'magic'. Many of the herbal remedies are used very frequently. The juice of a celandine[1] stalk is squeezed directly on to the warts, and this is repeated until the warts have disappeared. The milky juice of the dandelion is sometimes recommended for the same purpose. Sunspurge is a plant used, only more rarely, in the same way. One informant told the writer that sun-spurge was very effective, but great care was needed in its use. He had cured his own warts with the juice of this herb; but some of it had inadvertently got on to his face. The cheek became most painful, swelled up and remained swollen for nearly two days. But one of the most effective of these herbal remedies is undoubtedly the broadbean pod. The beans are shelled and the furry inside of the pod is rubbed gently on to the warts.

[1] The Greater Celandine (*Chelidonium maius*) is the effective variety.

Three well-attested cures by this method have come to my notice during the past few years: one was an architect's wife whose hands were covered by warts. Orthodox treatment failed to cure them; but she heard about the bean cure and after rubbing her warts with the white fur of the pod they quickly disappeared.

A rarer cure by means of a copper coin is worth noting. A coin is left in vinegar until it has acquired a fairly thick coating of green deposit. It is then taken out and rubbed on the warts which become smeared with some of the verdigris. An old lady who recounted this remedy told how she was cured. When she was a young girl she was kept out of ring games because the other children disliked holding her wart-covered hands. An uncle saw her crying on one of these occasions; and after finding out the reason for her tears he cured her warts by the above means.

But still quite as numerous as the cures of warts by herbs or substances is their treatment according to the traditional method of charming them. The charming can be done either by the patient himself or by a so-called white witch or charmer. Here are some of the ways used by the patient acting as his own charmer. Bacon or pork fat is rubbed on the warts and is then buried. As the bacon decays so the warts will disappear. A piece of steak must first be stolen and afterwards rubbed on the warts, then buried 'where no one is likely to walk'. The same principle underlies the following: 'Catch a big slug and rub it in the warts. Then impale it on a blackthorn bush. Your warts will go as the slug decays.' The next cure appears to be partly physical partly magical: 'Catch a black snail. Pierce it with a thorn—once for each wart. Anoint the wart with the froth that comes from the prick. Hang the snail on a thorn bush.' The cure using one's own spittle is of the same type; for spittle—as suggested in the Bible—is supposed to have magical qualities. And the last two in this group: 'Take a hazel stick and cut notches in it, as many notches as you have warts. Then bury it.' 'Count your warts then cut off the same number of buds from an elder tree and bury them.'

Imitative magic will be recognized in most of the above; but the injunction in one of the cures to 'bury the meat where no one is likely to walk' points to the principle of transference in which the contagious aspect of magic is uppermost. The above precaution was necessary to avoid giving the warts to another person. But there are also cures which aim at precisely this effect: 'Take a piece of string and tie as many knots in it as you have warts. Rub it in your warts and then throw it away. Whoever picks it up will catch the warts and you will be rid of them.' A similar cure is recommended using small stones which are thrown on to the highway in order to transfer the warts to someone else.

It will be seen that the number of warts a patient has is very important. In the charming of warts by a white witch the number is critical. If the patient does not give the correct number it is likely that the cure will not work—so he is told. The importance of this in East Anglia is shown by the use of the phrase 'Count your warts' as an equivalent to 'Cure your warts'. The procedure with most charmers is this: 'So you want to lose the wart on your face? Is it the only one you have?' After the correct number of warts has been given, the charmer says: 'They'll go. But don't be too impatient. Don't go counting them every morning.'

If you ask a wart-charmer where he got this power of healing he will tell you that he has had the power of healing passed on to him from someone else—usually a very old person. The power is his as long as he keeps it a secret. If he tells it to anyone, the power automatically goes out from him to the other person. If he accepts payment for his gift or skill he is also in danger of losing it. Nor must he advertise his skill unduly: this is the reason why many people who have lived in a village for years are often unaware that one of their number is a wart-charmer.

But whatever nonsense or hocus-pocus is used by the white witch —the careful counting of the warts, the silent recital of a mumble-jumble of words over the patient's hand, the atmosphere of secrecy— the cure almost invariably works. Often a wart-charmer is successful where a doctor has failed. Two instances of this have been encountered here during the last couple of years. Country doctors, moreover, gave evidence on wart-charming at the 1956 B.M.A. inquiry into spiritual healing; and one Devon doctor stated that 'the practice of charming away warts is extremely effective'. The research done by Dr Gordon, skin physician to St George's and West London hospitals, also shows that the medical profession tends to treat the charming of warts—in spite of its obvious quackery —with the seriousness its results deserve.

But the wart-charmer would not claim that his success is 'rational': it appears to lie in the subtle way he uses suggestion— unconsciously, of course. He is acting as part of a healing situation, and he rarely uses the direct suggestion of one man to another; a kind of suggestion which more often than not stimulates unconscious opposition. It is the very oblique suggestion offered by a combination of special circumstances which includes the knowledge that the charmer possesses a vague power which nevertheless has the sanction of long use. The power has been handed down to him in a mysterious or secret way, and now appears to operate almost independently of him as a man. The patient cures himself under the stimulus of a subtly impersonal suggestion that seems to by-pass the conscious mind and to operate independently of his reason. This, one supposes, is the same process that sometimes makes the curing of psychosomatic complaints so dramatic and so closed to rational explanation.

To sum up: although the content of traditional cures is usually

negligible there is still a great deal to be learned from the way they
operated. A large part of the old cures—usually the nonsensical
element to which modern science takes the most objection, but for
the wrong reasons—was directed not so much at the disease itself
as at the patient. It was the recognition of a total situation: it was the
principle underlying the witch-doctor's or clever-man's treatment,
the intuition that he was not dealing with a man with a sickness but
with a sick man.[1] All the hocus-pocus was an instinctive attempt to
stimulate the patient's own healing force. But the old medicine had

Sam Friend

the least success with the infectious diseases which modern medicine
has to a large extent tamed. Science isolates the bacillus or the virus
that causes the disease and then proceeds to render it ineffective.
And its very success in this field has caused a contradictory and
ultimately harmful trend in modern medicine, especially in hospitals
where various technical improvements, the specialization in different
skills, the better equipment, and improved drugs, are all tending to
emphasize the treatment of a patient as a more-or-less depersonalized
case, thus ignoring or undervaluing an important therapeutic factor
—the force within the patient himself that can greatly help his own
recovery.

[1] *v.* Brian Inglis, *Fringe Medicine*, London, 1964, *passim*.

Whatever the shortcomings of the old, pre-scientific medicine in attacking the disease itself, it had an instinctive grasp of the equally important technique of stimulating the patient's hope and desire to be well. And when we smile at the comic apparatus of this technique —the ritual to drive out devils, the supposed removal by sleight of hand of a stone from the afflicted organ—we must remind ourselves that technique is conditioned by the cultural level at which a given society finds itself. It is not so much the tools as the thought behind them which has relevance to present-day medicine; that is, it is more enlightened and scientific in psychosomatic and stress diseases for medicine to address itself as much to the man as to the actual disease —a very difficult thing to do at a time when the antibiotics and the powerful drugs have given medicine spectacular success in treating some diseases as absolute isolates.

Sam friend's boy

9

The Bees and the Family

THE close link of the bees with the household or family of their
owner is a feature of northern mythology; and the custom of 'telling
the bees' was practised in many north European countries until
recent years. It was a common practice among the old rural community in East Anglia, and here is a typical account of it taken from
a man who was born at Stonham Aspal, Suffolk:[1] 'If there was a
death in the family our custom was to take a bit of crepe out to the
bee-skeps after sunset and pin it on them. Then you gently tapped
the skeps and told the bees who it was who had died. If you didn't
do this, they reckoned the bees wouldn't stay, they'd leave the hives
—or else they'd pine away and die.'

It is clear from other sources that up to sixty or seventy years ago
in East Anglia the bee-keepers regarded the bees as highly intelligent beings and treated them as such: 'the wisdom of the bees' and
'the secret knowledge of the bees' were more than just poetic phrases
to them; they believed they were true to the letter. In the Suffolk
village of Debenham there was an old bee-keeper[2] who regularly
talked to his bees and claimed to be able to interpret their response
by the pitch of their buzzing. It is certain that bees are very re-
sponsive to different tones of the human voice, and this is probably
the reason for the country belief that bees are peace-loving beings
and will not stay with a quarrelsome family. Similarly it is likely
that it is the basis of the injunction that 'you must never swear in
the hearing of your bees'. A Suffolk man said:[3] 'My grandfather was

[1] W. H. Thurlow (born 1892).
[2] James Collins (born 1856, died 1917?).
[3] A. G. Addison (born 1910), Stowupland.

a bit of a rough diamond, and he wasn't above letting a few words fly in front of us children when he felt like it. But he would never use bad language when he was near his bees. He'd always be on his best behaviour then!'

Mr Thompson's bees

But to return to the old bee-keeper:[1] 'James Collins treated the bees as members of the family. He was a retired thatcher and he used to come and *work the bees*, as he said, at the saddler's where I was apprentice. This was well before the First World War. I used to carry the box up for him when he was going to smoke the bees out, and I was able to observe him pretty closely. If there was a tempest about—if the air felt thundery in any way—he wouldn't go near the bees. And at any time before approaching the hives he'd stand back and listen, to find out how they were getting on. Then he'd look to see which way they were travelling, so that he wouldn't get into their line of flight. He'd watch them quietly; and he often told me how he had a good idea where they'd been taking their honey: if they came to their hives low, they'd most likely have come off a field of clover. If they had been working on fruit trees they'd come in much higher. It wouldn't do to get in their line of flight:

[1] Recalled by Leonard Aldous (born 1900), Debenham.

you'd be sure to get stung. The old man told me in this connection: "If the bees come near you don't start beating the air: leave 'em. Don't fight the bees; the bees will allus win."

'It's true. The bees will stop a horse. And I thought of what Jim Collins said when I heard what happened over at Stonham. Just by the Maltings there was a man cutting clover with a cutter and two horses. Everything was going on well till the machine broke down. The worst part about it was that it stopped right in the line of flight of some bees who were working the field of clover. They attacked the driver and he straightway made a bolt for it, leaving the horses standing there. Both horses were stung unmercifully. One of them died soon afterwards; and the other one—I saw it myself—was so bad and its head so swollen up with the stings that it had to be supported in its stable by a kind of sling fixed to the roof.

'But Jim Collins was the cleverest man I knew at bees. He used to talk to them quietly when he was at the hives; and he reckoned he could tell when they were about to swarm by the different sound of their buzzing: how they answered his talk. As I say, he treated the bees as members of the family, as though they were friends; and I never knew him to be stung. Although the bees and the hives really belonged to Mr Rumsey, my master, Jim reckoned that he was their owner: the bees, he said, belonged to him. He could manage them; and he used to say that if he went away and left his hat hanging on one of the trees in the garden, the bees would never leave. If they swarmed they wouldn't go farther than the garden. He wore a hat with a veil when he was working his bees but often as not the veil used to be drawn back on his hat and nowhere near his face and his neck. There is a story that another Debenham bee-keeper once took a swarm of bees in his hat; and then put the hat on and walked home. And after knowing Jim Collins I can well believe the story's a true one.'

But the bees not only knew the voice of their owner but also his particular smell: one bee-keeper[1] told the writer: 'Whenever I go to the barber's I've always to tell him: "Nothing on, thank you." If he were to put lotion on my hair, however nice it smelled, the

[1] William Cobbold (1883–1964) of Battisford.

bees wouldn't think much of it at all. I know from experience that if I approached their hives with scented lotion on my hair it would make them angry.' The bees in fact should be treated at all times, so is the belief, as if they were people; and people who were very ready to take offence if not treated properly. They must not be bought or sold or even taken or given as a present. A bee-keeper may give away a hive, and later the recipient will find a way of unobtrusively repaying the kindness either with an appropriate gift or with some worthwhile service.[1]

Bee-skep

It is in this context of the close link between the bee-keeper and his bees and his high opinion of their intelligence that the custom of 'telling the bees' was practised, and it is against this background that it must be regarded. But it would be difficult to explain the custom other than by treating it as a true superstition, a remnant of an ancient and complex body of belief that was active in the old rural community until the First World War. The bees in classical

[1] *F.L.H.*, p. 28.

mythology had a close link with the *Ga Mater*[1] or the Earth Mother; and Melissa[2] (the Bee) was priestess to her under another of her titles, the Great Mother. Jupiter, also, favoured[3] the bees for the services they had given him when he was helpless in the Cretan cave. He, the Jupiter of the Underworld, had rewarded them with a portion of the divine nature, making them souls or carriers of souls to the hereafter.[4] 'The Zeus child of the Cretans, fed by a swarm of little creatures who were souls—the bees—had something of a God of the dead about him: his Cretan cave had the property of a place of the dead just as his other sanctuary had on Mount Lykaion.'

This special function of the bees in the old hierarchy of gods illumines a passage in the Fourth Georgic—lines 219 to 227, a passage that has been mistranslated at least since Dryden by a persistent reading of a kind of Christian pantheism into what is essentially pagan mythology. In the usual rendering of these lines there is a complete break of thought as compared with the original Latin, and the bees' function is ascribed illogically to *God*.[5] But it is clear from the myth itself, and the continuity given to the passage by paraphrasing the myth into its rendering, that the bees themselves were believed to carry the delicate filament of life from heaven or the gods—life that is given at birth to all living creatures including men. And at a creature's death they bear the filament or the soul back to that country where, as Virgil says, 'there is no room for death and where the souls fly free, ranging the deep heavens to join the stars' imperishable number'. This conception, although adapted and Christianized beyond recognition during the Middle Ages so as to make the passage even now a potential source of controversy like those lines in the Fourth (or Messianic) Eclogue,[6] has nevertheless been kept in its true, original form in the mythology of northern Europe.

[1] *Tinnitus cie et Matris quate cymbala circum. V.G.*, IV, l. 64.
[2] *Melissa officinalis* is also the name of lemon balm. There is an old belief that if this plant grew in the garden the bees would not leave the hive.
[3] V.G., IV, ll. 149–53.
[4] C. G. Jung and C. Kerenyi, *Essays on a Science of Mythology*, New York, 1963, p. 69.
[5] *deum* in line 221 is probably a genitive *deorum* and not a rather heavy *Deum* as it has been translated.
[6] *Ecloga*, IV, lines 4 ff. *v.* E. V. Rieu, *Virgil, The Pastoral Poems*, London, 1949, pp. 97–103.

In Scandinavia, for instance, the idea not only of the divine nature of the bees but also of their special function was preserved in a form identical with the old classical belief; and there is no doubt that the belief persisted in East Anglia, an area that for long periods was easily accessible to Norse influence. Osbert Sitwell has recalled[1] how the Sitwell family's East Anglian butler used to refer to the groups of cumulus cloud passing majestically across a blue sky as 'them great big Norwegian Bishops'. The Sitwell children were probably impressed but not enlightened—at least, not until many years later when a correspondent, referring to this passage in one of Osbert Sitwell's earlier books, pointed out that *Bishops* was a mis-hearing for *bee-ship* or *bee-skip* (*byskip*), and that the phrase Henry Moat the butler had used carried the belief that 'the souls of the dead are represented as bees and were supposed to traverse the sky in what was specifically termed a bee-ship'. And it should be pointed out that the old straw-plaited bee-hive could easily be considered as an analogue of a well-rounded cumulus cloud. Moreover, Virgil also compares[2] a swarm of bees to a dark cloud being drawn across the sky by the wind.

Thus when we look for the rationale or the explanation of the old custom of 'telling the bees' we can put forward the hypothesis that it stems directly from the pagan belief; and although this hypothesis is unlikely to gain general acceptance, it may serve as an example of how these apparently worthless and curious beliefs held by the old rural community—and derided by the ignorant—all had their own meaning, an ancient logic that should be material for the historian equally as relevant as a fossil, an artefact, an old building, or a valuable piece of parchment.

There is also another link between the bees in classical times and their discipline as observed in the old country tradition. This was the custom of *tinging* (or *tanging*) *the bees*. Here is an account of it from East Anglia:[3] 'Before he went to work on a summer's morning my father often used to tell my mother: "Watch the bees today,

---

[1] *Tales My Father Taught Me*, London, 1962, p. 63.
[2] *V.G.*, IV, ll. 58–61.
[3] W. H. Thurlow, Stonham Aspal.

Mother. It's a-going to be hot." And if later on there was a com-motion in the garden, us children used to run into the house and say: "The bees are out, Mother!" Then she'd get the key of the door and she'd say: "Go and get the dust-pan,[1] quick!" She'd then go after the bees a-tinging the pan with the door-key to make the swarm settle. They used to say that you could follow wherever your bees went if they swarmed across someone else's property. There was a clear right-of-way, as long as you did no damage.'

Mr. Thompson

There is also another belief about the bees that should be briefly recorded; a bee-sting has curative value for those who suffer from rheumatism or arthritis. A Suffolk doctor recently told the writer: 'Mr A. spent a number of years abroad. When he returned to this village he was crippled with rheumatism. He decided to keep bees in order to get rid of it. He became a bee-keeper and, in fact, he did cure himself.'

---

[1] Sometimes it was the frying-pan and the poker—*Matris cymbala*!

10

Perambulations

THERE is one custom that directly affects houses which straddle parish boundaries. These houses are by no means rare, even in the countryside; and it appears that parish officers still have the right of entry into private property not more than once in three years in order to establish the boundaries of the parish. The Perambulation or Beating the Bounds is an ancient ceremony that has its roots in the Roman festivals of *Terminalia* and *Ambarvalia*. The first was a sanctification by both owners of the boundary-stones between their properties with the sacrifice of a young animal, a libation of wine, and a crowning of the boundary-stones with garlands. It occurred in February. The *Ambarvalia*[1] was a joyful procession, at the end of winter, around the ploughed fields in honour of Ceres.[2] The ceremony included singing, dancing and the sacrifice of animals, also the symbolical driving away of evil from the cornland by a ritual beating with sticks.[3] These ceremonies aimed at two ends: the sanctifying of the boundaries, thus putting them above earthly dispute; and secondly, the blessing of the crops. This was the *rogatio*, an entreaty of the supernatural powers to preserve the corn that was fast coming to maturity.

Later, these two pagan ceremonies were Christianized and joined in a ritual[4] which was regularly celebrated at Rogationtide, the fifth Sunday after Easter. The Rogationtide procession was a means both of re-affirming the parish boundaries and of entreating God to send good weather and fair fortune to the growing crops. At the head of

---

[1] *Ab ambiendis arvis.*
[2] *V.G.*, 1, ll. 339–50.
[3] L. Whistler, *The English Festivals*, London, 1947, p. 152.
[4] It reached Britain early in the eighth century.

the procession was a priest; following was a crowd of people, some
carrying wands or sticks. The priest stopped at various well-known
land-marks–usually an ancient tree–and read the gospel for the
day, sanctifying the occasion and at the same time conferring the
incidental title of *Gospel Oak* on the tree which in many villages, for
instance the Suffolk village of Polstead, has long outlasted the
ceremony. Queen Elizabeth I ordered that Psalms 103 and 104
should be read, and that the priest should exhort the people to give
thanks and that he should say aloud such sentences as: 'Cursed is he
that transgresseth the bounds or doles of his neighbour.'[1]

The bearers of the sticks and the young boys in the procession
also had an essential part in the ceremony: at certain points of the
boundary–usually those susceptible of dispute–the men proceeded
to beat the land-mark with their sticks; then half in jest, half in
earnest, they transferred their beating to the boys; as an eighteenth-
century record has it:[2] 'whipping ye boys by way of remembrance
and stopping their cry with some halfpence'.

[1] W. E. Tate, *The Parish Chest*, p. 74.
[2] *Ibid.*

The Perambulation or Rogationtide ritual has been revived in many East Anglian parishes in recent years, more in the form of a *rogatio* rather than a beating of the bounds. The boundaries of most parishes have been definitively established for many years, following the successive ordnance surveys, and the only *walking* parish officers do officially today is the walking of the footpaths to establish right-of-way. But for centuries the beating of the bounds served a very practical purpose: the ceremony was essential at a time when maps were neither common or reliable. In many disputes over boundaries the oral testimony of those who had taken part in a perambulation was the only evidence the parties could appeal to; and even today in an age when maps have placed the physical detail of a parish beyond dispute, the detailed knowledge of use and custom held by the oldest inhabitant is sometimes invoked as a necessary and relevant supplement.

But apart from boundary disputes, from the earliest days of the church it was necessary for the parish officers to know exactly which houses or property lay within their jurisdiction, for each owner was liable to contribute towards the upkeep of the fabric of the parish church, and he in his turn could claim burial within the church's precincts. Yet for hundreds of years an exact determination of the parish boundaries was vital for one over-riding reason: the establishment of the parish as the unit of poor-law administration. The Tudor poor-law enactments, culminating in the 1601 Act—the basis for poor-law administration for over two centuries—combined with later enactments to set up the parish as a kind of closed compound. By making it chargeable for its own poor, legislation brought it about that the parish officers—the churchwardens, the constable and the overseers of the poor—felt it one of their main functions to see that they had as few poor as possible in the village. And in the event, this meant not so much an attention to the over-all economy of the parish as a determination to get rid of the poor they had by transporting them elsewhere, and by preventing any pauper or likely pauper from outside their boundaries from setting foot within. Before being eligible for poor relief a person had to *gain a settlement* in a parish, and in many cases this was as difficult as the entry of the proverbial rich man into heaven. A policy of excessive vigilance in carrying out this one aspect of their duties caused officers to hound the poor from one parish to another. The cost in actual expenditure following the constant law-suits about places of settlement and the cost in actual suffering was tremendous, and made a mockery of the word charity from which it has never recovered.

A settlement dispute concerning two places near the Norfolk-Suffolk border illustrates the difficulties of a house divided by a parish boundary; it also serves as an example of the absurdities into which a mechanical application of the law betrayed the parish officers. Almost the whole story of the dispute is told in a barrister's brief,[1] prepared for the appeal at Ipswich Trinity Sessions in 1830 by the churchwardens and overseers of the poor of the parish of Wortham against an order of two magistrates of the Borough of Eye, removing a pauper and his wife from Eye to Wortham. The Respondents were the churchwardens and overseers of the poor of Eye who had initiated steps to lessen the poor-rate by getting the man and his wife removed outside the parish. The barrister was briefed to put the case for the Appellants—the parish of Wortham:

'The Pauper, Thomas Woods, is 38 years of age and was born in

[1] Ipswich and East Suffolk Record Office, *Betts-Doughty Papers*, HD 7 9/A F 4/4/1.

the Respondent Parish (Eye) from whence he, at the age of 13, let himself on a Michaelmas day to a Mr Hammond for one year at the wages of 40s, and after serving a year and receiving his wages, again let himself to Mr Hammond as a weekly servant; and having lived about 9 weeks under the second hiring left the service and returned to the Respondent Parish where he continued about 3 years without, however, as he says, letting himself for a year. He then enlisted into the 12th Regiment of Foot and went abroad from whence he, in February, 1818 returned home with a disorder in his eyes which terminated in blindness. Ever since he has returned he has been resident in and constantly relieved by the Respondent Parish until he was removed to the Appellant Parish (Wortham) by the Order, now appealed against, having a short while prior to his removal, married a young woman, a circumstance which might lead to an increase of the charge on the parochial fund, and which there-fore increased the anxiety of the Respondents to settle him else-where.

'Mr Hammond, while the Pauper lived with him, kept a public house in Burgate, called the *Burgate Dolphin*, lying chiefly in that Parish and partly it is believed in the Appellant Parish (of Wortham). The Respondents, however, will contend that the room in which the Pauper slept is either wholly in the Appellant Parish or partly in that Parish and in the adjoining Parish of Burgate; and that in the latter case his *head*, as he lay in bed, rested in the Appellant Parish and the rest of his person in Burgate; and they will thus contend that where the person of an individual lies in two Parishes when he is sleeping his settlement is in that Parish where his *head* lies. On the part of the Appellants it will be contended that the room in question is wholly in Burgate or partly in that Parish and partly in the Appel-lant Parish and that supposing the Pauper rested in both parishes as he lay in bed he gained a settlement in neither. A model of the House in question and a ground plan and a chamber plan of it will be produced and given in evidence on the part of the Appellants; and a copy of the Plans accompanies this Brief: from which it will appear that the house is in height one story and that this story contains three bed rooms, in the middle room of which the Pauper slept. The house is copyhold and is described in the Court Books as lying in Burgate and Wortham; and in order to prove that it lies wholly in Burgate evidence will be given on the part of the Appellants that it is assessed to the Land and assessed taxes and to the poor's rate for Burgate, that the Constable of Burgate used to leave the Militia Schedules at the House, that in the Magistrates' and Excise Licences it is described as situate in Burgate; and the piece of land attached and belonging to the House is titheable to Burgate: while, on the other hand, the premises are not and never were assessed for any of those taxes or rates and pays no tithes to the Appellant Parish of Wortham and no Militia Schedules were ever left by the Constables of that Parish.

'Some pains have been taken by the Appellants to ascertain the boundaries of the two parishes and particularly as to the line of boundary adopted by the Parish of Burgate in their perambulations. It appears that they, on these occasions, entered at the front door opening into the Kitchen and proceeded in a straight line to and entered the Washhouse (a sort of lean-to erected within a few years) where they put a stick thro' a hole at the right hand corner of the Washhouse—that they then returned into the Kitchen; and going out at the back door went round by the Washhouse, taking a circle at the back of the house returned to the back door and again went out at the front. The track thus taken is distinguished by a dotted line in the plan. The front door and the door of the Washhouse are opposite each other and supposing the boundary line to run in the centre of the space between these doors and supposing (which appears to be the fact) that all that part of the house on the right of this line lies in the Parish of Burgate it will follow that the room in which the pauper slept is wholly in that Parish and that therefore the settlement is in Burgate.

'In this kitchen (as will be seen by the model) there is affixed to the ceiling a strip of wood about 2 inches in thickness which will be called a Beam but which it appears is nothing more than the head of a partition (which probably formerly existed but has since been removed) it not having the joists of the ceiling or anything else framed to it and giving no support or strength to the building. Be it

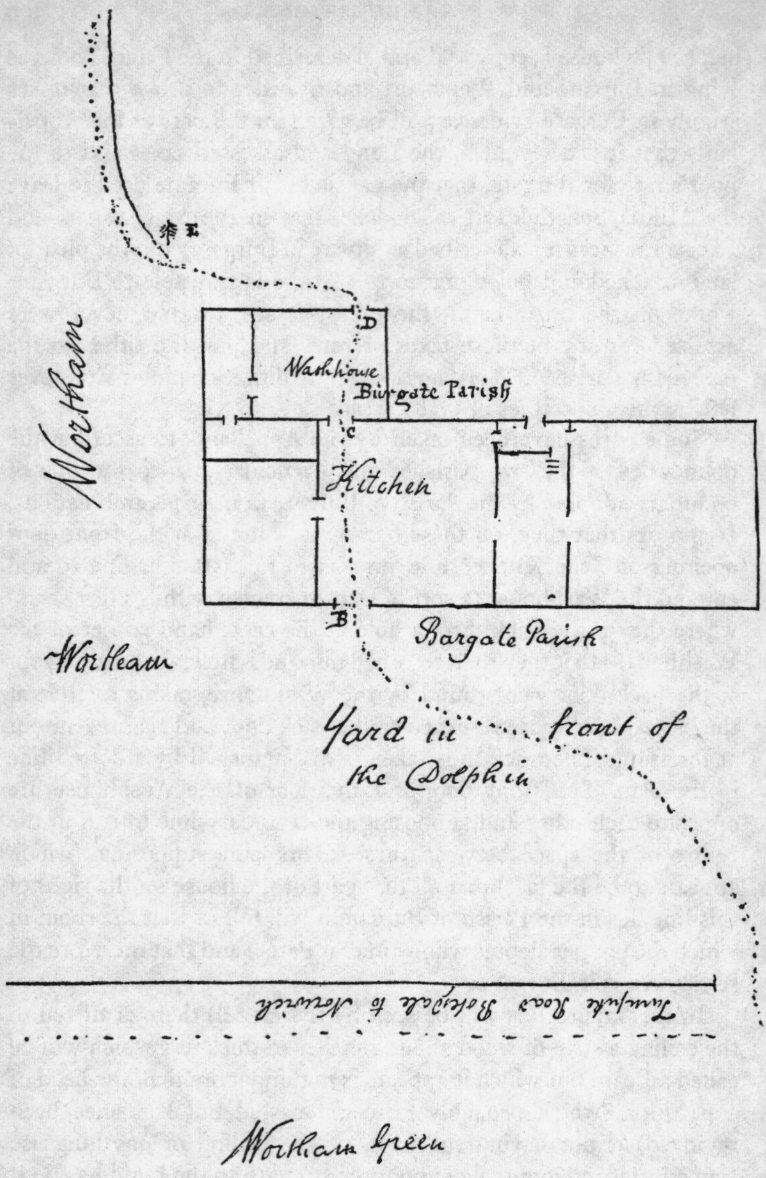

Wortham

Wortham

Washhouse

Burgate Parish

D

C

Kitchen

B

Bargate Parish

Yard in front of the Dolphin

Turnpike Road Botesdale to Norwich

Wortham Green

however a beam or no beam, the Respondents will, probably, contend that it marks the boundary line of the two Parishes and some evidence, though of a very slight nature, they will be enabled to give on that point. Admitting, however, this strip of wood to be the boundary the Case will stand somewhat thus: The wall against which the pauper's bedstead was placed is 11 inches from this partition head. The bedstead (which by the bye is now in the room at the same spot and in the same condition as when the pauper slept in it) has a head board to it. Then a bolster is to be placed against this head board, and making allowances for the circumstances the question will be: how much of the Pauper's head lay within these 11 inches? But the answer will be certainly not the whole of his head but at most only 4 or 5 inches of it; that is, supposing he lay with his head on the bolster; for if he lay with his head beneath the bolster (as boys are in the habit of doing) then no part of his head would lay within the 11 inches but his whole person would lie in Burgate. These niceties are, however, very absurd, and common sense would say they ought not to be entertained; but that the Court ought to decide that the Pauper gained a settlement in neither parish if it appear that he slept in both at the same time.

'A question naturally arises as to what line of boundary the Appellants have adopted in their perambulations; and the fact, which ought not to be concealed, is that they have always included this house as lying within their Parish. But as they have never assessed the house to any of their parochial charges and have in no other way supported their line of boundary, this fact becomes, it is contended, of no importance. Indeed, it is difficult to ascertain with any degree of certainty the boundary line of these two parishes for they (and Burgate in particular) have perambulated their Parishes so seldom that the oldest men living cannot remember the perambulations to have taken place more than twice in their lifetime. Thus doubts may be fairly entertained as to which Parish the House in question really lies in; and if the Court in the midst of this difficulty will reject all evidence of locality arising from the perambulations and will look only at the question of reputation they will decide that the house lies wholly in Burgate seeing that it pays land and assessed taxes and tithes to that Parish while it is described in the documents above referred to (especially the land tax assessments) as being there situate and that, consequently, the settlement of the Pauper is not in the Appellant Parish but in the Parish of Burgate.'

The outcome of the case was announced briefly in the *Ipswich Journal* for 17th July, 1830: '*Ipswich Quarter Sessions:* Wortham appellants and Eye respondents; orders quashed on debate.' So Thomas Woods, the blind ex-soldier, and his wife were allowed to settle where they had done so at first—in the parish of Eye.

The present Dolphin inn has been much altered, and now looks like a fairly modern brick house. But appearances, as usual in East Anglia, are deceptive; and a former occupant[1] of the inn remembers when the timbers and wattle-and-daub were removed and replaced by a brick front. The plans that accompanied the above brief show,

CHAMBER PLAN.

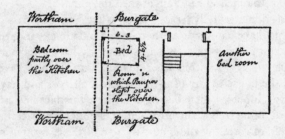

REFERENCE.

The line dotted in Black ink is the Boundary as Appellants contend.
The line dotted in Red ink is the Boundary as respondents contend.
The Black line between the 2 dotted lines, denotes the wall of the Bedroom against which the head of Paupers Bed stands.

[1] Miss Susan Smith (born 1892), Wortham.

in fact, a typical yeoman's house of probably the late sixteenth or early seventeenth century, with the stairs—as already described—opening straight on to a room or wide landing. The chamber plan shows the original arrangements of the bedrooms, one leading into another, the master and mistress sleeping at the end bedroom that had only one access. This was the usual arrangement in East Anglian houses until a passage was made against one wall to give separate access to each bedroom. The passage in the present Dolphin was constructed along the east wall, a natural development of the 'door-ways' with screens shown in the plan. To many of the old generation in East Anglia the seventeenth-century type of chamber plan was the usual one, the master and the mistress walking through the room where the apprentice or some of the children slept, perhaps jogging a child's elbow if he was sleeping on his left side—the wrong side—as the Blaxhall back'us boy was wont to do.[1]

There is a tradition in the villages of Wortham and Burgate that the ambiguous position of the Dolphin has been brought to notice on another occasion. Some years ago the Wortham constable was about to arrest a man who had gone to earth in the inn after a poaching or similar minor offence. As it happened the wrong-doer was in the Wortham part of the house when the constable approached; but receiving warning he quickly slipped into the bar on the Burgate side, thus putting himself outside the constable's jurisdiction.[2] There is also a tradition in these villages that the perambulation party used to confirm the boundary where a pond lay right across it: they took a farmer's twenty-two-yard measuring *chain* and dragged it through the water at this point.

An example from Suffolk shows that another similar device was sometimes used to prove the boundaries when a house lay partly in one parish and partly in an adjacent one. Such a house was Boss Hall which was once divided by the boundary line between the village of Sproughton and the borough of Ipswich. Boss Hall was originally a moated Tudor house and was one of the traditional places where

---

[1] *A.F.C.H.*, p. 26.
[2] That is, before the setting up of a county police force when the parish constable had no authority outside his own parish.

the perambulation party stopped when beating the bounds. They did this regularly at least up to the end of the last century. A Sproughton man[1] has described one of these perambulations: 'The schoolmaster and the parson took a whole class of us boys around to beat the bounds. We had sticks and we beat the bounds at certain places. We went all round, up to the Chantry and back again. We stopped at certain farms, and they gave us boys lemonade and the men had beer. I well remember coming to Boss Hall. The old boundary between Sproughton and Ipswich lay right across the house. So the only way to prove the boundary was to throw a rope over the roof of the house. Mr Freeman, the schoolmaster, did that. No, he never beat us boys when we went round. That had died out, no doubt, áfore our time. But I recollect when me and another boy got scrapping about something while we were going round with the party. We went at one another hammer-and-tongs—but we couldn't finish it. But when we got to school the schoolmaster finished it for us right well: both of us got a beating of a different kind. When this happened I had passed the fourth standard and I left school at eleven; so it was a tidy time ago—well over sixty year, I reckon.'

---

[1] Charles Woollard (born 1892).

11

The Rough Band

ALSO connected with the house in East Anglia was another custom called here the *Rough Band*. It was known throughout the British Isles as *Rough Music*, but each region seems to have had its own particular additional name: it was called the *Kiddly Band*[1] in Cornwall from one of the utensils most used by the band—a *kiddly* or pan, and it took part in the *shivaree* or wedding junketings there until the 'twenties. Its activities were known in Glasgow as *sherricking*. In other districts people called it *Riding the Stang*, *Riding*, *Stag Hunting*[2] and so on. The custom lasted until well into this century in East Anglia; and here is an account taken from a Suffolk village to illustrate what the Rough Band's activities were:

'A family used to live down by the forge: it doesn't matter much if I tell you their names; they're all dead now. But the woman was very short. We used to call her Mrs Dot. She was a Londoner and she had a brother who'd come up from London to live with her. He were a man some bit over sixty. After he'd been living there for some time he took up with a young girl who lived next door, daughter of a man who worked on Mr Durrand's farm. And though she were no more than eighteen he started courting her. Then we heard the couple were going to get married—had to, I reckon. Well, I was a lad just left school at this time; and when us lads heard about the wedding someone said: "Let's give 'em the *Rough Band*." So about twenty on us went down to the blacksmith's which was not far from the house where they were having the wedding party— dancing and singing and all manner of what-not going on.

[1] Robert Johnson, 62 Clinton Road, Redruth; and A. L. Rowse, *A Cornishman at Oxford*, London, 1965, p. 74.
[2] *E.O.S.*, p. 287.

'Now the blacksmith about that time had been repairing a lot of Dutch ovens. Everybody in the village had a Dutch oven, a big square oven with its sides made of iron sheets. Sometimes these sides used to get burned through, so they got the blacksmith to fit a new one. Well, there were half a dozen of these ovens lying about the smith's yard. We collared these and a few tin baths that were hanging up behind some of the cottages. But before we went out of the blacksmith's yard, a couple of the lads went along quietly to the house to prepare for us. As you know, the front doors in this village have no door-knobs or latches, just a big old fashioned twisted iron ring. It was dark, of course and the lads got a longish stake and fitted it through the ring, tying it so the ends of the stake were flush against the wall on each side of the door—which now couldn't be opened from the inside. Then the lads slipped round the back of the house and placed two bush faggots on the path just outside the back door.

'When they'd done this the *Rough Band* started. We took the owd baths and irons and started off round the village hitting blazes out of these tins and things with pokers, pieces of owd iron—anything we could get hold on. The whole village was out in no time to see what was up, but they could see it was the *Rough Band* and said nothing. Then we stopped outside the house where the wedding party was, and hit those owd things so you could hear the din for miles. Of course, those inside the house heard as soon as we started; but when they tried to open the front door they couldn't and the first man out through the back went sprawling very nigh down to the bottom of the garden path. But when we heard him swearing and shouting we knew the rest of the party would soon be after us. So we dropped the tins and things and made a run for it. I remember it well: the next morning when I went past the house the Dutch ovens, the baths and the rest of the stuff were still lying on the road-way.'

The Rough Band played on occasions such as the above, a marriage which the village considered reprehensible, or in cases of adultery, incest, wife- or husband-beating. Although its playing was nearly always reserved for sexual offences, unpopularity of any sort sometimes called out Rough Music. In one Suffolk district[1] it was used to 'drum a man out of the village' if his offence had been a gross one. Another sign of social disapproval in the case of wife-beating was the scattering of a bag of chaff on the front path of the house belonging to the offending man. Chaff, as an informant explained, is one of the less useful products of corn-threshing which in the dialect is usually *thrashing*.

Helmingham

The Rough Band has died out completely in East Anglia, as far as can be ascertained; but it is the sort of custom that may well be revived sporadically for some time to come. Before it finished, its form was considerably modified; and in East Anglia, at least, the Rough Band lost its old punitive function: it appeared outside the house at almost any kind of village wedding:[2] 'We didn't use to have big halls and things like that: when my brothers and I got married we packed as many as we could into the house. We had a really happy sing-song, you know; and the people used to come and give us a Rough Band. They'd say: "Oh, So-and-So is getting married;

[1] From George Garrard, born 1891, formerly of Stowupland and Gislingham. 'Drumming out' was also an Essex custom.
[2] Mrs. Grace Flack, Depden, Bury St Edmunds.

we'll have to go and give him a Rough Band." They'd pick up anything and they'd go down round the house and give us this sing-song,
rattling tins and old pails or anything you get hold of to make a noise
with. As soon as the people in the wedding-party heard, they'd say:
"Hello, some of the blokes outside are giving us a Rough Band;
we'd better call them in and give 'em a drink." That was the thing
to do.' In these weddings, as soon as the Rough Band had taken
their portion of the wedding meat and drink, they dispersed; and
latterly the custom seems to have been softened into a mild form of
blackmail, a method of obtaining a few cheap drinks.

But the original Rough Music was a most effective way of
ostracizing a person from the village community: and in some districts where a couple had been subjected to this music it was as good
as an ultimatum to them to leave the village altogether. Whatever
the offence, the punishment of Rough Music was both drastic and
cruel. For this reason some argue that it is a very ancient custom
whose dynamic is to be sought in pagan times when people believed
that fertility was undivided and that the same power controlled the
crops, the increase of animals and of human-kind. Therefore,
relations between the sexes were critical, not only in themselves, but
for the potential good or ill they had for the growth of the crops. It
is for this reason, as Jung reminds us, that a Swiss peasant—up to
fifty or sixty years ago—would embrace his wife in the freshly
ploughed furrows to ensure that the seeds he had sown on the land
would give an abundant yield. And it could well be argued that some
deep irrational drive is still operating in regard to society's attitude
towards sexual offences; for we still count them as a sin above, say,
greed and selfishness and pride, qualities that have done infinitely
more harm down the years—one would have thought—than any
amount of illicit or socially disapproved sex.

But whatever the theories about its remoter origins it would be
safe to infer that the custom is historically of long standing in the
British Isles. It is clearly at the back of one of Bottom's witticisms
in *A Midsummer Night's Dream*.[1] His perfervid wooing by Titania,
who in addition to being another man's wife was also inverting the

---

[1] Act IV, Scene 1.

woman's role in courtship, was the kind of situation which would have brought out an appropriately Rough Band in the old rural community. It will be recalled that in answer to Titania's question: 'What, wilt thou hear some music, my sweet love?' Bottom boasts: 'I have a reasonable good ear in music: let's have the tongs and bones.' We can assume that Bottom's quip was meant to be delivered with a salty gesture at the audience who would instantly take his meaning. For the First Folio stage direction is: *Tongs, Rural Music*. The tongs were either smith's tongs or the ordinary fireside implement; the bones were the sawn-off ribs of an ox used up to recent years—*teste me ipso*—by country boys as clappers. They were also part of the black-and-white minstrels' properties and the bones gave their name to one of the stock minstrel characters. But more to the present purpose, we have A. L. Rowse's evidence that the rattle of bones was a necessary accompaniment of the Cornish *Kiddly Band* or *Shivaree* up to this century.

Cretingham

Part Two

THE FARM

12

Magic on the Farm

IT HAS been pointed out more than once[1] that there were two religions in Britain for centuries after it had been 'officially' Christianized. These were the religion of the Church, and the old pre-Christian religion or cult followed by many of the people,[2] especially those in the remoter rural areas; and anyone who has lived for a length of time among the older generation of country people, survivors of the old rural community, will have recognized that the official religion of this country had not even at this late date penetrated very deeply into their psyche. Many of them cherished beliefs – beliefs, moreover that they acted upon – dating from a period well before the coming of Christianity. From one aspect this is not surprising, for these beliefs, most of which came from the old chthonic cult whose main concern was the fertility of both animal and soil, spoke directly to their condition: they clung tenaciously to their old practices which long before had become identified with their own remoteness.[3] For unless the soil gave abundant crops and the animals multiplied the primitive was lost; and the old beliefs and the practices that grew out of them were specifically aimed at preventing this. This is one of the reasons why early Christianity was forced to adopt and transmute some of the old pagan ceremonies and bring them within its ritual. But many of the old practices remained outside the Church and continued obstinately alongside its own, surviving into the twentieth century, unobtrusive

---

[1] Notably by M. A. Murray, *The Witch Cult in Western Europe*, Chap. 1, and G. G. Coulton, *Five Centuries of Religion, passim*.

[2] G. G. Coulton, *ibid.*, Vol. 2, p. 76: 'There is no doubt that the whole of the Church was on the lord's side. We have seen how Aquinas would have kept the peasant down.'

[3] *Pagani* that is the dwellers in the *pagus*, the village or remoter country areas.

yet resilient in a rural underground that, during the time the old traditional society flourished, was rarely suspected much less disclosed.

As Max Weber wrote:[1] 'Peasants have been inclined towards magic. Their whole economic existence has been specifically bound to nature and has made them dependent on elemental forces. They readily believe in a compelling sorcery directed against spirits who rule over or through natural forces or they believe in simply buying divine benevolence. Only tremendous transformations of life-orientation have succeeded in tearing them away from this universal and primeval form of religiosity.' Such a transformation has, of course, occurred during the last fifty years. Yet farming, even today, with all its mechanical, chemical and bio-chemical aids and complex subsidies and advisory services, is still tied to nature; and nature is the tremendous variable that has always to be taken into account. The weather, the haphazard movement of disease, whether of soil, plant or animal, are still unpredictable factors that cannot be absolutely controlled. Under the old, recently displaced farming, in conditions that had remained essentially unchanged for centuries, how much more apparent these variables were. A farmer might take all the care and make all the preparations humanly possible and yet be still aware of huge tracts of possibilities where he knew he was powerless. It was out of this awareness that the peasant clung to the old practices, irrational though many of them were: what he could not control at least he would attempt to placate. Therefore, he took precautions to appease the unknown powers, to fend off the evil ones he had perhaps unwittingly provoked: he poured his last drop out of the harvest cup onto the ground; he carried the green branches on the last load of corn; he made a corn-dolly to bring indoors and keep until the following year; he refused to begin work on a new job on a Friday; he hung a hag-stone over his stables—all for luck, as he would say, or to prevent ill-luck from entering onto his farm-land. For where technique is limited—and the basic techniques in farming remained the same for centuries—*chance* or *luck* plays a proportionately larger part; and chance has to be propitiated.

[1] *Essays in Sociology*, London, 1961, p. 283.

To say that these extra precautions could have had no possible effect on the farmer's situation is not to condemn them outright or to deny their usefulness in the social context in which they were practised. For, even though they did not and could not influence external reality in any way whatsoever, they had real pragmatic value: they helped to create a subjective climate that was ultimately beneficial. These old practices, irrational though they were, did at least give the operator the necessary heart; and unless a man, in the face of so many difficulties and uncertainties, had that heart, the conviction that there was a fair chance of his succeeding, he would probably not begin his enterprise at all. The primitive was as sound a psychologist as we know, and very rightly considered his own doubts and fears as threatening as any hostile environment; and it was to remove his own uncertainties that most of his irrational practices were mobilized.

cretingham

The farm, therefore, is the last resort of magic not by accident: it has earned this title because farming is—or was before successive governments elected, or were compelled, to play God—an essentially chancy business. As in acting in the theatre, or deep-sea fishing, a man did his job and waited: and reward or approval could be given or withheld by nature, by the whim of a fickle public, or by the seemingly haphazard movements of tide, wind and weather—all perhaps regimented by some remote but placable being. In these three occupations the area ruled by chance has always been formidable, and as we should expect the old beliefs die hardest precisely in these fields.[1]

But apart from all this, the farmer and farm-worker of the old pre-machine era in East Anglia had an attitude to the land that is characteristic of the primitive husbandman all over the world. It was enshrined in the proverb: *A farmer should live as though he were going to die tomorrow; but he should farm as though he were going to live for ever*. Between the farmer and the soil there was a bond that amounted, on his part, almost to veneration: the soil was something to be nursed and treated with the utmost consideration. This attitude was only one remove from animism and addressing the earth as *Mother*; and although in up-to-date farming countries it has been bawled out of court very loudly as *muck and mysticism*, it is still held in its original form by the farmers in the undeveloped countries; and those who have attempted to bring some of their methods up-to-date have found out this to their cost, as Margaret Mead has recorded.[2] In parts of India and the Middle East the primitive farmer regarded agriculture as a just partnership between himself and the cherishing earth. He considered it poor payment for the earth's generosity to inflict fertilizers and the iron plough upon it, and he refused to make use of the improvements which were offered to him free. It was only after he had been educated out of his primitive attitudes that any success in improving his farming technique became apparent.

Although no one can defend the outdated attitude of the primitive farmers and the farmers of the 'old school' and their resistance to change, it is understandable in the light of its origins; and it may still have its uses as a point of reference for the *scientific* farmer of today. And one would like to think that in his less harassed moments he would be able to pause and ask himself the question:

[1] A recent newspaper report shows that farmers still believe and practice sympathetic magic in its most ancient form: 'An effigy of Mr Fred Peart, Minister of Agriculture, was burned yesterday by Mayfield farmers on one of a chain of bonfires due to be lit at dusk across East Sussex. They built the fire on a hill near the village. The effigy, dressed in a black coat, striped trousers and a bowler hat, was placed on top; and as it burned the farmers fired their shotguns at it.' (*East Anglian Daily Times*. 15th April, 1965.) It was thus that primitive agriculturists used to deal with the god who omitted to send them rain.

[2] *Cultural Patterns and Technical Change*, Unesco, p. 197 ff.

'Who is nearer the truth?[1] The old school type of farmer with his near-veneration for the land as a living partner who must be nursed and humoured? Or the modern farmer who treats the land as an inert medium into which he can pour chemicals with impunity?'

If we grant that this old and world-wide attitude towards the soil existed in Britain up to the beginning of this century, it is understandable that many of the beliefs that grew out of this ancient seed-bed should remain active also. Some of them have lasted up to the present day in the minds if not in the practices of the generation that has survived the passing of the old traditional farming and the community which it nourished. Examples of these old beliefs and customs will be discussed in the following chapters.

moorhen's nest

---

[1] The truth, that is, viewed pragmatically as the best for the land and the people who consume its products.

13

Preparing the Ground

THE age, at least, of these beliefs cannot be questioned. 'That's been the same since the *Year Dot* when *Owd Hinery* were an infant' —so one of the writer's informants fixed the age of a custom under discussion; and when it was hinted that the date was a little imprecise he explained that Owd Hinery was the Devil; 'and as "dot" comes before 1, the *Year Dot* was somewhere right back at the beginning.' This was as precise as he could make it; and any estimate of the age of some of these old customs is not likely to come very much nearer to it than that. The custom, for instance, of pouring out a little drink onto the ground is as old as history. It was continued—mechanically perhaps without any appreciation of its origins —right into the present century in East Anglia when drink was taken out of doors, more especially at haysel or harvest time; a little beer, usually the last drop in the horn mug, was poured on the ground with indigenous phlegm, more of a casual than a ritual gesture. But it is recorded that in Herefordshire,[1] the purpose of the libation was openly acknowledged as 'a donation for the gods'; while the countryman in Ireland[2] poured out a little of his draught as a compliment to the 'good people' or the fairies; and the writer has seen a similar gesture on a Welsh hay-field of forty years ago.

A number of beliefs have centred in flints and flint fossils which are often turned up by the plough in East Anglia. Apart from the significance of unusually shaped stones or fossils to primitive peoples all over the world, it is likely that many beliefs accrued to flints in this region because we can say that in one respect flint is the only

[1] *F.L.H.*, p. 88.
[2] *I.F.W.*, p. 304.

truly native stone. Flints were automatically coming to the surface each time the ground was prepared for the seed-corn; and curiously shaped flints and fossils were usually kept; and even today a plough-man will pick up a fossil or a holed flint and keep it in his pocket 'for luck', or take it home and place it on the mantel-shelf of the living-room. But not long ago many of these flints and fossils were kept for more specific reasons.

sea-urchin fossil

One of these flints was the sea-urchin fossil or *fairy-loaf* as it was called in Suffolk.[1] It was polished and placed on mantel-pieces both as an ornament and a charm that was supposed to ensure there would always be bread in the house—a piece of imitative magic that grew out of the fossil's resemblance to an old cottage loaf. It was this resemblance, also, that caused the fossil to be used, especially, in north-east Suffolk where it was often picked up on the sandy heathlands, as a charm placed alongside the old brick-oven when the weekly batch of bread was baked. It was believed to be an induce-ment to the bread to rise and imitate the fossil's beautifully domed shape. The weekly bake of bread was critical under the old economy;

[1] *A.F.C.H.*, p. 212. This 90 million years old fossil was known as the *shepherd's crown* in some counties. *Country Life*, 7th October, 1965.

and if, after every precaution, the bread 'went dumpy'—as occasionally happened—the failure, like many other inexplicable accidents, was put down to witchcraft. Later mention will be made of a horseman's wife who attributed the failure of her bread to some of her husband's secret practices connected with his horses. And here is a witch-story from a west Suffolk village, an apocryphal story but one that illustrates the importance of the bread-baking at a time when if the bread failed one could not go to the shop and buy a substitute: The cook in a big house suddenly began to have difficulty with his bread-making. After a succession of failures he roundly ascribed his poor bread to a village woman who was employed part-time at the house. She was a witch, and it was she who was causing the trouble. It was arranged, therefore, that the priest should exorcise the oven, with members of the household staff standing about it. He had not gone far with the ritual when the apron of the suspected woman caught fire.

The attractive symmetry of a good specimen of a sea-urchin fossil, with its intricate and delicate markings, has ensured that the fossil has been valued since earliest times. Robert Graves suggests[1] that its magical significance explains why it is found in Iron Age burials. It is certain that curiously shaped stones have always had a fascination for the primitive mind; and were used magically in some of their ceremonies as aids to inducing hypnotic trances. Natives in certain parts of Australia,[2] for instance, were convinced that great power resided in unusual stones. It is worth noting that the fairy-loaf was sometimes known as the *pharisee-loaf* in Suffolk and this has been corrupted to *farcy-loaf*; and it has been suggested that the old farm horsemen who carried the sea-urchin fossil in their pockets did so as a charm against farcy—the disease of glanders in horses. But the word *pharisee* has no connection with farcy; and its other forms, known in Sussex as well as in East Anglia, *farissees* or *ferrishers* are derived from the word *ferrisheen* which is a development of the Gaelic *fear-sidhean* (*fear-sheen*) meaning fairy-men.[3]

---

[1] *W.G.*, p. 39.
[2] Ronald Rose, *Living Magic*, London, 1957, pp. 109, 163.
[3] Lewis Spence, *The Fairy Tradition in Britain*, p. 82.

Another type of fossil is often found on the sandy heathlands of east Suffolk: its name is *gryphaea incurva* and it is known locally as the *Devil's Toe-nail*. Its appearance does in fact suggest the nail of

devil's toe nail

some mythical beast, and although it is collected and kept as a curious stone no ascertainable belief is linked with this fossil. With the *Devil's Finger*, however, the belemnite fossil, a rich complex is associated. Belemnites are pointed flint cylinders varying from two to five or six inches in length: they are the fossilized guard of an extinct cuttle-fish and are frequently found in the soils of East Anglia where they are called *Thunderbolts* or *Thunderpipes*. The main belief linked with belemnites is still actively held by some of the older generation. One old horseman gave the following account of their origin: 'As the sun draws up water so the clouds draw up *substance* from the earth—the sulphur and so on. When there's a clap o' thunder, down all this comes as *thunderbolts*.' Another farm-worker recalled how he was working, singling sugar-beet in the spring of the year and there was a sudden thunderstorm. The lightning struck the ground not very far from the place where he was hoeing. On examining the spot later he discovered a small hole in the soil. His comment was: 'If I'd ha' dug down that hole, I'd ha' found a thunderbolt, you ma' depend.' Another farm-worker reported: 'I picked up one of those thunderbolts after a tempest, and it were right warm.' But this belief can be placed alongside what a research scientist[1] says about the idea of lightning generally held today: 'In the history of mankind, not many parallels are likely to be found to the concept of the "lightning bolt". Having appeared

[1] Dr R. H. Golde, *The Times*, 25th July, 1964.

in artistic representations or in descriptive terms for several thousand years, it persists in the vocabulary of modern man purporting to describe a material substance conveyed by the lightning discharge. Yet it has no physical reality but merely reflects the reaction of primitive man to a supernatural force which engenders fear. It is just one example of the many superstitions in connexion with lightning and thunder that continue to survive in our age, such as the ringing of church bells and the covering of mirrors to prevent lightning damage or the belief that beech trees are never struck, to mention a few outstanding examples.'

belemnite

The shape of the fossil, like the name belemnite, suggests a dart; and in one Suffolk village it has been called a 'prehistoric arrow'. Like the true neolithic flint arrowheads it appears to have been identified with fairy-darts or elf-shots which were at one time considered to be causes of disease in men and cattle. Elf-shots are frequently mentioned in the Anglo-Saxon leechdoms;[1] and Frazer confirms the link of the fossil with the artefact:[2] 'Among the peasantry of north east Scotland the prehistoric weapons called celts went by the name of "thunderbolts", and were coveted as bringers of success, always provided that they were not allowed to fall to the ground.' A horseman in the Suffolk village of Helmingham used to carry a belemnite in his pocket; and when asked the reason he said: 'For luck, I reckon.' But the belief that the belemnite was actually a product of the thunderstorm is recorded by Shakespeare and lends a much richer image to the lines which he gave to

[1] Grattan and Singer, *op. cit. passim. cf. The Arrows of Apollo.*
[2] *G.B.,* Part VII, Vol. 1, p. 14.

Cassius:[1] '(I) Have bared my bosom to the thunder-stone'; and to the sons of Cymbeline:[2] 'Fear no more the lightning-flash Nor th'all-dreaded thunder-stone'.

The absence of an indigenous rock in East Anglia has also invested with a special interest those boulder stones that have been exposed. One of these has given its name to a village in Suffolk; Chediston, from the Old English *Ceddes Stan*—Cedd's Stone; and another near the tower of Wortham church is called 'Wortham's Sacred Stone'. And if, as is likely, many of these stones were once regarded with awe, the early Church was careful to make a corner in veneration by having the stone either in the churchyard or even built into the church's fabric as at Shelley in Suffolk. For the Church's policy in this respect was quite clear, as we know from a letter[3] of Pope Gregory's giving the advice to St Augustine that pagan temples and shrines should not be destroyed but should be ritually cleansed and used for Christian worship. As well as legends of the sacredness of these stones there is sometimes a belief that a stone has grown on the spot where it has been always standing. A notable example of this comes from the Suffolk village of Blaxhall.[4]

In connection with ploughing the ground ready for the corn there is a very ancient custom that had its echo in East Anglia during the last century. This was the use of the plough to mark out a plot of land. At Battisford in Suffolk there is a straight length of road running through the parish: it is known locally as Battisford Straight; and there is a tradition that when the road was constructed one of the best ploughmen in the village drew a furrow as a guide to the roadmakers. A similar tradition exists concerning the village of Rickinghall which also has a *Straight*. Here, too, when the commons were taken in a skilled horseman drew a straight furrow to give the line of the new road. Certainly the ability of the old horse-ploughman to turn a long, straight furrow with only a fraction of an inch deviation commended itself on many occasions as a less troublesome method than the painstaking use of a theodolite; and—

[1] *Julius Caesar*, I, iii.
[2] IV, ii.
[3] *v.* G. G. Coulton, *op. cit.*, Vol. 1, p. 179.
[4] *A.F.C.H.*, p. 210.

provided a good ploughman drew the furrow—a method that was just as accurate. The use of the plough for this purpose is very ancient.[1] The original city of Rome was marked out in this way according to Dionysius of Halicarnassus: a primal furrow (*sulcus primigenius*) was drawn, and gave the rectangular shape of the city; but a plough was equally useful for marking out a circular boundary.

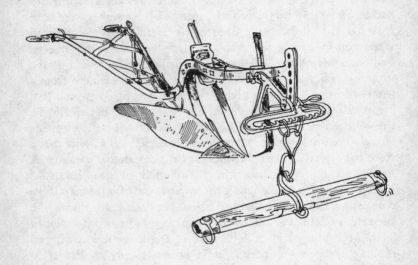

This ceremonial ploughing of the first furrow is also linked with another ancient tradition concerning the boundary of a piece of land. This is the custom which gave the name *hide* to a unit of land in medieval England. The custom was widely diffused, as it was considered the one method of unalterably fixing the boundary of an enclosure. It was done by cutting up the hide of an ox into narrow thongs and by distributing small lengths of the thong at intervals along the boundary. One of the earliest references to the custom is in Virgil who told[2] of Dido's founding a town in North Africa. Later

[1] Jung and Kerenyi, *op. cit.*, pp. 11 ff.
[2] *Aeneid*, 1. ll. 367–8.

writers elaborated on the story, and reported that Dido bought from the natives as much land as could be covered by a bull's hide. After the agreement was made she proceeded to cut up the hide into small thongs, enclosing a large piece of land on which she built a citadel. She called this fortified town Byrsa (βύρσα—a hide). But Frazer gave a different explanation of the cutting up of the hide. He suggested that the custom involved the sacrificial slaying of an animal, and cited the practice of a Bechuanaland tribe[1] who converted the hide of a bull by a long, spiral cut into one continuous thong. They then cut up this thong into small lengths which they distributed at the vulnerable parts of their own town or citadel in order to protect them from attack by their enemies. The protection was thought to emanate from the sacred beast which was slain and symbolically distributed around the confines. It is not implied that any such custom lasted until medieval times in Britain; but the name certainly did, and a *hide* denoted a fairly large piece of land the best estimate of whose extent is 120 acres.[2]

The plough was used, too, on a ritual occasion: on Plough Monday, the Monday after Twelfth Day, the end of the medieval Christmas holidays. On this day the ploughman dragged a gaily decorated plough from door to door in the village, asking for money to buy drink. The men themselves were also bedecked with ribbons, and they wore their shirts over their coats. If any householder refused to contribute to this foolery, the mummers put their shoulders to the plough and ploughed up the greensward in front of his door. There was also a lot of dancing and high-stepping antics performed by the mummers; and this gives the clue to the whole performance: the ploughing and the high leaping was another example of imitative magic, a fertility device to ensure that the corn for the coming year would be well bedded and would reach a good maturity.

It has been suggested that the ritual ploughing on Plough Monday anticipated the real ploughing which was to take place later. But in many parts of East Anglia, before the coming of the motor tractor,

---

[1] *G.B.*, Part IV, Vol. 2, p. 249.
[2] F. W. Maitland, *Domesday Book and Beyond*, Essay III, *The Hide*, London, 1960.

it was the aim to *complete* the ploughing before the advent of Christmas. This was especially so in the heavy clay of central Suffolk; and a horseman of the old school who worked in the Stow-market area remarked humorously that it was the unalterable law of the land that 'all ploughing must be done afore Christmas and the *brist* (breast or mould-board) of the plough must be polished up and put under the bed on Christmas Eve'. There was sound sense in this, as any ploughing done after Christmas in the heavy land districts of East Anglia would be a difficult business under the old horse economy; and there was no surety that any land left un-ploughed at this season could be worked into a good seed-bed in time for the drilling of the spring corn.

The Plough Monday jollifications were also used as an occasion to raise church funds, and plays were sometimes performed on this day.[1] The 'town' or parish plough was often used for the ceremony. It was kept at the church not solely for this occasion but chiefly to be hired out to those parishioners who wanted to use it for its ordinary purpose on their own land. In many Cambridgeshire parishes, Duxford, Bassingbourne, Dry Drayton, the plough was housed in the church: the plough at Dry Drayton was remarked on in a 1685 episcopal visitation and was transferred on the instruction of the bishop from the nave to the belfry.[2] Ploughs are still taken into church for blessing on Plough Sunday; and this January (1965) an old Norfolk 'gallows' horse-plough stood for the ceremony near the chancel arch in the magnificent parish church of Salle in Norfolk.

Also in connection with ploughing there is still in some villages a remnant of the belief that a piece of land in the parish should be left untilled. In English villages this is sometimes called *Jack's Land* or *No-Man's Land*.[3] This custom has its counterpart in many countries of the world: in India, for instance, such a piece of land had been a former burial-ground and it was left as a permanent habitation for the dead. In Nigeria the land was referred to as *Bad Bush* and was taboo.[4] But it is concerning Scotland, however, that

[1] W. E. Tate, *The Parish Chest*, p. 279.
[2] *East Anglian Notes and Queries*, Vol. VIII (1899–1900), p. 143.
[3] A. and B. Rees, *Celtic Heritage*, London, 1961, p. 203.
[4] Dilim Okafor-Omali, *A Nigerian Villager in Two Worlds*, p. 87.

we have the fullest evidence about this taboo piece of land. There it was called the *Gudeman's Fauld*, the fold or enclosure reserved for the Goodman or the Devil. Not to exploit this land was a kind of due paid to the Devil to divert his attentions from the rest of the farm, thus preventing misfortune befalling it.[1]

There was a piece of land called *Jack's Green* (now built on) in the Suffolk village of Creeting; and it is said to have given its name to part of the village. It is difficult to establish the truth of this but a tradition says there was a graveyard near here for seventeenth-century plague-victims: it also says that the land was infertile. 'That land wouldn't even grow damn paigles' (cowslips, or buttercups in some parts of East Anglia), a farmer said about this piece of land. There was also a *Jack's Pit* in the city of Norwich[2] at the beginning of this century when it was filled in as part of a building programme. A part of a Cambridgeshire village (Dullingham) is also called *Jack's Gallows* which appears to confirm the association.

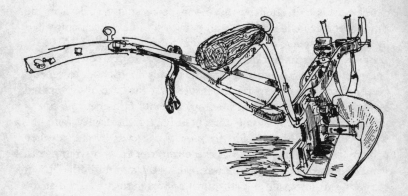

[1] T. D. Davidson, 'The Untilled Field', *Agric. Hist. Rev.*, Vol. III, Part 1.
[2] *East Anglian Notes and Queries*, Vol. XIII, p. 388.

14

Sowing the Seed

MUCH of the traditional knowledge and many of the old beliefs
and customs in East Anglia are concerned with the growing and
harvesting of wheat and barley. This is to be expected, as the region
is the natural corn-growing area of Britain: and wheat and barley
have always received special attention. The Romans grew great
quantities of both cereals in this region, and they identified wheat
and barley with Demeter in her role of Corn Mother. But barley is
probably an older corn than wheat and was the staple food of the
Greeks in the Homeric age. Some maintain[1] that it is one of the
oldest cereals cultivated by the Aryan peoples: it was used in the
ritual of the ancient Hindoos, and is known to have been cultivated
by the lake-dwellers of the Stone Age in Europe.

But whatever its antiquity, the care given to the sowing of the
barley by the East Anglian husbandman was almost akin to veneration. No trouble was spared to ensure that the carefully prepared
seed-bed was ready to take the crop. One old farmer in the Stowmarket area of Suffolk said that, ideally, for the barley (and the
wheat) crop the land should be ploughed east to west and then
drilled *overwart* (athwart) so that the *ringes* or rows of young corn
would lie north–south and be warmed by the sun on both sides of
the row. But he would not sow until he was perfectly sure that the
land was fit for drilling. He had his time-proven tests for this: one
was simply to walk over the land and to 'feel it through his boots';
then again he would take up a handful of soil, carefully crumbling
it to test it; or he would bend down and draw his fist backwards
through the soil. This method of deciding the right time to sow was

[1] *G.B.*, Part V, Vol. 1, p. 131.

recommended by Fitzherbert, the sixteenth-century writer on agriculture: 'Go upon the land that is plowed and if it synge or crye or make any noise under they fete, then it is to wet to sowe. And if it make no noyse and will bear thy horses, thanne sowe in the name of Godd.'

Some Suffolk husbandmen—up to the end of the last century, at least—took the advice to 'Go upon the land' in a very literal sense indeed. The husbandman's argument appears to have been this: he could easily determine by the above methods whether the seed-bed was ready for the corn and whether the soil was of the right tilth: but he could not be sure that the soil was warm enough to allow the seed to germinate. Therefore to make sure of this important condition he took off his trousers and sat down on the seed-bed, thus testing the warmth of Mother Earth through the most sensitive part of his anatomy. The writer has collected three instances of this practice: two in the Stowmarket district and one near Mendlesham where the farmer[1] who recalled it made the comment after the cold and wet spring of 1963: 'I don't know how those owd bors who used to set on the seed-bed would get on today: I reckon they'd get themselves right chilled.' But the test was, apparently, extremely effective: for if after this exercise the ground was judged right and the sowing proceeded satisfactorily, the husbandman expected the barley 'to be up in three days'.

Barley was undoubtedly *the* crop above all other crops in many districts of East Anglia; and its culture probably reached as high a standard of perfection here as in any other region of Britain. The two varieties grown in Suffolk during the nineteenth century were Chevallier[2] and Archer. One Suffolk farmer has said: 'There were really only two varieties of barley at that time o' day. Archer was a short-straw barley. We used to grow a lot of it; and at that time you used to keep account of how long your barley was in the ground. I recollect there was a man in Finningham who had his barley back in the barn for threshing thirteen weeks after taking it out (that is, as seed-corn). That must be something of a record.'

[1] Charles Brundish (born 1883), Tan Office Farm.
[2] *H.I.F.*, p. 105.

Whatever method was used for sowing the corn—broadcasting, dibbling or drilling—the care taken was considerable, as the result of sowing is only too plainly visible and remains so for months after the corn has come up. The broadcast sowing of seed, contrary to general opinion, was a particularly skilled job, especially if the sower was using both hands. A farmer was lucky if he had a man on his farm who could sow with both hands as it required an accurate synchronization of hand and foot: if a man missed his step and altered his rhythm his sowing would be immediately affected: there would be *missed bits*. These, in addition to being a lasting witness to a lapse in his skill, were also considered a bad omen in some districts of East Anglia. A missed bit in the sowing foretold a death in the parish. A similar belief existed in Ireland[1] and Herefordshire. Here, clearly, the principle of homeopathic or imitative magic underlies the belief; and it is frequently to be traced in customs connected with sowing in many parts of the world. In Malaya,[2] for instance, where there was a maxim that one must plant maize with a full stomach, using a thick dibble to ensure that the cob of maize would be large and bear abundant grain. The same principle is also at the bottom of many of the spring fertility rites where the lighting of bonfires and the ancient practice of dancing round and leaping over these was designed to induce the corn to grow: the fires helped the sun and the higher the leap, the higher would the corn grow. It is likely that some of the folk-dances, notably the candlestick dance where a woman tucked up her skirts and danced over and around a lighted candle, were the remnants of fertility dances.[3] This was danced in a Suffolk inn within the last few years.

Many sowing operations are connected with Friday. In Ireland this day was regarded as a lucky day to begin any operation not needing iron. The taboo against the use of iron on a Friday has been linked with the iron nails used on the Cross; but it is more likely another instance of the old prohibition against the use of iron being given an acceptable reason for its exercise. In Suffolk, however, there was—at least in one district—a strong disinclination to starting

[1] *I.F.W.*, p. 143 and *F.L.H.*, p. 118.
[2] *G.B.*, Part 1, Vol. 1, p. 130.
[3] *H.I.F.*, pp. 221–2.

any job on a Friday. This day was a *dies nefastus*, and to a certain extent the belief still exists: 'The farmer I work for won't start anything on a Friday. If a field of corn happen to come ready for cutting on a Friday, he'll get the binder out the day before and put it in the field ready, and perhaps he'd cut a little patch of the corn just to say he started. I don't know the reason, but we could never begin anything fresh on that farm on a Friday. Strange thing, though, about the only time this farmer went against his rule, he turned out his horses for the first time after the winter on a particular Friday. One of the horses got kicked and had to be destroyed.'

Good Friday in East Anglia used to be the traditional day for planting potatoes. It is difficult to say whether this was a fertility belief or whether this day was chosen simply because Good Friday was usually a holiday for the old farming community and therefore a convenient occasion for a workman to plant his own garden. It is likely, however, that there is some element of the old belief in the practice, as this day was specially chosen in many English counties[1] notably Devon: 'By many people potatoes are planted on Good Friday afternoon; in south Devon it was said: "We sow our potatoes at the foot of the Cross".' The basis of the Good Friday belief appears to have been that on that day the soil is redeemed from the

[1] Thomas Hennell, *Change in the Farm*, London, 1934, p. 89.

power of Satan—the old chthonic god of the pre-Christian religion—
and for this brief time he has no influence on it at all.

But the belief in the importance of the phases of the moon has
greatly influenced the husbandman down the ages in the sowing of
his crops. There are two aspects to the belief in the moon's influence. First, according to the age-old primitive reasoning, just as
the moon itself grows and diminishes so will it have an identical
effect on all growing things that are exposed to it. Therefore all
seed should be sown while the moon is waxing and everything that
has to be cut or gathered should be operated upon when the moon
is waning. Or as it was said in one district of East Anglia: 'Sow
when the moon is waxing: weed when it is waning.' Again, the moon
was supposed to be the source of dew and moisture. The argument
behind the belief was this: the dew falls most thickly on a cloudless
night. Where else could it come from but the moon? This belief was
enshrined in the old Greek myth that the dew was the daughter of
Zeus and Selene, the moon. The moon, moreover, was also believed
to influence rainy periods; and because of this and its influence on
the tides it was associated with water in many myths.

There are enough surviving instances of the moon beliefs to show
that they operated over the whole field of growth—plants, trees, and

Helmingham

animals: a surprising variety of instances have been collected in East Anglia. If you cut hair or finger-nails or corns during a waxing moon they will grow again very quickly. Cut while the moon is waning and they will grow slowly or not at all. Pigs killed in the waning of the moon will give meat of an inferior quality: moreover it will shrink in the cooking, a belief not dissimilar to the one held by the ancient Chinese:[1] 'The moon is the origin of *yin*. That is why the brains of fish shrink when the moon is empty; and why the shells of univalves are not full of fleshy parts when the moon is dead'. Under *September Husbandry* Tusser recommended: 'The moon on the wane gather fruit for to last'–advice that seems to have been followed up to recent years. Again, in the spring one should be careful to put eggs down for hatching while the moon is waxing.

An old Suffolk stallion leader observed: 'I used to get my horse to serve as many mares as he could while the moon was gaining– after the new moon. When it was wasting–after the full–it were no use. The mares would get foals; but they wouldn't be nearly so strong. I've proved it!' And at one time the moon influenced the activities of the farrier if de Solleysel's[2] advice was followed: 'You must continue the shooing of him after this fashion until his Heels be well-shaped and large which will be infallibly after twice or thrice shooing; do it at the change, or about the fourth or fifth Day of the new Moon.' The moon has also been associated with the horse in mythology through its link with Diana–especially in its form of the horned crescent, a frequent *motif* in horse trappings, and also one of the symbols of a secret society of horsemen. This will be discussed later, but it is convenient to mention here the link between the moon and silver. The new moon, the horned crescent, was the symbol of the goddess and silver was her own particular metal in Greek mythology, probably owing to the association of the colour of the moon and the metal; thus the turning of silver in our pockets at the sight of the new moon is a true superstition–a left-over from a very ancient belief; and at one time the practice was undoubtedly a gesture of worship like making the sign of the Cross.

[1] Mircea Eliade, *Images and Symbols*, p. 127.
[2] *The Compleat Horseman*, London, 1711, p. 104.

Most of the above instances can easily be recognized as the product of the primitive form of reasoning—like begets like. But empiricists all over the world—and here and there an occasional scientist—are far from being convinced that there is nothing more to the beliefs than this. While readily admitting that the *explanation* of the moon's influence is fallacious they argue that this does not in itself dispense with the fact; and some of them maintain that it has not yet been proven that the moon has, for instance, no influence on growth and the weather. The theory has been put forward tentatively by some scientists that as the moon affects the movements of the tides, so it may well influence the rise and fall of the water-table —that elusive but very real level which is well known to farmers and water-engineers who have to sink artesian wells in the drier parts of Britain especially in East Anglia; and no doubt many of them would not dismiss too hurriedly the contention of the old Suffolk well-sinker who never dug his wells while the moon was waning, simply because 'the water was going away from him'. But as far as is known no research has been done on this theory; and it is difficult to see how it could be done under suitable experimental conditions.

But an Italian scientist, Girolamo Azzi has approached with an open mind the universally held belief that the moon has an influence on plant growth; and he has done a great deal of work in an attempt to establish the truth or the myth in the belief.[1] Although his findings are not conclusive either way, his method of approach will undoubtedly be valuable as a basis for further inquiry; besides, the care and application he has given to the whole problem may induce us not to dismiss the whole complex of the belief merely because a large part of it is so patently myth. Azzi's main thesis grew out of the observation that it sometimes happens that a plant, in spite of apparently optimal environmental conditions of rain, temperature, and soil, does not develop as it would be reasonable to expect. He gives examples of varieties of the potato from the 'Equatorial-Andine' region of South America which cannot develop their tubers in Europe in spite of practically identical conditions of soil, tem-

[1] *Agricultural Ecology*, London, 1956, p. 123.

perature and rainfall, with those in the mother country. This, he says, is due to the difference in the length of the day. At the equator day and night are the same length—twelve hours—right throughout the year. Towards the Pole, at 60 degrees north the shortest day is six hours eight minutes, the longest eighteen hours seventeen minutes. At an intermediate latitude—Rome, for instance—the length of the day varies between nine hours four minutes to fifteen hours nine minutes.

near Framsden

This difference in the length of the day—Azzi claims, and he is supported by other scientists—has a definite influence on the development of the plant, anticipating, delaying or sometimes excluding the formation of the flowers—the organs of reproduction. Following these observations he divides agricultural plants into two categories: plants which prefer a short day that, in their case, encourages and accelerates flowering; and those plants which prefer a long day for identical reasons. Between the two categories is a number of plants that appear to be indifferent to the varying lengths of day and night. Among them are the plants of equatorial countries. To illustrate this he described an experiment with wheat—'the most outstanding example possible'. He calls the time when the plant is exposed to light the *photoperiod*, and concludes that we must assume for every plant the existence of an optimal photoperiod and of two photoperiodic limits (one for excess: too long a period of day), and one for deficiency (too short a length of day). By using artificial light (twenty-five candle-power) in his experiments he found that it frequently had a positive action in artificially lengthening the day. Although he considered that the light had no direct effect on the photosynthesis of the plant, it was responsible for lengthening the day and bringing forward the flowering of a long-day plant.

All this led him to pose the question whether the light of the moon does not, in fact, have some effect in accelerating the flowering of long-day plants, and conversely in retarding the process in short-day plants. And to illustrate this he gave an example of the result of practical observations on a long-day plant, the lettuce: 'According to experienced farmers lettuce sown when the moon is waning is well-developed vegetatively, producing a voluminous and juicy

head; if sown with a rising moon the plants rapidly go to seed without forming a good head.' In other words, sowing with a rising moon in fact artificially prolongs the day. Although photosynthesis does not take place, the mild lunar glow ensures that there is a connecting link between two successive days: the plant, that is, 'ticks over' and the vital processes are not abruptly interrupted as they are in conditions of total darkness. Azzi cautiously sums up his findings by saying, 'A certain analogy between the phenomena of photo-periodism and the effects of the moon seems to exist'; and, 'In these cases, as in many others which are empirically admitted, but not yet scientifically proven, it could be affirmed that the period of time between new and full moon is a favourable one for reproduction while the period between the full and new moons would be favour-able to vegetative growth'.

Some of the above experimental material was part of the tradi-tional lore of North America; and a record of this suggests that[1] generally speaking the waxing moon is the season for planting above-ground crops like grain and cereals; and the waning moon for underground or root crops. The same source gives an additional aspect of the moon belief. It was once thought that storing food below ground level helped to preserve it: silos were at one time not tall buildings but pits in the ground (the word itself is derived from the Greek word meaning pit). The ground, it was thought, helped to insulate the food against the harmful effect of moonlight. For the same reason pickling and canning were never done during the period of a full moon. This belief is not as ancient and 'away-out' as it appears, for there is a hard-to-believe report from the U.S. Weather Bureau (Department of Agriculture) in 1903:[2] 'That moonbeams or rays produce certain chemical results seems certain. It is known that fish and some kinds of meat are injured or spoiled when exposed to the light of the moon.' All of which seems to echo the Psalmist who implies that the moon can cause a 'stroke' at night equal to that of the sun by day; and it argues that the East Anglian housewife who spreads her stained white table-cloth on the grass on a moonlight night to get out the stains is not hopefully indulging in sympathetic magic but is using this power of the moon's rays to get it completely white for her.

The age-old belief that the moon affects the weather has also received examination in recent years by two groups of scientists

---

[1] Eric Soane, *The Seasons of America Past*, New York, 1958, *passim*.
[2] *Ibid.*, quotation.

working independently—one group in America, one in New Zealand. The two groups reported their findings in the American periodical *Science*[1] and their main conclusion is that there is a marked tendency to heavy rain in the first and third week of the lunar month; that is, in the period immediately following the new and full moons, and a corresponding tendency towards a lack of heavy rain in the other two weeks of the month. They were able to offer no explanation of how the moon causes these effects; and in the short space of three years their observations appear to have gained one of those shelves in limbo which are reserved for interesting scientific facts that either have not gained general acceptance or have not been harnessed to practical use.

[1] September 1962.

15

Harvesting the Crop

AFTER the crops were sown they were, as we have seen, sometimes ceremonially blessed at Rogationtide. But there was a continuous watching and waiting on the crop while it was growing: weeding—a slow and arduous job up to forty years ago when each thistle or dock was cut with a weed-hook or a *spud*—hedging, fencing, and ditching so that the crop was protected from stray animals and from the dangers of a water-logged soil. This need to watch and wait on the growing crop, and to take instant decisions, depending on the weather and the condition of the land and the young corn—whether to harrow or roll it and so on or, harder still, whether to do nothing to it at all—has given arable farming its distinctive character; and the difference between the corn and the grass farmer is still noticeable even today. A farmer who is a member of the committee of one of the national farming organizations illustrated this recently in a conversation with the writer: 'If we are together discussing some plans for a future date, the grass farmers can usually say definitely: "We'll be there. That date will suit us." And this is months in advance. But I've noticed that the arable farmers are much more cautious. They can only say: "Well, it depends on how we're fixed: what the weather's like; and what is the state of the crops." '

The seasons, in fact, have always had a rather different significance for the pastoral farmer of the west of Britain and the corn farmer of, say, East Anglia. In the Atlantic climate of the west the seasons are not as well contrasted as they are in the near-continental type of East Anglia with its greater range of temperature and its comparatively low rainfall in summer. But the essential difference—although this stems largely from the differences in the climate—

lies in the fact that the pastoral farmer specializes mainly in animals
while the arable farmer specializes chiefly in crops. This is to state
the obvious; but what perhaps is not as obvious is that spring and
autumn are seasons that are not of such great significance to the
pastoral farmer as to his arable counterpart. For the grass farmer
the year was traditionally and essentially divided into two seasons:
the time when he could turn out his animals to graze, and the time
when he was compelled to keep them indoors.

combine harvesting - Stour Valley

This gave the old Celtic division of the year: winter and summer.
The animals were taken out on 1st May and returned to their
winter shelter on 31st October—dates which still have their significance as May Day and All Hallows Eve but which were once the
most important divisions of the year in the Celtic calendar. These
also were the ancient divisions of the year in all parts of Britain
before the coming of agriculture, and these festivals were still
retained in those areas in which agriculture developed; and the corn
festivals proper were later grafted on to them. Thus in East Anglia
we still find remnants of the old, pastoral division of the year and
the festivals and beliefs connected with it as a sub-soil to the corn-

myths which came with arable farming from the Middle East and are essentially the myths of classical Greece and Rome. The two main pre-agricultural festivals were held on these important dates, May and Hallow E'en; and it is significant that they have always been associated with witches whose chief festivals they were. There is strong evidence that the witch cult dates from the period before the coming of agriculture to Britain; and this suggests that it is a survival of the primitive rites whose original purpose was to promote increase in animals.[1] The two cross-quarter days, 2nd February and 1st August, were also witch festivals; and it is very likely that originally both these lesser festivals were also connected with animals. For the Christian *Candlemas* festival was essentially an adaptation of the old Roman festival of *Lupercalia* which was held in early February in honour of the god Pan, the god of shepherds, who was responsible for protecting sheep from the rapacity of the wolves. In this festival naked youths, representing the god, paraded round the streets slashing passers-by with whips made from the skin of a sacrificed goat; burning torches were also carried; and both these were undoubtedly apotropaic devices, symbols of the actual methods used by shepherds to keep away wild animals. The *Lammas* festival was also connected with animals—at least in East Anglia. For this was the date when animals—sheep especially—were allowed to graze on the land that had just been cropped for hay. This was a fixed custom and fell at a natural time at the end of the hay-harvest. It was called *Lammas Shack* in Norfolk to distinguish it from *Michaelmas Shack* which was the custom allowing the animals to feed on the stubble after the corn-harvest had been taken.[2]

Some evidence will be brought forward later to support the suggestion that the witch cult was a survival from the pre-agricultural period and was concerned chiefly with the fertility of animals, as were the rites of all those primitives who depended on their animals to keep them alive. But there is also day-to-day evidence of the regard with which some of these festivals were once held: this is the

[1] M. A. Murray, *The Witch-Cult in Western Europe*, p. 12.
[2] K. J. Allison, *Agric. Hist. Review*, Vol. V, Part 1, 1957, p. 19.

place they hold in traditional weather rhymes and sayings, the Candlemas rhymes, for instance, like the following:

> *If Candlemas Day is bright and fair*
> *Half the winter's to come—and more.*

and sayings such as: 'If we get three frosts before 11th November (All Hallows Eve under the old Julian calendar) we'll be sure to have a mild winter.'

To sum up: the particular nature of arable farming in the past, arising out of its main task of the careful and protracted tending of the corn-crop and its ability to regiment a strong labour force at certain definite periods like the corn harvest, has made for a more rigid and hierarchical social structure. It has also helped to condition the folk-life of the region, making for a direct correlation between the old customs and beliefs and the demands of the actual growing and harvesting of corn. To give one example: knowing the ancient belief in the link between plant growth and the phases of the moon we would expect to find numerous aspects of the belief here in East Anglia. We found that this was so. We should also expect to find a rich complex of beliefs relating to the myths of corn growth and abundant examples of the customs connected with its harvesting.

This again is true; and these beliefs and customs once enlivened and profusely decorated the villages of East Anglia; but it is not proposed to list them here as they have already been described elsewhere.[1] Yet it should be added that many of these old customs have lasted up to recent years, and may still be observed where corn is still harvested and carted in the old manner and stored in the stack. Within the last year or two the old fertility practice of decorating the last load of corn with green boughs still went on. The green bough, moreover, was then placed in the stack of corn and remained there until it was threshed, perhaps six months later. 'It got pressed down,' one old farm-worker related, 'like green leaves put inside a book.'

Harvest customs have also shown a remarkable continuity with regard to their form; and there is no need to search for abstruse reasons for their survival for centuries almost unchanged. They mirror the structure of arable farming which in its reliance on animal power and cheap and easily available human labour remained up to sixty years ago essentially the same since the Romans farmed in Britain. Harvesting under the old economy was a quasi-military operation: disciplined labour had to be brought to bear quickly and efficiently at a time chosen by the weather. It was like an attack to beat an ancient enemy; and for hundreds of years it was organized on these lines. The corn harvest was gathered in by a regiment of workers marshalled under a Lord. As we know from the fourteenth-century Luttrell Psalter, the harvest Lord summoned up his workers in precise army fashion by blowing on his horn. The Lord of the Harvest used exactly the same method down to the early years

[1] *A.F.C.H.*, chapts. 11 and 12.

Framsden barn

of this century in south Cambridgeshire; and in Mendlesham, Suffolk, during the same period, a substitute harvest horn—a hollow hemlock stalk—did service to summon up the women and children to bring their *elevenses* and *fourses* into the harvest field. The Mendlesham farmer[1] who recalled this added: 'The hemlock was a very tall plant with a grut thick owd stem which we used for a horn. It's a very rare plant now round here. You hardly see any. It was done away with because it was poisonous to cattle. If a cow ate hemlock, she was finished.'

Frazer has suggested that the harvest-supper had a sacramental character,[2] and that the flesh eaten on this occasion was once regarded as an embodiment of the Corn Spirit that inhered in the

[1] Charles Brundish.
[2] *G.B.*, Part V, Vol. 1, p. 303.

green bough just mentioned or in the Maiden or Corn Dolly, a more sophisticated form of the same belief. Whatever the original significance of the meal, the harvest supper or *largesse-spending* was the most memorable occasion of the year in East Anglia; and the meat—usually beef—was rarely eaten at any other time of the year by the men; not because there was some sort of taboo on it but simply because their wages at that time rarely allowed the enjoyment of any meat other than pork or bacon which usually came from an animal they, or their neighbours, had reared themselves. Under the old pre-1914 economy, workers and small-holders in many Suffolk villages formed little 'pig groups' and made arrangements to supply one another with pork. Thus by killing their pigs at pre-arranged times each member of the group would be ensured of meat over an extended period. 'A quarter of pork' was usually the amount sold or exchanged; and the custom is illustrated by an entry in a small farmer's[1] account book for 1899: ¼ *pork—18s. 4d.* This preponderance of pork in the Suffolk farm-worker's diet has left its mark in the dialect where a *chowpork* (chew pork) was an old synonym for a *clodhopper* or *swede-basher*—that is, a real country dweller.

But certainly one of Frazer's suggestions[2] regarding the extraction of money from any strangers who came near the harvest-field gives a deeper meaning to the custom in East Anglia of '*Hollaing Largesse*'. Originally, it is suggested, the stranger was considered an embodiment of the Corn Spirit. This was a dubious role for anyone to have thrust upon him, as we know from those counties where there was a competition in the harvest-field to see who cut the last sheaf of standing corn.[3] The reapers stood with their backs towards it, and turning round threw their sickles without properly sighting it. The man whose sickle actually cut the corn was roughly handled because it was considered that the Corn Spirit had migrated from the last sheaf to his person. It is suggested that the rough handling was the vestige of what was once a fertility sacrifice. And though, as far as is

[1] Charles Garrard, Stowupland.
[2] *G.B., ibid.*, pp. 227–9.
[3] *F.L.H.*, p. 104.

known, there was no rough handling in the *Largesse Crying* as practised in Suffolk, there was indeed a threatening aspect to it; and it appeared that passing strangers would refuse to contribute to the Largesse fund only at their own peril. This is confirmed by an old farm-worker[1] from the parish of Framsden: he recalled that whenever a stranger passed the harvest-field all the reapers downed tools and crowded to the hedge and shouted humorously but with half-serious undertones: 'Largesse or revolution!' This was extortion under threat, however playfully covered up; and the extraction of money for their harvest-supper from total strangers does suggest that they were acting under the licence of an ancient custom that had been harnessed to a more practical and understandable occasion.

In Suffolk the largesse-spending usually took place in the long room of the village inn, or sometimes in the *Lord*'s cottage when tables were set outside for the meal. Afterwards there was singing and dancing—*stepping* it was often called in East Anglia. Occasionally the jollification took place on the *knoll*, a small piece of green which many villages seem to have had before the coming of the motor age.[2] The name knoll is directly connected with a communal occasion such as this; and the village green was called a knoll either because it was situated—ideally—on an eminence, or because a small mound of earth was raised near its centre as a seat for the fiddler or accordion player who provided the music. Villages on the Welsh border possessed a similar knoll or green, known there as *twmpath chwarae* or playing hillock.[3]

Selling the corn crop was the last activity in the farming year;

[1] Samuel Friend, born 1888.
[2] e.g. Blaxhall and Little Glemham.
[3] Trefor Owen, *Welsh Folk Customs*, p. 96.

and this did not altogether escape the application of that primitive form of reasoning that had been applied so liberally to the rest of it. In west Suffolk, it is said, certain farmers once maintained that the corn market could be gauged by the rise and fall of Barton Mere—a stretch of water not far from Bury St Edmunds. A direct sympathetic relation was assumed between the level of water in the mere and the level of corn prices in Bury market. The same principle underlay a method of divination, performed on New Year's Day, of corn prices for the ensuing year. It was used by a seventeenth-century farmer from north Suffolk:[1] 'Take twelve principall graynes of wheat cut of the strength of the eare, and when the harth of your Chimney is most hot, sweep it cleane. Then make a stranger lay one of these Graynes on the hot hearth: then mark it well. And if it leape a little, the corne shall be exceeding cheape. If it lye still and move not, then the price of corn shall stand, and continue still for that moneth. And thus you shall use your twelve Graynes, the first day of every moneth one after another; and you shall know the rising and falling of Corne in every moneth all the yeere following.'

---

[1] Katherine Doughty, *The Betts of Wortham*, London, 1912, p. 80.

16

Animals on the Farm

IF OUR thesis is right there should be in this arable farming region not only an abundance of old customs and beliefs relating to the cultivation and harvesting of corn but also a corresponding lack of those concerned with animals. This is true if the writer can judge from his own experience of collecting these beliefs in East Anglia. Compared with the richness of the corn and ploughing customs those relating to animals are meagre. (An exception is the horse; and we should expect this to be so, for the horse was for centuries the chief means of power[1]—apart from human power—on the arable farms of the region, and therefore the most important animal on most farms. He remained so even after the coming of steam power to the farm about the middle of last century; it was the motor tractor, within the last twenty years, that displaced him almost entirely.) We have only to compare the rich cattle lore of the traditional pastoral regions of Britain[2]—roughly the Celtic countries—to realize that the way the land has been farmed was a powerful determinant of yet another element in the folk-life of the region.

Nevertheless, there were a number of interesting East Anglian practices relating to cattle; they were similar to practices in other regions and they should be recorded if only because they illustrate the principles that underlie these practices everywhere. The first is the placing of a cow's afterbirth on a thorn-bush. The same custom was practised with sows and mares. In clearing up after the birth the horseman or stockman took the placenta and threw it over a white-

[1] The horse displaced the ox comparatively early in East Anglia. v. p. 197, also Robert Blomfield's *Farmer's Boy*: 'No groaning ox is doom'd to labour there'.
[2] v. Thomas Davidson's, *Rowan Tree and Red Thread*, London, 1949, and *Cattle Milking Charms and Amulets*, Gwerin, Vol. II, No. 1, 1958.

thorn, usually on a remote part of the farm where it remained until it had rotted away. The dynamic of this belief is pure contagious magic. While the placenta was on the thorn-bush there would be an unbreakable link between the animal and the bush; the thorn-bush was the *quickset* which as its name implies is always abundantly alive. This would ensure that the animal would still remain *quick* or fertile and would breed again next season; or alternatively, that the offspring of this particular birth would grow into a fine foal or calf, which was only a different application of the same principle.

Suffolk horsemen of the old school invariably followed this practice; and many stockmen also. One stockman[1] said: 'We allus used to do it, take it away from the *nethus* and throw it over a thorn hedge, somewhere out of sight. But then the milk inspectors started to come round. One on 'em saw us a-doing it, and they didn't like it. So we left off.' The custom was world-wide, and Frazer lists numerous examples. He also gives instances of the careful disposal of the human afterbirth and the navel-string in order that no harm should come to the mother through a dog or any other animal devouring it.[2] This belief was also held in East Anglia; and the writer recalls a Cambridgeshire woman giving a warning about the disposal of the placenta: 'You got to be very careful to bury it deep enough so that the dogs won't get hold of it.' A district nurse in Suffolk has noticed a reluctance, especially in country areas to burn the placenta. Burying is the accepted way of disposing of it, chiefly —she believes—because this has always been the practice, and probably not because many people believe in the continuing link between the mother and the severed part of her. But even in this apparently neutral practice the old principle of contagious magic persists in the suggestion that the best place to bury the placenta is under a grape-vine.

An analogous custom was once practised in Montgomeryshire:[3] *foul* or foot-rot in cattle was cured by a similar form of magic. If a cow had *foul* and lay down to take the weight off her affected feet, she must be observed as she got up. Then the piece of turf on which

[1] Caleb Howe, born 1886, Helmingham.
[2] *G.B.*, Part I, Vol. I, p. 182 ff. and *Aftermath*, p. 53.
[3] J. E. Jones, Dollas, Berriew.

she had placed the bad foot must be cut out of the ground and thrown into a thorn hedge. This would ensure that the disease would soon disappear.

At one time the practice of burying a beast to stay the plague in a herd was widespread in Britain and it survived in East Anglia into this century. Undoubtedly the beast was once buried alive as a sacrifice or propitiation to the powers the farmer had inadvertently offended:[1] '(They) caused ane hole to be made in Maw Greane; and the cow was put quick in the hole and all the rest of the cattle made thereafter to go over that place, and in that devilische manner by charming they were cured.' In more recent years the beast was either first killed or buried after it had died from the disease. In both Suffolk and Norfolk it was buried in a gateway so that the other cattle would in their normal route pass over it. This was a fairly common practice on Suffolk farms within living memory; and if a cow *slinked*[2] her calf, the carcase was buried in a gateway as a matter of course, as a precaution against contagious abortion.

In some regions of Britain farmers introduced a billy-goat into the cowshed to prevent the spread of abortion among the cattle; and it is likely that this practice still survives. A search in East Anglia has not revealed that it was followed here; but there is a recorded instance of a billy-goat being housed recently in a racing-stable at Newmarket. A horse called *Golden Fire* was so nervous that it proved almost impossible to train him;[3] 'His (the trainer's) head-man suggested that a goat might have a calming influence. Soon afterwards a goat called *Munsy* was introduced to *Golden Fire* who quickly reformed.' The horse reformed to such purpose that he immediately won two handicaps. There is a theory that the first case of contagious abortion always gives rise to an epidemic; that the smell of the dead foetus triggers off a physiological mechanism in the other cattle in the cowshed so that they are immediately affected. The theory sounds far-fetched but it is worth examining later in connection with the sense of smell in the horse. Yet it can be stated

---

[1] Thomas Davidson, *op. cit.*, p. 49.
[2] Aborted—an East Anglian term applied only to cattle. The mare *slips* her foal; the ewe *warps* her lamb.
[3] *The Times*, 9th May, 1961.

here that biologists have turned their attention to animal odours by extensive research only in recent years; and the field is such a large one that it would not be too much to say that work on it has only just begun. If this theory is true, then the prevention of abortion spread could be explained in this way: the malodorous flank gland of the billy-goat would cancel out the inhibiting odour caused by the first abortion and thus prevent its spreading. In the case of the race-horse it could be maintained this is just another instance of a nervous horse taking a liking to an unusual stable companion (a donkey often served the same purpose). On the other hand, granted that a horse is extremely susceptible to odours, it may well be that the goat's smell masked another odour, undetectable by the human nose, but which was particularly offensive to the horse, and would, as we know from other instances, be a sufficient explanation for his extreme nervousness.

Cretingham

Some ingenious applications of the principle of sympathetic magic were to be found in animal breeding. One Suffolk horse-leader for instance, was always careful that the sun did not shine into his stallion's eyes while he was serving a mare. If this happened, the foal, he maintained, would be born with four white feet, a most undesirable trait which always made a horse suspect. This is similar to the device observed in Wales (Carmarthenshire)[1] where

[1] J. V. Price, Agricultural Education Centre, Witnesham, Suffolk.

a cow about to be served by a bull was placed in front of a white-washed wall or barn to ensure there would be a preponderance of white in the coat of the resulting offspring. This, again, was a universal practice; and one of its most detailed examples was to be found among the Nez Percé Indians of North America: this was the tribe which bred the Appaloosa strain of horse.[1] To ensure that the spots were well placed on the colt, the pregnant mare was marked with a special kind of paint, prepared from a secret formula and applied at the correct time with the aid of certain magic words. This practice of attempting to control the markings of an unborn animal has a long history, and recalls the resourceful Jacob's peeling of the rods of green poplar, hazel, and chestnut and placing them in the gutter of the water troughs when the flocks and herds came to drink:[2] 'And the flocks conceived before the rods and brought forth cattle ringstraked, speckled and spotted.'

Not many unorthodox remedies for the cure of sick cattle have been found in this area, and the contrast with the abundance of horse-cures is noticeable. But here is one from Wetherden near Stowmarket: the date is the last part of the eighteenth century. It is of interest because it implies the importance of a sweet-smelling *nethus*.[3] 'For the use of Cattel: Take rue, sage, wormwood and lavender—a handful of each. Infuse them in a gallon of whit wine vinegar in a stone pot covered close. Set on wormwood ashes (?) for four days, after wich strain the liquid through a fine flannel and put it into bottles well corked. Into every quart bottle put a quarter of an ounce of Samphire, the herb the Liquor is mad from. Set it in a tub in the cowhouse. The cows are fond of the smell, and every morning and night when the cows come to be milked Dip a Sponge in the liquid and rub the Nostrils and Mouth of the Beast well.

'If a man or woman would keep a box with a Sponge Dipped in the liquor when they go where any infection is, only rub their temples, nose, mouth, and palm of the hands and (they) will not catch any Disorder. It is therefore propere for nurses who attend the sick, physical gentlemen and Judges who try prisoners coming

[1] Frank Gilbert Roe, *The Indian and the Horse*, New York, 1955, p. 154.
[2] *Genesis*, 30.
[3] From the papers of Benjamin Batt, Ipswich and East Suffolk Record Office.

from a jail. This is a fine thing for those troubled with the hiddake to smell on.'

Not much material about pigs has been found in this area, but there is a well established belief in Suffolk that pigs can see the wind; or at least they have, by some means or other, fore-knowledge of the coming of high winds. A pig-farmer in west Suffolk said that he had noticed that pigs are extremely sensitive to wind and generally have no liking for it: it is possible that they react bodily to a change of air-pressure before the wind actually begins to blow. Physio-logical explanation or none, many people still believe in the pig's traditional gift as the following story shows: 'They say round here (the Stowmarket district of Suffolk) that pigs can see the wind. If they go wild and go a-rooting at the straw there'll be a gale, sure enough, before the end of the day. I once knew a man named Buckle who was up sawing off the branch of a tree. The tree was a hedgerow one, next to a field with a lot of pigs. Suddenly, for no reason at all, the pigs tossed up their heads and went running around like mad things. A bit later this man Buckle fell off the tree; got on the wrong side o' the branch he was sawing, or suthen like that. Anyway, down he come. His mates saw him fall and ran towards him. As they came up to him he was a-picking himself off the ground. And one of them said to him: "Why did you come down, Buckle?"

' "Well," he say, "I see the pigs a-tossin' up their hids and a-caperin' about, so I know they'd seen the wind. So I thought to myself I'd better git down right quick afore it gits properly a-started." '

It is difficult to throw any light on this belief by referring it to any principle like sympathetic magic; and it is fairly certain that it is a true superstition—a *stand-over* from an ancient religious cult. Robert Graves suggests[1] that pigs were sacred to the ancient Mother Goddess who also had charge of the four cardinal winds. This is probably the original reason for *pig* being a taboo word among fishermen when they are afloat. The importance of the pig in ancient Ireland is significant[2] and it is evident from the old Welsh tales of the *Mabinogi* that the pig had a powerful numen in early Britain.

But other animals were believed in this region to give indications of coming bad weather: 'If a thunderstorm is brewing the cows get uneasy, and often they run round the meadow as fast as they can go, their tails sticking right up.' 'Before the rain comes cows in the field will often lie down together with their heads in the same direction—into the wind.' Horses are always uneasy before rain, shaking themselves frequently; and this has given rise to the saying: 'It's a-going to rain. Listen to the horses a-rattling their chains (traces).' A gamekeeper[3] said: 'When I was at Livermere I used to notice that not long after the cattle had moved over to the shelter of a belt of trees on the other side of the lake, rough weather would soon follow. You can forecast it, too, by watching the birds. One evening the

[1] *W.G.*, p. 435.
[2] *I.F.W.*, p. 117.
[3] William Baker, Woolpit.

partridges wouldn't settle down. They kept rising and dropping, rising and dropping. Then suddenly a covey rose and made straight for some high ground not far off. Then covey followed covey to the same spot. The pheasants went running alongside the hedge and made for low ground where they perched on the bottom branches of some pines. I went home that evening and said to my wife: "We'll have some weather before long." About three o'clock that morning we had the worst thunderstorm I've ever experienced.'

17

The Smith and the Old Beliefs

THE richest combination of beliefs and customs relating to the farm
in East Anglia is undoubtedly centred in the heavy horse. Up to
recent years when horses still worked on the farmlands, the blacksmith was a key figure in the phalanx of craftsmen who were concerned with the horse directly or indirectly—the wheelwright, the
harness-maker, the horseman himself, and the country tailor; and
we should expect some of this richness to crystallize around him and
around his forge. But the smith was a great figure of interest in his
own right even before horses were his chief concern. Moreover, the
fact that he was deified or highly honoured in so many cultures—
Tubal-cain, Hephaestos, Vulcan, Wieland or Volundr—is a measure
of the awe with which he was regarded in early times. At first, too,
a man who could hammer sparks of fire out of an object was looked
upon with fear, as someone who was in league with the Underworld
or the Powers of Darkness. For this reason, and from their ingrained
fear of iron, primitive people preferred to let travelling smiths, the
early ancestors of the tinkers, risk their souls by working in iron and
having traffic with the Devil.

In spite, too, of the archaeologists' dating of the Iron Age as
beginning about 500 B.C. in Britain, iron was a very costly and a
comparatively rare metal for centuries afterwards. It was only
when the rich mines of northern Europe were opened in Carolingian
times that iron became material for really common use, ceasing to
be a precious metal reserved chiefly for arms and the more costly
tools.[1] This period—the sixth to the ninth century—is a stamping
ground for guess-work, but it seems tolerably certain that this access

[1] Lyn White, Jr., *Medieval Technology and Social Change*, p. 40.

of iron was at least partly responsible for the winning of the farm-lands of Britain, particularly those on the heavier clay soils. For during this period the Anglo-Saxons used their heavy plough with its share, coulter, and hake—all made of iron—to such purpose that by the eleventh century they had given these farmlands a form that in some counties lasted right up to the present century.[1]

The smith, therefore, even when iron had become plentiful and he had outgrown the superstitious awe that surrounded him, still remained a special figure in an economy that depended so much on iron ploughshares and iron coulters, iron queues or tips for the hooves of oxen and shoes for the horses; and some of his ancient eminence in the order of the countryside has remained to this day in many of the legends surrounding him and his craft. 'The smith,' a Suffolk blacksmith said, recounting one of them, 'is the next best man to the Lord. For the Lord changed water into wine and the smith changed old iron into new; and if you ask a smith how he got the frills at the bottom of his leather apron he'll probably tell you something like this: The blacksmith was once considered the most important man next to the King. So when the King gave a feast to all his craftsmen he had the smith sitting next to him in the place of honour on his right hand. There was a little bit of jealousy among the other craftsmen because of this; and the tailor who was sitting opposite the smith particularly didn't like the favour shown to him. He said nothing, though, but while the feast was going on he quietly took out his scissors and slyly snipped the smith's leather apron under cover of the table, putting his malice into every cut in the leather.

'Of course,' the blacksmith explained after he'd finished his story, 'you haven't got to believe one word of it! I myself cut the frills in the bottom of this leather apron I'm wearing; and I did it for a very good reason. Often when I'm hammering a piece of hot iron, the scales drop off on to the anvil and mess up the work. To get rid of 'em, I only have to lift up the edge of the apron, bunch it in one hand, and I've got a brush that'll sweep the anvil clean with one flick.'

[1] W. G. Hoskins, *Provincial England, The Highland Zone in Domesday Book.*

The smith's difference from other men is also shown by the privilege he alone has of mounting a horse-shoe with points downwards. Any other person who uses the charm mounts it points uppermost: it would be at his own peril to do otherwise, so it is believed. And the smith's privilege is confirmed by the mark of his trade; for the badge of the Worshipful Company of Farriers is a pyramid of three joined horse-shoes each with its points downwards.

But many smiths, even in modern times, occupied a privileged position in the countryside because they shared the old farm horsemen's apparently magical secrets. Whether there was a tight organization of horsemen in this region similar to the *Society of the Horsemen's Word* in north-east Scotland, or whether there was merely an informal inner ring of the most knowledgeable, the blacksmith—or at least some blacksmiths—was admitted to their secrets. In the initiation oath of the Scottish horsemen the smith or farrier is mentioned as the only person other than a true horseman who is entitled to share their lore. This was probably no more than a recognition of what became in time an accomplished fact; for the forge and the *travus*, the little annex where the horse is actually shod, were the very stage and spotlight of that horse-control in which most of the skills and secrets of the Horsemen's Society were concentrated.

But to turn to the role of the smith as skilled craftsman, or artist-craftsman such as the smith we are considering now.[1] He had to go through the rigours of a long apprenticeship of seven years, following the medieval pattern. He spent five years with a master smith

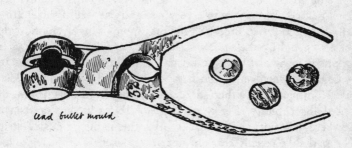

lead bullet mould

after which he had to pass a practical test. He then went for two years as an improver to another smith, a stage corresponding to journeyman in other crafts or trades. After this term he returned to his original master, as a master of the trade, qualified to set up as a smith in his own right. The smith has described some of the customs linked with his apprenticeship. There was a kind of initiation ceremony similar to the harvest-field initiation and the ceremony of First Nail.[2] A new apprentice was seized by the men in the smithy, and a nail was driven into the heel of his shoe until he shouted, 'Beer!' This word was his bond of agreement to pay for a pint of beer for every man working in the smithy: it was a kind of token payment on entry into his apprenticeship. In the Brandeston forge there was a four-and-a-half gallon barrel of beer always kept under a bench; and the men got their allowances, such as First Nail, from

[1] Hector Bradlaugh Moore (The Forge, Brandiston) who has kindly given most of the material for this chapter.
[2] *H.I.F.*, pp. 203–4.

here. As the boy grew accustomed to the gruelling work at the forge, and his muscles began to harden up, he was given one of his first tests. He had to bend down, put both forearms under the anvil and lift it off the floor of the smithy. If at first he was unable to do this, he kept trying during the course of his apprenticeship until he had successfully completed the test. This, no doubt, was a device to emphasize to the lad that he needed not only skill and intelligence but main strength to follow the craft of smithing.

Hector Moore told an apocryphal story[1] about an apprentice which nevertheless points to a very necessary aspect of the smith's craft—the need for accuracy. At the beginning of his apprenticeship a boy was told by the master-smith: 'If you follow this job, your working day will always begin with a big W; but dew you stick to it, my boy. And when you've finished your time, I'll give you a Golden Rule.' This promise either stirred the young lad's imagination or excited his cupidity. For a *rule* in Suffolk, as among craftsmen elsewhere, is a ruler; and a blacksmith's rule is the graduated strip of brass that he usually keeps in a narrow pocket along the leg of his trousers or overalls. The boy said nothing further, as he had already built up a picture of a kind of ceremonial ruler of gold, something of great value that would be presented to him as soon as he finished his apprenticeship—something he could keep in an honoured place on the mantel-shelf, or wherever the family treasures were shown, as an earnest that he had truly served his time. But when, however, he came to the end of his apprenticeship, the smith told him: 'You have finished your time to my satisfaction. You are now a master-smith and I can give you the Golden Rule. Here it is: *Measure twice and cut once*'; astringent advice to the young smith but advice that would have a wider application than simply to the niceties of his own craft.

The skill of a good smith needs no paeans here; but the standards he set himself and the care he took to carry them out are epitomized in the story from another village. It concerns a wheelwright, a

---

[1] Many such stories were once told in the smithy—the gossip-shop or news exchange-mart under the old community. This, it seems, was the smithy's ancient reputation; as it is reported (C. Kerenyi, *Prometheus*, p. 74) that, according to an old Nordic law, a man was not held responsible for what he said at the forge.

fellow craftsman whose shop was usually next door to the forge in most East Anglian villages. A wheelwright who specialized in making farm-tumbrils and wagons could tell if one of his own vehicles was passing on the road merely by the sounds it made. It could be dark, and he could be indoors but he had only to hear it to say: 'That's one o' mine.' The same wheelwright, as soon as he had finished a wagon, made a practice of having the horses harnessed to it immediately. He then had someone to drive it out on to the road, he himself walking behind the wagon for a few miles, listening intently all the while to the sounds it made to make sure it was running true. If he detected an unfamiliar noise, he would have the wagon taken back to his yard; and he would not let it go to its new owner until he was satisfied he had remedied the fault.

One of Hector Moore's skills which gets little exercise today is the *crystallization of axles* belonging to wagons and tumbrils from the farms. *De-crystallization* would be a more apt description of the process; for before the use of modern bearings in a wagon wheel it was necessary after a time to treat the axle—to de-crystallize it. Owing to the intense friction and the resultant heat in that part of the axle near the collar, there was a re-alignment of the iron molecules which tended to crystallize. The axle then became so brittle at this point that a sudden jolt—the wheel dropping into a pot-hole or encountering a large stone on the highway—often caused it to snap off completely without warning. Occasionally a farmer brought in a wagon for repair and took the precaution of telling the smith: 'Do the axles at the same time, will you?' By this he meant that the smith should treat the axles so that the weak, crystallized sections should regain their former temper. The following recipe for the process was given to Hector Moore by an old craftsman. It is headed: *Crystallization of Axles*. 'All forge pieces should be brought to a white heat and then plunged into a receptacle filled with raw Flax Oil. I have applied this process for many years to the Axles and Springs of common Vehicles and it has always proved successful.' Raw flax oil was unboiled linseed oil: the boiled or refined oil was the kind often used for horse-draughts.

Brandeston smithy

When the smith made wagons and tumbrils with the wheelwright one of his jobs was to weld the axle. An axle came from the foundry in two sections so that it could be welded together at its centre to give the exact length required by the wagon or cart it was to serve. But it was no use preparing one end of the section without first tying a sack tightly round the collar end and dipping the whole into water. If this were not done, when the section was hammered the vibration would cause a re-alignment of the molecules at the collar end, and it would fly off exactly as it did after being subjected to the friction of a fast moving wheel as described above. Dipping the sacking into water caused it to contract, thus tightening itself round the axle and preventing the vibration from reaching the collar. It is worth noting that the place of salt in the welding process was often not recognized by some of the older smiths. They used to maintain that sand out of the pit was no use for welding: it had to be sand from the seashore. Pit sand, however, was equally effective if a little salt was added to it. Sand, it appears, is used as a flux in welding, and the presence of a little salt in the sand facilitates the process, keeping the temperature down and preventing oxygen from mixing with the carbon in the steel.

Brazing—the making of a joint in metal with the aid of brass or *spilter*, brass with a high proportion of tin in it to give it a low melting point—was another process that relied on traditional skill. A clear fire was essential: 'Whatever you do, don't put the *green* coal on it—plenty of cinders, that's all. Heat the iron till it's cherry-red then sprinkle borax on it: as the spilter runs it fuses the two faces of the metal to form a joint.' One old smith who worked with Hector Moore some years ago used to insist that the borax must be rubbed into the metal with a piece of cherry-wood; and he kept a piece of the wood in his pocket just for this purpose. Commenting on this example of sympathetic magic the smith said: 'If I'd asked him why he had to do this, he'd probably have knocked me down. It would have been like questioning his whole way of life!'

Another process in the smithy attracted a good deal of speculation up to a few years ago; and it was wrapped round with much mystery and secrecy. This was the tempering of *mill-bills* or -*picks*, the steel wedges used for *dressing* a mill-stone, making the grooves in it more deep and roughing or *cracking* the grinding surface. This implement is about eleven inches long with a cutting edge at either end. It was fitted into a wooden holder or *thrift* which was usually turned from a piece of wych-elm. After the millwright had used the bill for some time, the cutting edges became blunt and the bill lost its temper. He then took the bill to the smith to have it re-tempered and

sharpened.[1] This was a skill that few smiths possessed; and in
recent years, at least one East Anglian farmer who used to have a
mill in his barn for grinding grist for his cattle, has had to discon-
tinue this: he dismantled his mill and sent it away for scrap chiefly
because no smith in the district could temper a bill satisfactorily
so that he could keep the mill-stones properly dressed. Most mill-
stones in East Anglia were made from French burr; and to cut this
stone the steel at the tip of the bill needed to be hard enough to
scratch glass; that is, it had to be almost as hard as diamond. Some

millwright's bill and thrift

of the smiths who knew how to temper mill-bills liked to surround
their skill with a little mystery; though undoubtedly many of them
believed in the efficacy of their secret tempering mixtures which
were said to be essential to their skill. The following letter is
a comment on this belief: it is from Reginald Lambeth, Rural
Industries Organizer for Cambridgeshire: 'I thought I saw your
ears prick up the other day at Bury St Edmunds when I mentioned
Bills and Thrifts. The story is that, when I was working in Cambridge University Metallurgical Laboratories during the war, out of
curiosity I took a Vickers Diamond hardness test of a bill, and I was
astonished to find that the centre core which is made of silver steel, as
a rule, gave a higher reading than any nickel chrome armour-piercing
bullet. I mentioned this to Dr Tipper, Mr Douglas Searle and one
or two other professional metallurgists, and they asked me to bring
some more along for testing.

[1] *H.I.F.*, p. 201.

'On testing we found that they all gave an equally high reading. This has never been explained, neither had the professional metallurgists any theory or explanation to offer and dismissed it as just a freak or a piece of folk lore, as scientists naturally would. I might mention that Dr Tipper was probably at the time one of our most distinguished metallurgists: she also had no explanation.

'I returned these to Mr Ruffell, the blacksmith of Horseheath, with a request for information; and he told me that the secret lay in quenching the steel. As you know, a bill is made up of a piece of sheet silver steel sandwiched between two pieces of mild steel and forged together by a fire-weld. This keeps the inside hard and the outside remains ductile, which means that in use the bill more or less sharpens itself by the mild steel outsides wearing away and exposing the silver steel. When this is all welded together in a sandwich and roughly ground up, it is put in a fire to about 650° C. which is in colour a dull cherry red. It is then quenched in water from his own well that contains certain chemicals which made it specially hard. This, of course, from a scientific point of view is absolute bunk: it has no scientific foundation whatever. Nevertheless, Mr Ruffell gets results with a piece of steel which will cut millstone grit or French burr stones. I have heard of other smiths who quenched in either horse urine or even cabbage water.

'To harden a piece of steel you quench to reduce the temperature drastically and suddenly; and it doesn't matter quite what you are quenching in as long as the temperature is reduced suddenly. Often if you want a piece of steel not too hard—that is, brittle hard—you quench in paraffin or oil. It may be that in this case it quenches the silver steel not quite as drastically as hard water would. Owing to the chemical properties of either the water from the well, horse urine or cabbage water, there may be some tempering effect: the two latter do, of course, contain considerable chemicals, but what I do not know as I am no chemist.

'Mr Ruffell has a great reputation for making all edged tools; and the people in the neighbourhood swear by his billhooks. Very often a blacksmith will make an edged tool out of an old wagon strake, that is the segment of iron which covered the joins in the felloes of a wooden-axle armed wheel. This is because the iron made before a certain date, say before the Industrial Revolution, was smelted with charcoal. When a blacksmith is using real iron for wrought iron work he has to be careful not to quench it in water, but to let it cool off gently; as this too would harden up if the temperature was reduced suddenly.'

One Suffolk farmer, however, had no doubts where the secret lay, and put his money on the tempering mixture. A blacksmith was known to have great skill in sharpening mill-bills, and it was generally agreed that his tempering liquid held the secret. The smith naturally declined to discuss the question. Therefore the farmer called on him one morning, determined to break the secret. The ostensible reason for his visit was to pay a five shillings account he had with the smith; and he purposely offered him a £1 note in payment. While the smith was out of the forge getting the change, the farmer took an empty bottle out of his pocket and quickly filled it with the liquid from the tempering vat. He later sent the specimen to be analysed for which the analyst charged a fee of £5. The result of the analysis was interesting, though perhaps not to the farmer: the water contained no appreciable amount of any substance except iron rust.

After hearing the question of the critical factor in tempering mill-bills so often debated, Hector Moore determined to settle it to his own satisfaction once and for all. He sought the help of his friend, Jesse Wightman of Saxtead, the last millwright of the old school in Suffolk. He first of all unearthed two old recipes for secret quenching mixtures, both of which claimed to be able to give bills the best possible temper. One was for preparing a mixture of ground borax in a quart of hard water and then adding the mixture to a gallon of ordinary water—and so on. Another was for a mixture made with potassium ferro-cyanide which had the very necessary warning *Beware of Fumes*. He had used both these formulas before but after long experimenting over the years he had come to the conclusion that he could do as well, even better, without any of the so-called secret mixtures. He determined, however, to try one more experiment, and he asked the millwright to bring him twelve bills for sharpening and re-tempering. Jesse Wightman soon brought the mill-bills and the smith divided the bills into two lots, marking six of the bills with a mark of his own. These he tempered using one of the old traditional and secret remedies—the borax and hard water, as it happened; the second, unmarked, six he tempered using nothing but water from the tap. Then he gave them to the millwright:

'You take these two lots, Jesse,' he told him. 'Don't pity 'em. Give 'em a good testing, and tell me afterwards which lot you think the best.'

Jesse Wightman was working full-time on dressing mill-stones at that time—about fifteen years ago—as most of the bigger farmers used to grind the grist for their animals and had oil-driven mills of their own on the farm. It was not long before he returned with the used mill-bills. His verdict was:

'These six bills are as good as any I've used,' he said. Then pointing to the six unmarked bills: 'But this lot is much better: and I shan't hope to find any more bills to equal them.'

They were the bills the smith had treated according to his own method and they confirmed his theory that there was no mystery about it and his opinion that the tempering mixture was not critical. As he explained afterwards: his method was simply an appreciation, arrived at through long experience, of the right temperature at which to quench the bill. His way of testing the temperature of the heated

steel was lightly to run his thumb and fore-finger over the end of the bill, just touching the metal. From experience he could feel the right temperature and choose the right moment to make his quenching. He also pointed out: 'Once you've dipped the end of your bill into the pail of water, you have to make sure to change the water before quenching the other end; for the first dipping of the bill has raised the temperature in that water by a few, very important degrees.'

Some smiths tested the time for quenching the heated bills by observing the changing colour of the metal. Cherry-red was also the important colour here; and as it could easily be missed in daylight and the right temperature accordingly exceeded, the process was best performed after dark—a circumstance which would be likely to increase the mystery in the eyes of the uninitiated or the casual observer.

The technique of horse-shoeing[1] has remained virtually un-changed for centuries although the early medieval shoe was fashioned from plate-iron as distinct from the bar-iron of the modern shoe. But each county, and often different districts of a county, had a characteristic shoe of its own, or a shoe with its own peculiar mark. The clip is one of these marks: this is the tab of metal which is turned up from the shoe itself onto the side of the hoof to give the shoe stability. The position of the clip depends on the tread of the individual horse, but even more so on the type of surface he works on. A horse puts his foot down on a hard surface in the same way as on any other. But there is a big difference in the result: if the shoe hits an obstruction the hoof tends to continue its forward motion, thus bending or even breaking the nails that hold it to the hoof. The clip is made on the toe of the shoe to prevent this; and where the dangers of an uneven surface are greater two or more clips are put on each hoof. Conversely, in those counties or regions where the going is fairly soft and even—the Sussex downs or the downs of Dorset—no clips are needed: for the same reason a race-horse requires no clips on his shoes. In very stony country a shoe with a broad web—a much wider shoe—was used to protect the horse's foot from the stones; and, in general, early shoes were

[1] Lyn White, Jr., *op. cit.*, pp. 57–8.

much broader than modern ones for the same reason. The calkin, the wedge of iron at the heel of the shoe, often had a design peculiar to the district; and in the north, even up to modern times, smiths made shoes with calkins on the toes as well as the heels, probably to suit the hard conditions under which they worked. But an expert smith could tell the mark and style of a fellow smith in the same county, merely by a glance at the shoe; and this was particularly true of earlier times when communications between one area and another were not as good and individual and county styles tended to become more differentiated.

We know this from an account of the escape of Charles—later Charles II—after his defeat in the battle of Worcester. He was in disguise, trying to reach the south coast and a ship to take him to France. He got to Charmouth near Monckton Wylde in Dorset:[1] 'Meanwhile my Lord Wilmot's horse was being shod, and the prick-eared blacksmith Hamnet viewing the remaining shoes said: "This horse hath but three shoes on, and they were set in three several counties, and one of them is Worcestershire;" which speech of his fully confirmed the ostler's suspicion that one of the inn's guests was the King . . .' Another incident in this escape has a link with villages in East Anglia. To complete his disguise Charles had

[1] Quoted in A. C. A. Brett, *Charles II and His Court*, London, 1910.

previously rubbed his hands on the back of a chimney and then on to his face. Now: 'My Lord Wilmot cut his hair, untowardly notching it with a knife.' Charles, who was supposed to be an ordinary villager, looked less like one than ever: 'Then Richard came with a pair of shears and rounded the King's hair.'[1] Richard Penderel was a Cornish countryman who was helping the royal party to escape. He knew the proper drill and the proper instrument for cutting hair country fashion—that is, with a sheep shears; a method that lasted in East Anglia[2] and in other regions, notably Sussex, until the beginning of this century.

[1] *Charles II and His Court*, pp. 52–3.
[2] *A.F.C.H.*, p. 50.

18

Hag-stones and the Evil Eye

AT THE beginning of this century some farm horsemen in East
Anglia hung a flint stone with a natural hole in it on the door of the
stable. They often tied a piece of iron such as a key to the flint:
sometimes they suspended the flint by a piece of string or wire just
above the horse's head or back as he stood in his stall. The two
following accounts hint at its purpose. The first is from a Suffolk
harness-maker who was born in 1900:[1] his business specialized in
making and repairing farm-harness: 'In a farm about two or three
miles from this village a gentleman told me that one of his mares was
very upset during the night. Every morning when he went in, she
was all covered in lather—all of a sweat, as we say. And one of his
friends told him to try and get a flintstone—a round flint to hang up

in the stable. He found the particular flint that he required and hung
it up in the stable nearly over the centre of the mare's back: I should
say, roughly about eighteen inches above head height. And he
assured me that cured the mare. In the morning when he went to
the stable his mare was quiet and calm; and he assured me, as I say;

[1] Leonard Aldous, Debenham.

"Blast, bor, that done the trick." The flint had a hole in it and was hung up by a piece of wire.

'Since this occurrence at this particular stable I took notice when I went into the other stables, because I used to go round to collect the harness repairs. And in several other stables I noticed this flint hanging up. I took particular notice then, because after this one or two people told me that it was to keep the horses calm at night.'[1]

The second account comes from an eighteenth-century veterinary manual:[2] 'I have been surprised at the Stupidity and Ignorance of the Vulgar who believe that their Horses are rode in the Night by Sprites and Hobgoblins because they find the Creature all of a damp Sweat in his stall, as if he had been a Journey; never considering that if the poor Horse did not sweat thus and Nature throw off the Superfluities of the Grass Food he (through want of care in the Owner) lives upon, that he would soon be in a much worse way than sweating in the Stable. But when the Piece of old Iron or Hollow Stone has been over his Back a week or a Fortnight on a String, and the Horse better taken care of with respect to Food and Exercise, the Filly Bitch-daughter leaves him; although he is in far better order for her riding than he was before. But I leave the Reader to judge in what the Remedy consisted: that is, whether it was the Charm or the other Requisites I have spoken of, namely, good Keeping and Exercise which performed the Cure, if it may be said to be a cure; which I apprehend it may, seeing all Creatures that are not at the proper standard of Health may be looked upon as diseased.'

The practice was once common, also, in other parts of Britain: in Sussex[3] the flint was hung in windmills as well as in stables; and it was much used in Scotland[4] and Ireland. Frazer records[5] its

---

[1] *cf.* Herrick's *Hesperides: Hang up hooks and sheers to scare*
    Hence the hag that rides the mare,
    Till they be all over wet
    With the mire and the sweat.
    This observed, the manes shall be
    Of your horses all knot free.

[2] Henry Bracken, *The Travellers's Pocket Farrier*, London, 1755, p. 32.

[3] R. Thurston Hopkins, *Old Water Mills and Wind Mills*, London, 1931, p. 172.

[4] Thomas Davidson, *Gwerin*, Vol. II, No. 1, and *I.F.W.*, p. 304; also *The Holed Amulet and Its Uses*, J. G. Dent, *Folk Life*, Vol. 3, 1965.

[5] *G.B.*, Part VI, p. 162.

use in eastern Germany where it was believed that cattle were especially exposed to the attacks of witches on Walpurgis Night (May Eve): 'To protect their animals prudent farmers placed crosses on the door of the byres, also three horse shoes and holed flints.' The flint had various names in different areas of Britain: a holy-stone, a ring-stone or a hag-stone. The last name is the most descriptive of the purpose of the stone, for a hag is another name for a witch. Aubrey wrote in his *Miscellanies*: 'To hinder the Night Mare they hang on a String a Flint with a hole in it (naturally) by the Manger; but best of all, they say, hung about their necks. . . . It is to prevent the Night Mare *viz*. the Hag from riding the Horses who will sometimes sweat at Night. The Flint thus hung does hinder it.' Attaching iron to the stone gave it additional potency, it was believed, in repelling witches and all evil influences.

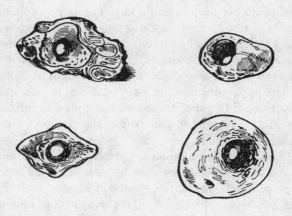

But what was the significance of the holed flint and what principle was supposed to make it effective? There can be no doubt after examination of some of the flints so used in East Anglia that the hag-stone is a symbol of the eye, the hole standing for the pupil. It is, therefore, equivalent to the All-Seeing Eye which has always been an apotropaic device all over the world; this gives the flint its power as an amulet. It serves the same purpose as the painted eye or oculus on the prow of boats belonging to Mediterranean fishermen, especially Sicilian, who use it to this day. The square-and-compasses symbol once common on Scottish boats is very similar to the oculus if it is turned on its side; and it is suggested[1] that the triangle enclosing the All-Seeing Eye, used in Freemasonry, is the design from which the square-and-compasses symbol derived. This is confirmed from another source:[2] 'The lamb, the dragon (or serpent), the dove above the altar, the triangle enclosing the all-seeing eye (common to Freemasonry) as well as the sacred fish-symbol . . . are the silent witnesses in the modern Christian churches of the symbols of paganism.' In the Egyptian traditions the eye is a symbol of Horus who is identified with the moon, a very significant link when we are discussing the use of the eye-symbol in connection with horses. The myth[3] records that Horus, the son of Osiris and Isis fought with his uncle Set and lost an eye in the combat. Thoth restored the eye of Horus by spitting on it; the eye thus became a symbol of all sacrifice. Its use as a symbol may, therefore, be a propitiatory one, a protection against evil influences not by the sacrifice of an eye but some object that will serve for it; or it may be a direct attempt at identification with the god as is suggested in its use by fishermen: by painting the eye on the prow of the boat they hoped to induce the god to take part in the enterprise in person, thus assuring themselves of success.

The symbol was also worn on the person, as a costly stone; and Westermarck, the Finnish anthropologist, has pointed out:[4] 'The splendid ornamentation in the Alhambra is in a great measure founded on designs which are at the present day still used in Morocco as amulets against the Evil Eye; conventionalized images of eyes or eye-brows and various combinations of the number five, representing the five fingers of the hand with which the evil influence emanating from the eye is thrown back on the eye itself—is, in a

[1] T. C. Lethbridge, *Boats and Boatmen*, London, 1952, p. 60.
[2] W. Y. Evans-Wentz, *The Tibetan Book of the Dead*, London, 1957, p. 4.
[3] *G.B.*, Part IV, Vol. 2, pp. 121–38.
[4] Quoted by H. R. Hays, *From Ape to Angel*, London, 1959, p. 186.

symbolic manner, put out.' Belief in the evil eye and the use of the
palm of the hand with the five fingers extended to ward it off is still
to be found in Greece and Italy today.[1] The eye-symbol as used in
primitive art has also been taken over by painters of the modern
school, though not out of any regard for its original ritual or
apotropaic properties but for their own purposes of design; and
probably, too, for the shock synthesis in one picture of both modern
and primitive elements as though the artists are painting an instinctive and symbolic commentary on the presence in modern,
technological man of large areas of primitivism or irrationality.
They seem to be drawing attention by these symbols to an aspect in
himself which twentieth-century man persists in ignoring; and in
so doing they are making a kind of visual or plastic counterpart of
the work of Pareto, Freud, and Jung. Picasso,[2] for instance, in more
than one painting or drawing has used the full, front-elevation eye
in the profile of a face (just as the Egyptians did for ritual purposes);
a device that would seem to have been the starting point for the
fusion of two angles of a head on the same canvas.

[1] See also: F. T. Elsworthy, *The Evil Eye*, p. 127.
[2] *v. The Sculpture Studio* (Etching, 1933); *Les Demoiselles D'Avignon* (Oil, 1907);
Young Woman Drawing (Oil, 1935); see also Marc Chagall's *The Green Eye* (1944).

The holed flint has been used as an amulet up to this day in Suffolk, and in a place other than the stable—although the principle behind it is the same. In the village of Woolpit it is hung on a bed-post as a preservative against *nightmare*—a use which emphasizes the origin of the word. A woman from the nearby village of Beyton also recalls that her grandfather used a similar precaution about fifty years ago. It is evident that the flint was used against something more specific than ill-luck or evil influences. Who, then, or what was the Mare whose night visitations were so dreaded and against which action had to be taken?

19

What Was the Mare?

BEFORE trying to answer this question it will be necessary to turn aside to consider the history of the horse from earliest times. The true or, caballine, horse evolved on the plains north of the great mountain ranges of Asia; and there is general agreement that primitive man first hunted the horse for food. Cave pictures which he drew to give him magical power while hunting these horses still survive; and prehistorians who have studied the paintings of palaeolithic man in the caves at Lascaux in the south of France have pointed out that there is a similarity between the horses depicted and Przevalski's, the most primitive type of horse, a few specimens of which still remain wild in Siberia. But the hunting of wild horses may have gone on long after the horse was domesticated. This, we are told,[1] occurred at some time in the third millennium B.C., and reached Macedonia by 2500 B.C.; it is certain that by 2000 B.C. the horse-drawn chariot had made its appearance right across western Europe, a picture which argues a long preceding period of domestication.

From this early domestication of the horse, it has been suggested, there grew up so strong a link between the horse and man that the horse became sacrosanct: his flesh became taboo and he acquired a sacred or exalted character. This was attributed to his swiftness and the difficulty—as opposed to other domestic animals—of breaking him in. But it is more likely that the horse acquired this 'sacred' character long before domestication; and this is confirmed by what has happened to other animals which have been held sacred in man's history. For the sacred character was acquired irrespective of the

[1] F. E. Zeuner, *A History of Domesticated Animals*, London, 1963, p. 313.

animal's attributes. The pig, for example, is an admirable and very intelligent animal, but no one could say that it has such noble and exalted attributes to merit a claim to a special or ritual regard. Yet the pig, as already inferred, had this distinction in man's history; and even today among certain peoples the pig's flesh is taboo. It seems then that the explanation for the horse's sacred quality is to be sought in that time prior to his domestication, when his flesh was food and, therefore, life to those peoples who eventually sanctified him and held magical ceremonies for his increase.

Food and shelter, the basic essentials of survival, were man's chief concern during that remote period when he existed in the primal undifferentiated horde. He lived where he could get food and if he lived chiefly on a herd of animals he followed the herd about until it dwindled or removed beyond his reach. But the indiscriminate hunting of one species of animal and the over-cropping of one kind of plant must have caused a gradual dividing up of the horde, an apportioning of one plant or animal to a family group or clan within it.[1] The very necessities of surviving dictated a rudimentary differentiation; for starvation was the certain result of a haphazard use of a limited food supply over an extended period. As

[1] George Thomson, *Aeschylus and Athens*, London, 1941, pp. 11 ff.

soon as this dividing off occurred man had made an important step
in his evolution as a social animal: a new organization emerged—the
tribe which could consciously direct a process that had already
begun to evolve of its own momentum: for disputes, rivalries,
seasonal shortages, and the pressure of natural events would have
existed from the beginning and have suggested their own solution:
an agreed apportioning of the available supply of food. And it was
this trend that the tribe eventually embodied in a system.

Thus the animal or plant which had come to be the 'share' of each
family group or clan became in time the clan's *totem*. The clan
developed a direct symbiotic relation with its totem and each member identified himself with it.[1] At definite times of the year—the
breeding time of the animal—they congregated at the breeding place
and performed magical ceremonies to promote the animal's increase.
Australian aborigines who had reached the same stage of evolution
as we are now discussing held exactly the same ceremonies in recent
times: in the Aranda[2] kangaroo-increase ritual, each clan or totem
group was responsible for the fecundity and plentifulness of the
animal or plant it stood for. It was a great responsibility, and magical
aid was sought to help the group carry it out. For the clan was tied
up with its totem, flourishing when it flourished and starving when
the species failed to reproduce itself in adequate numbers.

But this arrangement or differentiation into groups or clans also
had its disadvantages: it meant that a clan, if tied solely to one
animal or plant, would not only have an unvarying and, therefore,
monotonous diet but it would not be much better off than before if
its totem animal failed it completely. Here, however, came another
of those advances forward which moved imperceptibly step-by-step
in response to the pressure of an uncontrolled environment, until it
reached a stage when it became consciously recognized that a new
disposition of the tribe was not only possible but inevitable. This
was the point when it was realized that it would be better for the
tribe as a whole if each clan, instead of *killing* and eating its totem,
consecrated itself to *preserving* it for the use of all the other clans

[1] This is the non-differentiation between subject and object which Levy-Bruhl, in
How Natives Think, calls *participation mystique*.
[2] Ronald Rose, *Living Magic*, London, 1957, p. 75.

in the tribe. Thus the clan which had formerly lived on the horse ceased now to eat its flesh and became concerned primarily with its multiplication, themselves existing on the various other plants and animals preserved by other clans in the tribe. Horse-flesh became for them taboo, forbidden by direct injunction from their headman or priest, and their main function as a totem clan in relation to the horse was to celebrate the magical ceremonies and to implore the ancestral gods – the personification of the tribe with whom the clan became identified – to grant its increase. The animal became identified with one of the gods; and often the theriomorphic ancestor was believed to have been born of the god who was also an animal.

But an important question remains: why did the horse-totem reach such predominance over all the other cults associated with animals at this stage? It is suggested that the main reason is this: when man emerged from the hunting stage and acquired the technique of taming the animals he had formerly pursued, the totemic taboo on eating horse-flesh attained a new economic significance. The extended group, no longer a clan in the totemic sense, would live in part on mare's milk and its derivatives – kumys, cheese and dried curd, exactly as did the Scythians[1] – and mare's flesh particularly remained taboo. Again, the increasing use of the horse as a means of quick transport and as a draught animal, both essentials for a nomadic people, emphasized its social importance. It was natural that this importance should be celebrated in the retention of the original totemic rites long afterwards, when an entirely different stage of social evolution had been reached; and when, indeed, the primitive origins of the cult had long been forgotten.

This, it is admitted, is an over-simplified and over-formalized treatment of the growth of horse-worship: but it is perhaps justified here as a first step to answer the question we proposed, and as a prelude to one of the earliest references to the horse in history: the horse-sacrifice performed by the king or a royal person as recorded in early China.[2] Horse-sacrifice also played an important

---

[1] *Cambridge Ancient History*, Vol. III, p. 196.
[2] Joseph Needham, *Science and Civilization in China*, London, 1954, Vol. 1, p. 90.

and symbolic part in early Indian religion; and, as Jung records,[1] following the teaching of the Upanishads the sacrifice had a cosmic significance: a new state beyond the human was to be reached through that sacrifice. The sacrifice of the horse, in other words, was an analogue of the renunciation of the world, with which it was identified.

Now the sacrifice in its later sophisticated or cosmic form, stems directly from the ritual eating of the horse's flesh at the totemic level. For the clan at its increase ceremonies broke the taboo by ritually eating the flesh to renew their essential identity with the totem: the totem was the clan and the clan was the totem. And the royal horse-sacrifice later retained this feature: the flesh of the sacrificed stallion was afterwards cooked and eaten by those taking part in the ceremony.

The horse-sacrifice has lasted into historical times in many European countries: in Scandinavia,[2] where the horse's blood was sprinkled on the altar and toasts were drunk in a form of communion which linked the worshippers symbolically with the gods of war and fertility and with their dead ancestors; in Ireland[3] horses were sacrificed in the twelfth century; in Wales,[4] even later. At a shrine near Abergele in Denbighshire—Llan Sant Sior—horses were offered to St George. The rich gave a horse to secure the Saint's blessing on all the other horses they possessed. The cult had obviously been Christianized here; and it is significant that near this spot is *Parc-y-Meirch* (The Park of the Stallions) where the earliest and most extensive hoard of horse-trappings in Britain was unearthed[5] during the last century. The hoard dates from the Late Bronze Age.

In the earlier sacrifices the participants, or just the priest alone, symbolically 'took the totem inside him'—ate it, in plain words—thereby joining himself with a wider reality; for the horse was considered as a link between the day-to-day life in this world and the life of the ancestors who had gone to another world, and were

[1] *Symbols of Transformation*, p. 420.
[2] E. O. G. Turville-Petre, *Myth and Religion of the North*, p. 251.
[3] *W.G.*, p. 384.
[4] T. Gwynn Jones, *Welsh Folklore and Customs*, London, 1930, p. 112.
[5] T. Sheppard, 'The Parc-y-Meirch Hoard', *Archaeologia Cambrensis*, XCVI, Part 1, June 1941.

responsible for preserving the animals' increase. But at a later stage, the horse-sacrifice represented a generalized fertility and became the medium through which its spiritual guardian the Earth Goddess could be reached. She was the Ga Mater, also the Mother Goddess who has appeared in various guises and under various names throughout history: Artemis, Diana, Hecuba, the Great Mother, the White Goddess, Hecate, Epona. The names are repeated here because the relation of some of them to the horse will be easily recognized.

The horse, too, now came to be regarded not merely as a spiritual link with the Goddess but also as a kind of psycho-pomp who served to conduct the soul of the departed to the next world and also to see to his needs when he got there. This is the reason why the horse was slaughtered and buried with the chieftain—a practice which archaeologists have confirmed from eastern Asia to Scandinavia.

But in northern mythology the horse's association with fertility is most marked[1] and there were numerous survivals in Britain up to recent times which pointed to this aspect of the cult. Probably the most outstanding is the ceremony of *Crying the Mare* which used

[1] E. O. G. Turville-Petre, *op. cit.*, p. 56.

to be practised in Herefordshire. Here the Mare was directly linked with the Corn Spirit. Reapers left a small patch of corn standing in the field and then fashioned it into the shape of a horse by tying it into four bunches to represent the legs which were then fastened together at the top. The reapers then tried to cut it by hurling their sickles at it. The man who was successful was honoured by sitting opposite his master at the harvest feast;[1] and the 'Mare' was plaited in a variety of ways and kept in the house until the following harvest. The hobby-horses that appear in many countryside ceremonies and ritual dances, notably the *Hodening Horse*, and the *Mari Lwyd* in Wales, also refer to the fertility aspect of the horse cult, and recall the primitives' impersonation of the totem animal at their increase festivals—the wearing of the animal's skin and its most characteristic mark, for instance, the horns.

The *Mari Lwyd* ceremony lasted in Glamorgan to well within the present century. The phrase probably means 'Grey Mare' as Dr Iorwerth Peate has suggested;[2] and refers to the horse's head that was worn by a member of a wassailing party. His companions took him from house to house during the Christmas season singing and reciting their requests for alms. The grey colour in the name of this ceremony is significant and suggests a direct link with the Celtic horse cult. The Celts originated in the areas round the Caspian sea, in the grasslands which formed a natural habitat for the horse; and they were in close contact with the Scythians who were *the* horsemen of antiquity. The Celts, as befitted a nomadic people, prized the horse highly: theirs was essentially a horse-culture; for the horse had carried them across Europe, was venerated as their chief link with the next world, their glory in peace and their pride in battle. It seems likely that some of the horse monuments carved into the chalk downs of southern England, especially those at Uffington and Westbury, were made by the Celts, the worshippers of Epona, the horse goddess. Her name is said to be Gaulish for Mare;[3] and it was in this form that she was worshipped by the auxiliary (Celtic)

---

[1] *F.L.H.*, p. 104.
[2] Quoted by Trefor M. Owen, *Welsh Folk Customs*, p. 55.
[3] T. C. Lethbridge, *Witches*, p. 115.

regiments of the Roman army. The figures of horses in the white chalk of the downs ensured that the goddess would see her creatures' handiwork, especially when the sun was upon them. But the site also provided that these horses, dedicated to the goddess, would be of the right colour—white or grey, the colour linked with Epona under her name of the White Goddess who took another form, as Rhiannon, in the Welsh *Mabinogi*.

farrier's gag

The Germans, too, as we know from Tacitus[1] also kept sacred white horses at public expense, and paid particular regard to their haphazard neighings and whinnyings which they interpreted as a guide to action. This veneration for the horse was kept alive in northern Europe until late in medieval times; and it is probable that this thread in the complicated myth of the horse is most relevant to East Anglia and to the question which this chapter set out to answer. Many horse burials have been discovered in Scandinavia, and their purpose was to provide mounts for the dead to ride to Valhöll. In northern myth[2] Odin, the most powerful of the Norse gods, rode a grey horse called Sleipnir to take him to and fro between the earth and the World of Death. Sleipnir was depicted as an eight-legged beast, probably to emphasize his speed as in a modern cartoon. Like the Valkyries he was the *helhüst* or death horse, and bore the dead swiftly to the other world where they were beyond mortal reach. It was for this reason that the horse-apparition, or a dream that figured

---

[1] *Germania*, X: *hinnitusque ac fremitus observant. cf.* Heroditus, Book III, 84–7.
[2] E. O. G. Turville-Petre, *op. cit.*, pp. 57, 71.

a horse, was always attended with great dread and looked upon as a premonition.

This, then, is the horse or mare which has remained alive in country beliefs and customs up to today: the horse in its role as death messenger, confused—it appears—with the image of the Mare Goddess, Epona, or any other one of her various names. And what were once valid religious images have become debased, in their long passage through time and the buffetings of a newer and stronger religion, to the monster which troubled horses at night and rode them till they were white with lather, or settled on innocent sleepers: an incubus or lamia that gave them bad dreams. But this is the usual course of old discarded images and dogmas: they sink into society's unconscious, the old traditional and unbroken rural culture; or they are kept alive in the games and practices of children who are still inadvertently keeping Epona's memory green by spitting on their finger and wetting the sole of their shoe on those rare occasions when they meet a white or grey horse.[1] But the old cult has left a trace at a more exalted level. It has come through the Middle Ages right up to the present in a form that is seldom recognized, but which can still be traced back to the horse-sacrifice of prehistoric times. As the economic value of the horse became greater, instead of sacrificing the horse itself a substitute sacrifice was made. Clay images of the horse were burnt; or, as in ancient Gaul, instead of burying horses with the deceased,[2] images—rows of horse-heads— were carved on the lintels of the burial chambers to furnish a symbolic escort for the deceased to the land of the dead. This substitute practice survived in England until medieval times; for it was then the rule[3] that on the decease of a tenant the lord of the manor had a right to appropriate his best beast as a heriot. The priest claimed the deceased man's second best beast as a mortuary. But people of substance, on the death of one of their number—the lord of the manor himself, for instance—often walked his best horse, as a customary death due, to the church; and the horse complete with

[1] Iona and Peter Opie, *The Lore and Language of School Children*, London, 1959, pp. 206–7. Spitting is the ancient device of spitting out evil (*despuere malum*).
[2] A. A. Dent and D. M. Goodall, *The Foals of Epona*, London, 1962, p. 15.
[3] W. E. Tate, *The Parish Chest*, Cambridge, 1951, p. 69.

trappings and the dead man's armour followed him in procession to the grave.[1] Although the horse was later sold and the money donated to the church, its presence with harness and trappings at the funeral is patently a ritual one; a link with the time when the chief's horse followed him right into the grave, his mount for his last journey. Today it is not unusual to see a riderless horse following the cortège of a well-known soldier or a person of national repute.

[1] If we should express surprise that the medieval Church tolerated a custom that was manifestly pagan, we have only to note that the Church itself had issued a clear interdict under Canon Law against breaking the taboo on eating horse-flesh. *v.* J. P. Clebert, *The Gypsies*, p. 101.

20

Horse Bones

WE DISCUSSED the taboo on horse-flesh in the last chapter; and what is the most convincing evidence of the former power of the horse-cult is that the taboo has lasted in Great Britain—especially in Ireland—up to the present day. There is still a strong repugnance here to eating horse-flesh, although continentals tell us it is tasty; and an attempt during the last war to popularize it failed completely. But more evidence of the cult comes from East Anglia than any other region of England, and it is worth trying to find out some of the reasons why this is so.

In one of his books[1] T. C. Lethbridge derives the name *Iceni*—the Celtic tribe who occupied eastern England before the coming of the Romans—from an old Celtic word *Eachanaidh*, meaning people of the horse; and he also suggests that the Icknield Way also took its name from the same tribe. Whatever philological support is brought for or against this derivation, it is true that the name of a Scottish clan, the *MacEacharns* who come from the Mull of Kintyre and the nearby islands, is Gaelic for 'Sons of the Horse'; and it is also true that in the eastern counties, the territory traditionally occupied by the Iceni, the breeding of horses has been highly developed throughout historical times. In this region horses made up full plough teams long before other regions changed over from their teams of oxen; and it is recorded[2] that in Suffolk the horse was harnessed to the plough as early as the beginning of the twelfth

[1] *Witches*, p. 79.
[2] v. Lyn White Jr., *op. cit.*, p. 64: '. . . but c. 1191 we discover Abbot Samson of Bury St Edmunds granting lands equipped in one case with a plough of two oxen and three horses (presumably one of them for harrowing), in another case a team of six oxen and two horses, in another manor two more teams similarly made, and a third ploughteam of eight horses.'

century. In this region, too, there evolved one of the best known and most successful of the heavy breeds of farm- and draught-horses: the Suffolk. There is, moreover, enough evidence—as will be shown later—coming from the old farm horsemen themselves for us to infer that the horse tradition in East Anglia is a very ancient one.

The related objects most frequently found in the region are horse-bones placed in buildings for a specific purpose. It may be disputed what in every case the purpose was; but in many instances there can be no doubt that the bones were placed in the buildings to serve as amulets to keep away a visitation from the Mare. Horse-bones have been discovered in the foundations of houses in the Fens and some of them are now in the Cambridge Folk Museum. A horse's leg-bone was found in the flint and rubble packing of a Suffolk farmhouse;[1] and where a horse-bone has been unearthed in a house-floor it is now generally explained as a foundation sacrifice. But horses' skulls were frequently buried under the floors of houses and public buildings for acoustical effect: in Ireland skulls placed under the flag-stones of a house improved the sounds when the occupants danced on them and the following is quoted in Professor Estyn Evans's book[2] on Irish folk-life: 'A good thrashing floor should bend to meet the flail, and in Scandinavia, for instance, great pains were taken in the old days to construct floors which would make the flails sing. They were occasionally strung with wires, and to magnify the echo of the clay floors a horse's skull was buried under each corner.'

A seventeenth-century house in Bungay,[3] Suffolk, once had about forty horse-skulls neatly laid under the floor, the incisor teeth resting on a square of oak or stone. On discovery it was assumed that they had been placed there for improving the acoustic properties of the room; and it was pointed out that skulls were sometimes placed for this purpose under the choir stalls of a church. In Llandaff Cathedral, for example, skulls were embedded in the choir stalls of the south aisle (east). A similar find is reported from a Yorkshire village where horse-skulls were discovered under the flag-stones of cottages that were being restored. 'According to local

[1] Bright's Farm, Bramfield.
[2] *I.F.W.*, p. 216.
[3] Ethel Mann, *Old Bungay*, London, 1934, pp. 253-5.

tradition, if one had a good horse and it died or was put down, it was the custom to take the head and bury it under thus, in order to retain some measure of the virtue and protect the house from evil.'[1] This, it seems likely, was the original purpose of burying skulls in the foundation and the echo effect was at first, at least, subsidiary; and it is relevant to add that later on earthenware jars, sometimes Bellarmines, served as substitute echo-makers for the horse-skulls.

Great Bradley church

Evidence from other sources suggests that the original purpose of horse-bones or skulls concealed in the house was to keep away evil; and the discovery of bones in other parts of the house—even in the roof—points away from the theory that they were symbols of a foundation sacrifice. Horse images as well as bones are to be seen on the roofs of some houses, and they remind us of the mouldings of animals on the ridge tiles of medieval buildings[2] (not very different in their intended purpose from the gargoyles on medieval churches). A notable example is from Old Manor Farm, Fen Drayton, Cambridge, a late sixteenth-century house with corby gables. On its chimney-stacks the head and shoulders of a horse were moulded or

[1] Halton East, Shipton-on-Craven: personal communication from J. G. Dent.
[2] Dr Peter Eden, Cambridge.

cut in brick. T. E. Tegg of Beccles, a former official of the Ministry of Housing, has taken between seven and eight hundred photographs of Tudor houses in Suffolk; and he discovered that many of these had horses' heads carved in brick, usually on the chimney. (The photographs now form part of the National Buildings Record.) He points out that similar horses' heads in brick, rendered with cement to make it resemble stone, are to be seen in the outstanding brick porch of Great Bradley Church, Suffolk. In one of the houses Mr Tegg photographed, Hill Farm, Great Wenham, the owner called the horses' heads *squirrils*.

This, it appears, was also a common practice in north Germany where the horse-beliefs were so strong. C. G. Jung, the psycho-analyst, who was deeply interested in old country myths because he so often found them buried in the unconscious of many of his patients, mentioned the horse myths particularly. He wrote[1] of the belief in the lamias who *rode* their victims, and 'their counter-parts the spectral horses who carry their riders away at a mad gallop'. He also quoted an eighteenth-century Dutch writer, Hendrik Cannegieter of Arnhem, who said: 'Even today, the peasants drive away these female spirits (Mother-goddesses, *moirae*) by throwing the bone of a horse's head upon the roof, and you can often see such bones on peasant houses hereabouts. But at night they are believed to ride at the time of the first sleep and to tire out the horses for long journeys.'

But we must distinguish this, which we might call the use of bones as amulets, from their use to serve a more mundane purpose: the strengthening of mud floors in medieval houses to give the floors a more resistant surface. R. C. Lambeth who lives in a timbered house at Fulbourn, Cambridge, has discovered that the floor in that part of the house which was once an open hall was thick with sheep bones. This was not due to the slovenliness of the early dwellers but to their wish to have a sound, durable floor to their living-room. The practice is well documented, and C. F. Innocent[2] wrote that it was common in the eighteenth century; and he gives an example from

---

[1] *Symbols of Transformation*, p. 249.
[2] *Op. cit.*, p. 159.

a seventeenth-century house (now destroyed) in Broad Street, Oxford, with a floor of trotter bones tricked out whimsically in patterns. The practice is undoubtedly the reason why floors in minor 'follies' such as bizarre summer-houses, have been laboriously built up or patterned with horse-teeth.

No discussion of horse lore could leave out the Gypsies who have been active agents in keeping the old beliefs and practices alive. The Gypsies came into Britain in the early fifteenth century:[1] Wales between 1430 and 1440; Scotland between 1492 and 1505; and they made their appearance in England at the beginning of the sixteenth century. One of the first records of English Gypsies comes from Suffolk where the Earl of Surrey entertained a party of *Gypsions* at Tendring Hall about the year 1520. The Gypsies, coming originally from the Malabar Coast of India, preserved at that time — as to a certain extent they still do today — many of the aspects of the horse-cult which was an integral part of ancient Indian religion. Jean Paul Clebert,[2] the French historian of the Gypsies, says that to them the horse is 'a funerary and psycho-ceremonial animal'; and they practised the two customs peculiar to those peoples who were usually or originally nomads: the taboo on eating horse-flesh (the breaker of the taboo bringing on himself the penalty of madness); and the use of the horse as a funerary animal. In this, as we have seen, the horse suffered ritual slaughter and was buried with his master. In later times the Gypsies appear rarely to have killed a dead man's horse, probably for economic reasons; but they burned his wagon and his effects and sold the horse out of the family. Clebert shows how the ritual burial of the horse was sublimated during the nineteenth century in a Caucasian Gypsy's funeral. For several days after the funeral the dead man's horse was led to his grave fully saddled, and the servant who led him had to call the deceased three times by name and ask him to come to dinner.

As well as being bearers of the cult aspects of the ancient tradition, the Gypsies in Britain have also carried the practical lore that

[1] Brian Vesey-Fitzgerald, *The Gypsies in Britain*, London, 1944, p. 28.
[2] *Op. cit.*, p. 101.

is associated with it—as Brian Vesey-Fitzgerald has so convincingly shown. No people are more skilled in curing (or disguising) a sick horse and few people know more about horse psychology. This is important for our purpose because it will be suggested that some of the old farm horsemen in East Anglia and Scotland also carried much of the old horse cult—not necessarily directly connected with the Gypsies; and as well as following some of its ritual were also out-standingly skilled in the practical application of the ancient lore to the farm-horses that came under their charge.

Clebert has also picked out another facet of the horse tradition in Britain, indicating at the same time that it was one result of the strength here of the ancient horse-cult:[1] 'Let us finally mention that in England the love of horses (which moreover came from the Islamic Orient) gave birth at Chester in 1511 to the first horse-races. The turf remained an exclusively British sport until the nineteenth century.' The Frenchman is probably using England here as a synonym for Britain, because no one could exclude specific mention of Ireland in this context. This statement about the love of horses prompts one to draw attention to the well-defined social caste which is associated with the horse and is strong even now a considerable time after the eclipse of the horse as a transport and draught animal. It is unlikely that historians would recognize the class; but social satirists and cartoonists who used to delight in depicting the *horsey people* would disagree; and the fact that this class appear to be surviving a social revolution argues a tenacity that has its roots in something deeper than the privileges of a ruling minority whose riding on a horse gave them in every sense a claim to a higher station.

Mention has already been made of C. G. Jung's interest in horse myths. He discovered numerous symbols of the old cult in the unconscious of many of his patients: unknown to them they shared these symbols in common; and from long experience of this phenomenon Jung postulated a racial, or collective unconscious as he named it. Using the hypothesis of the collective unconscious he repeatedly demonstrated the correspondence between the figures he

[1] *Op. cit.*, p. 105.

detected there—the archetypes—and the phylogenetic myths transmitted down the ages either orally or in writing. Many of these were
horse myths, and they were—as he pointed out—only another facet
of the horse's appearance as a numinous figure in myth and folk
story. In more than one place[1] in his works he illustrated the
coincidence of ancient horse myth and modern dream. He brings
out, for instance, how in a dream the horse represented 'the dynamic
and vehicular power of the body'—the libido, and was also linked
with death and, paradoxically, with the Mother who is life and
fertility exactly as he was in the historical myths discussed in the
previous chapter.

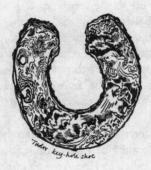

Tudor key-hole shoe

[1] *Symbols of Transformation*, p. 420, and *The Practice of Psychotherapy*, p. 159.

21

Jading and Drawing a Horse

THE last three chapters have been a long but necessary preamble to a discussion of the ancient customs that have survived among certain farm horsemen in East Anglia particularly, but also in north-east Scotland, right up to the recent past. Many of the horsemen who followed and believed implicitly in these practices are still living, and some of these practices and customs have been recorded elsewhere.[1] But much information has come to light since that book was written; and now, in order to put this information into a more clear perspective, it would be as well to restate the underlying principles of the customs and the rationale of the beliefs on which they were based.

One of the most interesting and spectacular devices of the old farm horsemen was the stopping of a horse dramatically so that it would not move. This was called in East Anglia *jading* a horse; and it was from this practice more than any other that the horsemen sometimes earned the name of *horse-witches* because they were able to make the horse stand as though it were paralysed or bewitched. A note in Gibbon[2] shows how ancient this practice was. It concerns the sixth-century Gothic king, Clovis:

'After the Gothic victory, Clovis made rich offerings to St Martin of Tours. He wished to redeem his warhorse by the gift of one hundred pieces of gold, but the enchanted steed could not move from the stable till the price of his redemption had been doubled. This *miracle* provoked the king to exclaim: *Vere, B. Martinus est bonus in auxilio, sed carus in negotio.*' (Indeed, St Martin may be a

---

[1] *H.I.F.*, Section IV.
[2] *Decline and Fall of the Roman Empire*, Vol. 6, chapt. 38.

good friend when you're in trouble, but he's an expensive one to do business with.) It is evident that the priests who served St Martin knew how to jade a horse and to attribute its state to the Saint's intervention; and if Gibbon had had the slightest suspicion of how the *miracle* had been performed he would have used a much stronger form of irony than a mere italicizing of the word itself. For the priests, in fact, were doing exactly the same trick, and probably by exactly the same means, as the old East Anglian and Scottish horse-men who made out and actually believed that the horse's immobility was the result of some secret and magical device they had resorted to. This incident concerning the Saint is also an example of early Christianity's adaptation of the old pagan beliefs, with politic fore-sight, for its own purpose; and, as already shown, traces of the sacred horse-cult remained in Christian ceremony for centuries after this event recorded by Gibbon.

A later instance of the practice of jading a horse is quoted by Margaret Murray:[1] 'Another man-witch, who was sentenced to the galleys for life, said that he had such a pity for the horses which the postillion galloped along the road that he did something to prevent it, which was that he took vervain and said over it the *Pater Noster* five times and the *Ave Maria* five times, and then put it on the road so that the horses should cease to run.' A more recent instance comes from the Suffolk village of Polstead[2] towards the end of the last century: this shows also the same identification of the practice with witchcraft: 'A harvest wagon was coming in from the field when suddenly the horses stopped and refused to go any further. Then someone suggested beating the wheels of the wagon with branches of broom. But still the horses wouldn't budge: they were fixed as if something was holding them to the road. They didn't move either until they got one of the old horsemen: he got them away without any trouble.' The broom plant, it may be noted, was supposed to possess magical qualities as well as being a useful imple-ment at home: the broom stick—that is, the green broom—could sweep out a room or carry a witch. The broom, according to the

[1] *The God of the Witches*, p. 154.
[2] Mrs Kate Rose (born 1881 at Polstead).

witch tradition, could give or blast fertility. Mrs Leather gave a similar instance of jading a horse from Herefordshire[1] but without deducing anything from it except that the old woman concerned was thought to be a witch.

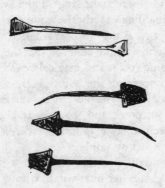

The following example of horse jading happened in Suffolk just after the First World War. It is typical of how an older horseman[2] who had in his possession most of the ancient secrets, was able to deal with a situation that had baffled a younger man. The older horseman tells the story: 'I was coming home with three lovely black horses which we always used on the road; and I used to glory in trimming them up, because they wore the worsted—red, white and blue—and they used to look lovely. I found I'd come to the Wetherden *Maypole*, and there was a chap there with his horses. He said to me:

' "Hullo, Charlie. You're just the chap I want to see."

'I said: "What's the matter now, mate?"

' "Somebody's been *a-doing the saddle up* on my horses and I cannot get these horses away. The trace-horse is backing and the *fill'us*[3] is going another way!"

---

[1] *F.L.H.*, p. 55.
[2] William Charles Rookyard.
[3] The shaft-horse.

' "Wait here a minute, bo'," I said; "I'll tell you what: you've been a-braggin' again, haven't you?"

' "No," he say, "I haven't said a lot."

' "I told you," I said, "you must not brag what you can do, because there's allus somebody as good a man as yourself. Here now," I said, "wait a minute. . . ."

' "What about your horses?" he said.

' "I ain't frightened my horses will run away: it's yours I'll have to look after."

'So I just went a-front there with my milk and vinegar; rubbed it in my palm and fingers; and then I rubbed it inside the horses' nose and then round their nostrils. I then said to this young horseman: "Now hop on your wagon and be off!" and he done so.'

As can be inferred from the above account there is no magical practice involved. Someone had played a trick on the young horseman and had put down a substance that was so obnoxious to the horses' delicate sense of smell that they would not move. The older and more knowledgeable horseman knew exactly what had happened and took immediate steps to neutralize this smell. The substance or substances were placed down either on an object in front of the horse or somewhere on the front of the horse himself. Until the smell of the substance is neutralized the horse will not move forward an inch, resisting all kinds of persuasion and even force. One horseman revealed that he could jade a horse standing, say, on the sandy apron outside an inn simply by walking round him and unobtrusively dropping one of the obnoxious powders in the sand, especially in front of him: 'You didn't have to touch the horse, but that would stop him.' The same horseman also revealed that if this particular device had been used there was no need to use a neutralizing substance. A well-informed horseman simply had to grasp the horse's head firmly and give it a sharp turn and *back* him out of the area that had been contaminated by the jading substance.

One cunning old horseman used to jade a horse simply by pretending to feel the horse's fetlocks, but with the palm of his hand covered with the repellent substance. Later when he wanted to release him he had only to go through the same motion but this time having his hand covered with a substance that would neutralize the smell. And he gulled, and also impressed, the bystanders by lifting up one of the horse's front hoofs, giving it two or three sharp taps with his knuckles and saying confidently: 'Right! He'll go now.'

Many of these secret jading substances are organic; and their number is added to by, for instance, an observant horseman adapting something for his own use. While out ploughing a horseman had noticed a stoat some distance away stalking a rabbit. The stoat was gradually moving round unobserved by the rabbit. But as soon as the stoat got into the wind and the rabbit scented it, the rabbit set up a shriek and remained as though paralysed. It was easy then, as the horseman saw, for the stoat to make its kill. The incident remained in his mind and was reinforced by another experience he had shortly afterwards. He was ploughing a *stetch* not far from the headlands when his two horses suddenly stopped dead. He was too wise and experienced a horseman to attempt to force them to go forward: instead he turned them short and proceeded to plough another *stetch* A little while later he gave his horses a rest, and returned to the spot they had refused to pass. He found a dead stoat lying near the hedge. Reasoning from this he made himself a jading substance compounded of stoat's liver and rabbit's liver, dried and powdered up and added to *dragon's blood*[1] which was a code name among the old horsemen for one of their more powerful jading substances. The same horseman, a stallion-leader, gave another instance of how he made use of the horse's hyper-sensitive power of smell. When his horse staled he kept some of the urine. He corked it down in a bottle until the smell was particularly aggressive. If he wanted to keep his horse away from a certain mare he had only to rub some of the liquid on the stallion's bridle or on the mare to ensure that the horse would not go near her.

In addition to the repellent or jading substances there are the *drawing* or *calling oils*. They have the opposite effect: they *draw* or *call* a horse towards the horseman; but they, too, depend for their effect on the horse's keen sense of smell. The drawing oils are nearly all aromatic oils to which the horse is attracted. The following will

[1] The actual substance is red-gum resin which exudes from a kind of palm-fruit.

show how the name *drawing* arose: To catch a frisky horse or a young colt in a field the horseman placed a little of the mixture of oil of origanum, oil of rosemary, oil of cinnamon, and oil of fennel about his person. The instructions with this recipe which came from an old horseman's notebook were: *Set this mixture by the wind*; that is, the horseman was advised to stand in the wind so that as soon as the colt or horse scented him he would advance towards him. On a warm day, the instructions said, it would be sufficient for the horseman to place a few drops on his perspiring forehead to *call* his horses from a fair distance without saying a word, or making any sound. Another device was to bake sweet-scented cakes to give to the horse as tit-bits:

'*It is For Catching Wild Colts and Vicious Horses on Aney Feild or Common* (For a long distance)

'You must get by the wind and take with you scented cakes made as follows: half lb of oat flower mixed with Treacle and slack baked. Then sweat it under your arms. The cakes to be scented with the oil of origanum, oil of cinnamon, oil of fennel, the oil of rosemary and the oil of vidgin. If you have not time to bake the cakes you must scent a peice of gingerbread and give him that, and it will answer the same purpose.'

The castor or wart that grows on the inside of horse's foreleg was also used as the basis for a drawing powder: 'Dry it in your pocket; great it into powder with a bright file or rasp. And it will be a pure white powder. Put it in a verey Close Box for the purpose. This powder has a great attraction for all animals, and the horse itself. The oil of rhodium possesses peculiar properties: all animals cherish a fondness for it and it exercises a subduing influence over them. Oil of Cumin: the horse has an instinctive passion for this. Both are natives of Arabia. With this knowledge horse taming becomes easy, and when the horse scents the odour he is drawn toward it.'

Drawing oils and jading substances were sometimes used with spectacular effect. A Norfolk man answered an advertisement for a horse-leader in Essex. He went down to the farm and applied for the job. They told him that the horse's previous leader—an old man —had died suddenly. He asked to see the horse and they took him to the stable. When he got to the horse's stall he found it was locked. Then the farmer admitted that there had been many applicants for the job already, but each had been driven out of the stall by the horse. Latterly they had been feeding him by dropping his fodder from a loft above the stall, and lowering down pails of water on a string. The farmer warned him of the danger of entering the stall. But the Norfolk man said: 'Never mind. Give me the keys.' He opened the door, took off his cap and threw it into the stall: 'If that's welcome,' he said, 'so am I.' In a short time the horse came to the door: they put the bridle on him and shortly afterwards the Norfolk man was taking the horse to the smithy to be shod.[1] A similar incident happened in the Hartest district of Suffolk. A vicious stallion had 'got the master' of his leader who could not do anything with him. Someone sent for the narrator's[2] father: 'My father said: "I'll come later on tonight: I'll catch him for you." They couldn't catch this stallion: it was in a loose box and it got on top of the chap who'd been leading it. The chap had tried but he daren't tackle him any longer. That night my father went out after it, but he did something before he left. As soon as he got to the loose box where they had the horse he pulled a little bit of stick about six inches long out of his pocket and threw it right up into the manger. The horse went up to the manger and stood there. Then my father went in and put his headstall on and led him out. But he never did tell me what he'd put on that stick.'

Drawing oils were also used in a more quiet way. A stallion leader had a walking stick which he invariably carried with him when he travelled a horse. The stick had a special feature about it; the horseman had split it at the end, just above the ferrule, and he had inserted a piece of cotton wool which he impregnated with a drawing oil mixture. A similar device can sometimes be seen at a pig-judging ring in a show. An old horseman pointed it out: 'You'll notice at a show that one man's pigs may be standing quite still, though it's natural for pigs to be a-rooting about all the time. The man has something at the end of his stick you may depend—some of the oils

---

[1] From Albert Love, Wortwell, Harleston.
[2] George W. Sadler, Whittlesford, Cambridge.

–and he keeps holding it in front on 'em. You'll notice the difference when you see someone at the other side of the ring with the sweat all over him trying to keep his pigs somewhere in position.' A similar appreciation of the horse's acute sense of smell induced an old blacksmith to keep a bunch of violets in the forge whenever the season permitted.[1] He believed that the smell of the flowers had a soothing effect on the horses brought to him to be shod. In this connection it is worth adding that it was once considered the fashion to wear a little bunch of violets in the coat when riding to ·hounds.

Many of the drawing oils were allied to the conditioning powders which were sold in great quantities up to recent times. These powders helped to keep the horse in good condition; and their essence or oil was often the kind of tit-bit that made an effective drawing substance as well. An advertisement in an eighteenth-century newspaper[2] shows that in East Anglia they have varied hardly at all over a period of two hundred years:

Advertisement

Having fix'd up two large Mills which I work with Horses, for grinding the following Powders with which I'll supply Country

[1] From Miss H. A. Beecham.
[2] *Ipswich Journal*, 3rd November, 1739.

Shopkeepers, upon Cheaper Terms than any Man in London; I sell for Ready Money, and no less Quantities than 14 lb of a Sort; and to any Person that takes 56 lb of an Sort at a Time, I'll allow 2s for every 56 lb on Account of Carriage, or 4s for 112 lb.

Fine Powder Liquorice at 6d per Pound	Powder Gentian at 7d
Ditto second sort at 3d	Powder Bay-berries at 6d
Powder Elecampane at 4d	Root of Liquorice at 5d
Powder Turmerick at 6d	Powder of White Helle-
Powder Fenugreek at 4d	bore Root at 16d
Powder Horse Spice at 4d	Fine Powder of Ginger at
Powder Aniseeds at 6d	34s per cwt.
Powder Cummin seeds at 6d	Ditto second sort at 18s
Powder Diapente at 6d	per cwt.
	Pepper Dust at 30s per cwt.

N.B.: Please to direct for JOHN ROWLEY, Druggist at the Red Cross in the Poultry, London; where may be had all Sorts of Drugs, Chymicals and Galenicals upon Reasonable Terms.

In support of this hypothesis that the horse's sense of smell is the critical factor in most examples of so-called magical control, evidence is forthcoming from biologists who have lately turned their attention to a field that has been comparatively neglected.[1] They point to the great variation in olfactory perception in vertebrates: birds, for instance, have poor sense of smell but excellent vision, and this has a great effect on their social behaviour and their response to their environment. But among mammals smell is the most important sense; and odours can have a direct neural effect on certain animals, and have caused physiological changes in some animals tested in the laboratory. The horse is one of those animals whose nostrils are specialized for high sensitivity; and it is likely that much of a horse's behaviour is conditioned by this highly perceptive sense of smell. In man, however, the sense of smell deteriorated during the later stage of his evolution and now 'it is not so much rudimentary as vestigial'. This will explain why in the use of drawing oils and jading

[1] A. S. Parkes and H. M. Bruce, *Science*, 13th October, 1961, Vol. 134, No. 3485.

substances the horse will react strongly to an odour which a human being cannot detect.[1] Research has also been going on in the University of Georgia on a chemical repellent which, it is hoped, will have early practical application:[2] it will be used to discourage savage dogs, and the United States Post Office Department have already experimented with the mixture.

As a coda to this account of the more sophisticated ways of controlling a horse, here is the down-to-earth method of an old Suffolk farm-worker who thus managed most of the horses that came under his charge:[3] 'You don't stand for any nonsense from the young colts when you put them to work. You got to let them know the first letter of the alphabet, and that's *Whoa!* But if you got a young horse on the plough, and he thinks himself a bit of man at first "go off" and kicks about a bit and get himself into a mess and throws himself down, let him lay there. Then when he's said *Amen*, liberate him; and if you got the *mother-of-a-sloe*[4] draw him one across the *wallows*[5] with it and he'll wonder what's come over him; and he won't trouble you no more. Some people used to have whips. But I niver had one. I used to put my *whip* in the manger – give 'em plenty o' *tooth-powder*,[6] that's as good as any whip you can think on.'

[1] *V.G.*, III, 250. *Nonne vides ut tota tremor pertemptet equorum Corpora, si tantum notas odor attulit auras?*
[2] *The Times*, 23rd March, 1963.
[3] Sam Friend, Framsden.
[4] The sloe is the fruit of the blackthorn: the *mother* is therefore a stout blackthorn stick.
[5] The withers (East Anglian dialect); sometimes also *wallis*.
[6] That is, bait or food.

22

The Milt and the Frog's Bone

BOTH these objects were used as fetiches in connection with the two classes of practices described in the previous chapter—the *jading*, and *drawing* or *calling* of horses. The horseman, that is, who had been initiated—either formally or informally—into these ancient practices believed that in the milt and the frog's bone inhered some power that enabled him to control, enchant or bewitch his horses.

The milt[1] was usually combined with the drawing oils to attract or allure a horse. It is a small oval-shaped lump of fibrous matter like the spleen (milt is, in fact, another word for spleen) and can be taken from the foal at birth. The milt lies on the colt's tongue when it is in the mare's womb: it is very rarely discovered in the afterbirth because the colt almost invariably swallows it. The old horseman was careful to extract the milt from the foal's mouth with his finger the moment it was born. Veterinary surgeons, when they know of the existence of the milt, appear to disagree about its function—as do the horsemen themselves. Some horsemen say its purpose is to prevent the foal's tongue folding back before and during the birth: if this happened the colt would be suffocated almost as soon as it was born. Others say it has no particular purpose at all. But the most convincing explanation of the purpose of the milt comes from a Welsh horse-breeder[2] who said that the milt lies length-ways along the foal's tongue until the colt either ejects it or swallows it. The tongue is slightly folded around it; and the function of the milt is to act as a former to cause the growing tongue to develop a longitudinal fold, or the ability to fold easily in this way when the foal suckles at

[1] Also called the *milch* or *melt* in Norfolk and Suffolk, *meld* in Cambridgeshire, the *pad* in Scotland, the *mummy* in parts of Wales.
[2] J. E. Jones, Dollas, Berriew, Montgomeryshire.

the mare's teats. Without some such former as the milt the tongue would tend to develop in the 'round' and make suckling extremely difficult.

A Suffolk horseman who was born towards the middle of the last century wrote down how he prepared the milt. He included it in a carefully written note-book where he put down all his secret methods: 'Now for all natural Causes I shall give you a alurement. For it is thus: when a mare foale her first foal get the milt. It must be a mare foal for a intire horse and a male foal for a savage mare. Everey living foal spue it up directly they are foaled. First rap it up in a pice of thin white papper jest as it comes from the foal; then put a pice of Brown papper over that. Put it in to a old Baken tin; put it in an oven after the Bread is drawn out when it is not to hot, and perhaps it will have to be put in the oven twice. And when it become cold it will become hard and like a peice of pitch. Let it keep in the papper till you want to use it. Keep it very dry; and when you use it Beat it up into a verey fine powder: mix a smal quantity of oat flower and lunis powder and mix it with pure olive oil and slack bake it in the oven after the Household Bread is drawn. When it is not to hot. After it is baked put it in to a mussiline Bag and sweat it under your right arm. Let him or her get the sent of it, and if he be ever so savage you can take him under your Charge and do aney thing with him: only be kind and gentel to him or her. Sometimes if you put a few drops of rhodium on the cake and then sweat it under your arm it will improve it when you first go to them. But you must not put aney thing Else on it but pure rhodium. The pure rhodium has a portion of the natural scent of the sweat of a man's under his arm, only stronger and it does not take the natural scent from the milt; but all other ingredients will take away the natural Scent. This is the most useful and precious Recipt in the world for savage horses that are so by natural Causes.

'Another Alurement made from the same thing: take the milt and put it in a stone jar. Put a little olive oil on the milt then put a peice of Brown thick papper over it and bind it down tight and plaster it over the white of an egg to prevent the Steam coming out. Set it in the Oven after the Bread is Drawn out, and it will Draw forth an

Oil out of it. Pour the Oil into a small vial. When warm, put a few drops of the Oil of Rhodium and a few Drops of the Ottar of roses in with it and Cork it up air tight. And when you feed or handle your Stallions put a glove on your right hand, and 3 or four drops on the palm of the glove; and you can do what you like with them. For they have a distinctive passion for it; and so they have for them that use it. It is a good thing for Colts of all kinds to make them kind and good tempered. Give them 2 drops on loaf sugar.'

The milt, as one can gather from the above, was not of much effect if used by itself. But in addition to its practical use in this manner it was carried about by some farm horsemen simply as a charm. They believed that possession of the milt ensured that the foal would always be attracted to them and follow them about even when it reached maturity. This belief in the powers of the milt is of very ancient origin. It is indubitably the *hippomanes* of antiquity. Both Pliny and Juvenal mention its use in love potions. It was described as a small black membrane on the forehead of a new-born foal. Virgil mentions it as something different:[1] Robert Graves[2] cites Aristotle and says that the mare normally eats the membrane as a means of increasing her mother-love. Most farm horsemen in East Anglia, however, believed that it was the foal that swallowed it; and unless it was taken from the foal's mouth at the moment of birth it would not be found: it is rarely discovered in the afterbirth itself. It will have been noticed that these accounts are contradictory; but it should not surprise us that the ancients were uncertain about the exact location and purpose of the milt and the reason for its scarcity when it is far from being 'scientifically' established even today what the milt is for and what usually happens to it at the time of birth.

The milt then was normally mixed with some of the drawing oils and used as an *allurement*. But one Suffolk head horseman described how he used the milt as a jading substance when one of his horsemen went out of his place in the hierarchical order of turning out of the

[1] *V.G.*, III, 280.   *Hic demum, hippomanes vero quod nomine dicunt pastores, lentum distillat ab inguine virus, hippomanes, quod saepe malae legere novercae miscueruntque herbas et non innoxia verba.*

[2] *W.G.*, p. 386.

stables for the morning ploughing: 'I used the milch only once to rub on the door when one of the under-horsemen, a youngster, kept a-turning out in the morning out of his proper order. I said to myself: "I can't have that!" So I used the *milch*. His horse wouldn't come out of the stable, and that was the end of that caper: he stuck to his turn after that.' This exceptional use of the milt strengthens the theory that it was used as a fetich, because either drawing or jading substances could be added to it; and it could be equally effective in either case, so it appears. But almost invariably the old farm horsemen in East Anglia used the milt with the drawing oils to allure the horse and to establish rapport with him in accordance with the ancient usage.

In the writer's experience of recording the practices of old farm horsemen the frog's or toad's bone was nearly always linked with the jading of a horse, and they used the repellent substances with the bone, which was either powdered or whole, in this practice. Like the milt it has wide and ancient associations. Many of these have already been described elsewhere,[1] but here is a description by a Norfolk horseman[2] of his way of getting and preparing the toad's bone. It is unusual for two reasons: he used the powdered bone of the toad with drawing oils and substances instead of with jading substances as most horsemen in Suffolk did; again, the description of the actual ritual of getting with all the attendant circumstances is of the deepest interest. He described the whole process as *The Water of the Moon*, presumably referring to its happening in a running stream when the moon was at the full:

'Well, the toads that we use for this are actually in the Yarmouth area in and around Fritton. We get these toads alive and bring them home. They have a ring round their neck and are what they call *walking toads*.[3] We bring them home, kill them, and put them on a whitethorn bush. They are there for twenty four hours till they dry. Then we bury the toad in an ant-hill; and it's there for a full month, till the moon is at the full. Then you get it out; and it's only a

---

[1] *H.I.F.*, chapt. 23.
[2] Albert Love (born 1886), Wortwell.
[3] The natterjack (*bufo calamita*) v. W. A. Dutt, *Wild Life in East Anglia*, London, 1906, p. 203.

skeleton. You take it down to a running stream when the moon is at the full. You watch it carefully, particular not to take your eyes off it. There's a certain bone, a little crotch bone it is, it leaves the rest of the skeleton and floats uphill against the stream. Well, you take that out of the stream, take it home, bake it, powder it and put it in a box; and you use oils with it the same as you do for the milch. While you are watching these bones in the water, you must on no consideration take your eyes off it. Do [if you do] you will lose all power. That's where you get your power from for messing about with horses, just keeping your eyes on that particular bone. But when you are watching it and these bones are parting, you'll hear all the trees and all the noises that you can imagine, even as if buildings were falling down or a traction engine is running over you. But you still mustn't take your eyes off, because that's where you lose your power. Of course, the noises must be something to do with the Devil's work in the middle of the night. I've been lucky enough to get two lots through, but with the third lot I didn't succeed. I think what really happened then [the third time] there was a sort of crackling in the noises as if someone was falling down. It makes you take your eyes off it. Then there was no answer: he [the bone] had no power. He wouldn't answer. But once you got the bone, you take it home, bake it, dry it well, and break it up into powder. You preserve it in a tin or bottle till you want it. Or you can mix it in the bottle with the oil so it's always handy in your pocket if you ever have occasion to use it. You put it on your finger, wipe the horse's tongue, his nostrils, chin, and chest—and he's your servant; you can do what you like with him.'

We shall return to the second part of the old horseman's description: here it is necessary to emphasize that he used it in an exceptional way. Most horsemen in Suffolk did not powder the bone but used it whole and also as a device to jade and not to draw the horse. They also went to a running stream at midnight at full moon, after going through the same procedure with the frog or toad. But after extracting the bone from the stream they cured it in jading substances. They then wrapped it in linen and concealed it about their person: to jade a horse they touched him in the pit of the shoulder with the frog's bone: to release the horse they touched him on the rump. The bone itself is probably the ilium, one of the bones in the toad or frog's pelvic girdle: some say it was the breast bone. Whichever bone it was, it was a *crotch* in shape; that is, a forked bone like a wish-bone, and having precisely the same shape as the frog— the horny elastic pad—in a horse's hoof.

But what is the meaning of this apparently nonsensical ritual of going to a running stream at midnight at the time of a full moon? One thing is clear to the present writer: after talking to many of the older horsemen who had performed it—men born before or about 1890—he became convinced that they were totally involved in the ceremony. They believed implicitly in the effectiveness of their method of preparing and getting the bone, and they were certain that the bone's power stemmed as much from the special treatment it had during the ceremony as from the actual jading or drawing substances with which they afterwards impregnated it. It was no empty show or flippant rehearsal of an ancient practice: they were in deadly earnest, serious and secret about everything concerning the frog's bone, mainly because they felt they were dealing with something that was dangerous. This is identical with the reaction of primitives to a fetich: it is animated by something they cannot understand. And as Levy-Bruhl had pointed out,[1] they cannot distinguish between the fetich and the effective substances that are sometimes associated with it. If, for instance, poison were used with something, harmless in itself but merely used as a carrier, a primitive would think that the fetich is just as effective in killing as is the poison. In the same way, the old horsemen believed that the milt and the frog's or toad's bone contributed almost wholly to their skill in drawing or jading their horses. The situation for them was a total one: and it was from this totality—the ritual killing of the frog, the dismembering and the unusual behaviour of the bone in the running stream—that they gained their conviction.

It is very likely, however, that this ceremony whereby East Anglian horsemen visited a stream at midnight is a vestigial one, and that at one time it was attended by other horsemen who observed

[1] *How Natives Think*, p. 67.

the participant and saw to it that he carried out the ritual correctly. The main support for this theory is that similar initiation ceremonies are being carried out to this day in north-east Scotland where there still exists a tight organization of an ancient horsemen's society or craft guild called the *Society of the Horsemen's Word*. Only in relating the ceremony to what was undoubtedly its original form can we explain the apparently nonsensical and irrational. And it is incumbent upon anyone who studies rural history to make an attempt at a rational explanation because, too often, the marginal or apparently superficial has been impatiently swept aside as negligible and not worth examination, when often there is underneath a hard core of historical fact and enlightenment. Academic fashion avoids the dark and 'way-out' places where no kudos, or at least no kudos that will pay immediate dividends, is to be gained; and much that is valuable to an understanding of our rural culture has already been lost either because it is not considered worthwhile investigating or because academic reputation is too flimsy a covering to risk a few rough journeys into country thickets and morasses. It is in the belief that the marginal is worth spending time over, and in the conviction that a hypothesis—even a wrong one—is better than none at all that the writer offers the following explanations. The truth, after all, is more likely to emerge from honest error than from the present confusion of a subject which is contemptuously dismissed as folklore by many people who—to judge from their position—should know very much better.

The frog, as C. G. Jung has pointed out, is a symbol of initiation. After listing a number of animals so linked, he wrote:[1] 'The frog, on the other hand, stands on a higher level and counts because of its anatomy as an anticipation of man on the level of cold-blooded animality.' It is clear that the frog, because of its similar anatomy, was a surrogate for a human being: it was a sacrifice and also a reminder to the initiate that he would, after the ceremony, become a new human being. He was undergoing a second birth, a birth and entry into a group that would for ever afterwards be his sworn brethren. Some support for this comes from the remnants of the

---

[1] *The Integration of the Personality*, p. 93.

Horsemen's Society in Scotland. For here 'a bone of a more sinister origin' was once used in fairly recent times in the Society. Initiation was one of the most important and notable ceremonies in the Scottish Society; and there is a strong probability – though actual testimony is naturally lacking – that the 'sinister bone' was one of the fingers of a dead child's hand.

A constant thread in the descriptions of the frog's bone ceremony in East Anglia is that great care must be taken in performing the ritual as 'the Devil is looking over your shoulder'. The devil here has nothing to do with the ecclesiastical Devil who is, as far as the evidence goes, a symbol or extrapolation of subjective evil that is in man himself. The devil in this context is undoubtedly the man who was in charge of the ceremony of initiation, the priest or Head Horseman, exactly as he is today in those branches of the *Horsemen's Society* still existing in Scotland and Orkney. He is the man who has the most outstanding or leading personality in the group; usually, too, who is the most intelligent; and he is responsible for the proper carrying out of the ritual by the initiate. To confirm that this interpretation of 'devil' in this setting is the correct one we can again refer to the Scottish society. Here the officiating horseman, or the devil, is vicar for the ancient horned god of fertility, the 'Auld Chiel' who was long ago written down by the Church as the Arch Enemy. He was the old pre-agriculture, fertility god and was maligned and castigated by the Church when it was fighting to establish its ascendancy. To underline this relation to the ancient cult a stirk's (or steer's) foot is used in the Scottish initiation ceremony: the initiate has to grasp the Auld Chiel's hand and the stirk's foot is used for this purpose. The priest of the god took his form, dressing in his skin or using one of his significant marks: the symbol of the horns is also used in the Scottish ceremony, linked in meaning with the crescent moon, which also forms an essential mark. The meetings in north-east Scotland and Orkney are secret, and the place of meeting is carefully guarded by two of the brethren who stay on watch for 'cowans and intruders'. The group rarely meets in the same place on consecutive occasions.

The use of this unusual equipment in the Scottish ceremony

sometimes brings about an amusing situation. A hut in Orkney where a branch of the Society had just met was accidentally burned down shortly after the meeting. The next day the police were calling on farmers in the district to ask which of them had lost a stirk because the remains of a stirk's feet had been discovered in the ashes. They were very puzzled when no one came forward to say that one of their beasts was missing.

Another aspect of the Norfolk account already quoted on page 218 will probably have been remarked by those who are familiar with the form of the primitive initiation ceremony. This is the noises: 'as if buildings were falling down, a traction engine is running over you'. Noise is an essential part of the primitive initiation ceremony because it is the most effective means of impressing or frightening a blind-folded initiate.[1] The old Norfolk horseman gave it as his opinion that the noises 'must be something to do with the Devil's work in the middle of the night'. And he was speaking true, though probably not in the sense he meant. For the leader of the group, the devil, in the Scottish ceremony today provides a certain ordeal chosen by him to test the blindfolded initiate: to determine whether he has absorbed his instructions to trust implicitly in his own sworn brethren in the group, whatever happens to him. One such ordeal at a fairly recent meeting of a group of the Scottish society is related by one of its members:

'The ordeal can involve whatever they've thought up for you. On this occasion I know the meeting was being held not far from a very ancient and very well-known kirkyard where – because it was old – most of the stones were flat. Now at the initiation the entrant was told that if he would leave the room or barn, or wherever they were, and follow a certain path until he came to this kirkyard, and walk down one of the paths in the kirkyard and – say it was a tombstone, number five on the right – grope in there in the dark he would find a whip that would give him for ever more power over any horse that he was likely to meet. He did so, but in the meantime they had already planted one of the boys below the stone so that when he reached in to gather the whip he was immediately seized. Well, you

---

[1] cf. The sudden beating of a gavel on the table in the Freemasons' ceremony.

can imagine in a kirkyard in the black of night what the effect would
be on the entrant. But again here, he was in the hands of a brother,
although he didn't know it. And this is typical of what happens:
they can frighten you but nothing will happen to you provided you
believe in what you're undertaking.'

Here it was not necessary to blindfold the entrant as he was
operated on at night, but the shout in the dark and the seizure of his
hand was aimed at stirring him to the depths. Noise played a great
part in the initiation ordeal of most primitive tribes; and the *bull-
roarer* is an implement designed specifically for that purpose. It
became the frightening noise made by the God, and it was one of
the main instruments for penetrating deeply into the consciousness
of the initiate and clearing the ground for a new alignment. For it is
evident that the initiation ceremony was not simply a rather super-
fluous test of manhood, which undoubtedly it was, but only incidentally. Its main purpose was to align the individual to a new
group consciousness, and this was done not simply by precept but
by first attempting to shake him to the core of his being. For now
he has ceased to be an immature individual and has become a
member of a group each of whom had to a large extent to submit to
the group's will. In return he got the assurance, emphasized by the
ceremony, that nothing would really harm him if he trusted to the
power of the group and to the aid that his fellows, his sworn
brethren, could bring him.

Therefore, the initiation, 'going through the ring', was more than
the symbol of a new life; in many respects it was a new life for the
initiate in a really primitive society. Ronald Rose,[1] a pupil of Dr
Rhine of Duke University, U.S.A., spent six years living among a
primitive tribe in central Australia. His wife and children were with
him. As a trained psychologist he noted particularly the function of
the initiation ceremony from a psychological point of view. The
aborigines were extremely suggestible and the witch doctors were
able to practise hypnosis to gain a variety of effects. The initiation
ceremony, it appears, actually aimed at producing this highly suggestible uniformity in the group; and it is instructive to note that if

[1] *Op cit.*, pp. 161, 215 ff.

a youth did not submit to the conditioning ordeal he was led off into the bush to die. It is possible that the show of violence given to candidates in modern initiation ceremonies when they do not carry out the instructions of their conductor to the letter is a vestige of this final exclusion that was once offered to them. This aspect also comes out in the Scottish society's initiation where the initiate can get slightly hurt if he does not carry out the instructions faithfully. 'At the initiation ceremony, too, while the entrant is equipped to face life, not only is he equipped with a lot of secret and special lore, he is also disciplined, both towards his horse and towards his fellow horsemen. He must, at all time, render aid if called upon to do so. There are special signs which we can give, if we are in trouble with our horses or need a brother's help in any way we make that sign and the brother must assist.'

The noises mentioned by the Norfolk horseman were patently not real but hallucinations, a folk-memory of the time when the initiation ceremony was performed as it is in Scotland today, in the classical manner with blindfold initiates and a hidden band of assistants who supplied the *works*—the whole apparatus of perturbation. The injunction that 'you must keep your eyes on the bone, else you'd get no power' was the prelude to the hallucination. Like the primitive shaman the initiate was hypnotizing himself by staring into the running stream: the noises were what folk-memory told him he would hear; and, expecting to hear them in his highly suggestible state induced by staring into the water, he actually heard these noises; and that they were all, in fact, subjective did not make them any the less terrifying. A similar account of the frog's bone ceremony complete with 'all manner of noises' comes from the Hargrave district of west Suffolk.

One aspect of the frog's bone has not been commented upon. This is the horseman's practice of keeping it under the arm-pit. After it had been cured and kept in this place, if he used it on a horse the animal 'couldn't pull a duck off its nest even if he wanted to'. It is possible that the horseman did this for the same reason as the New Guinea magician mentioned by Frazer.[1] The magician kept the hair

[1] *Aftermath*, pp. 48–9.

of an intended victim in a little bamboo tube which he placed in his arm-pit to keep warm and to ensure that it retained the energy of the unfortunate victim. But it is more likely that the horseman kept the bone and the milt there for more practical reasons—for the same purpose as he kept his slack-baked oatcakes there—to impregnate them with the scent of his own person. The horse he managed would then be conditioned to associate his individual odour with the other scents on the cake or the bone, and he would respond effectively to that particular horseman and to him only. There was, one imagines, nothing mystical in specifying the right arm-pit as a Suffolk horseman did in his recipe. The right arm was the one more often used and therefore the one that would generate the most sweat.

Another method of horse control which is assumed to be of primitive origin is the blowing down a horse's nostrils.[1] Strangely enough, this method was used by an old Sheffield blacksmith[2] in fairly recent times. He trained all his apprentices to breathe into the nostrils of any horse brought to the forge in order immediately to establish friendly relations with it.

But whatever methods they used—breathing down the nostrils, frog's bone, milt, native intelligence or use and intuition—some East Anglian horsemen could control their horses to a degree that hardly seems credible today, as the following stories will show.

A Suffolk farmer once told his head horseman rather peremptorily: 'Tomorrow morning I want you to put three horses in the wagon and take 'em to Ipswich market. I'll follow you with the pony and meet you at the *Fleece*.' The horseman said nothing: he did not like such short, unvarnished orders. So at six o'clock next morning, out of pique or simply out of devilment, he harnessed a horse to the wagon and backed it against the *muckle* (muck-hill). He then took the horse out of the shafts, led him up the *muckle* and then onto the wagon. He did the same thing with the second horse, packing him neatly alongside the other in the wagon. The third horse he led up the *muckle* and left him standing there, motionless while he went to wake the farmer. Having aroused him by gently pulling a bell

---

[1] *H.I.F.*, pp. 242–4.
[2] From Miss H. A. Beecham.

which was fixed outside the farmer's window (a not unusual method in East Anglian farms) he called up: 'I got two the horses in the wagon, Maaster, but I'm durned if can git the third 'un in.'

The farmer came down in a fury: 'Call yourself a horseman! What is the matter with you?' But on seeing the horses, each weighing nearly a ton, standing immobile in the wagon with the third horse posed alongside on the *muckle* like a carefully contrived tableaux, he had a second and more effective awakening.

The second story is told by a Cambridgeshire farmer:[1] 'My grandfather used to stop at a certain pub used by other horsemen and he'd take the horses out of his wagon and go inside; well, they'd get arguing the toss, what they give their horses and what they don't give them; and the tricks they know, and the tricks they don't know. And one day my grandfather bet some of them in there a gallon of beer—he'd got four Suffolk horses; he'd been to the maltings, I suppose with about forty sacks of barley—that he could go out and get the horses out of the stable, put 'em in his wagon without the halters or without touching their heads, get in the wagon and drive round in front of the pub. They bet him a gallon of beer he couldn't. Anyway, he went and he called these two horses to go in the shafts out of the stable, backed them in—told them to back into the shafts—fixed them in. Then he got his two trace horses out, yoked them on, got in his wagon and cracked his whip and drove them round in front of the pub. And he left them outside there, while he went in and had the beer; and they never moved; wouldn't move. And in fact they daren't move.'

[1] G. W. Sadler, Whittlesford.

23

North-east Scotland and East Anglia

THE reader will no doubt wonder, after the copious references in the last chapter to the north-east of Scotland, what this region, apparently so different, has to do with East Anglia. But is north-east Scotland – and the Scottish carses, for that matter – so very different from the subject of the present study? Both in East Anglia and in these Scottish regions arable farming is of primary importance: it has been historically the chief work and it was developed and given its characteristic stamp by the same waves of people from the Continent in the centuries after the departure of the Romans. The dialect spoken by the people of both regions has the same basic roots – Anglian to use a comprehensive term. The Scots themselves recognized this and once called the language of the Scottish lowlands, the north-east and the east coast *Ingliss*, reserving the term *Scottish* to mean Gaelic or Erse. The fourteenth-century Scottish poet, Barbour, called the language he wrote in *Ynglis*; and W. W. Skeat[1] has shown that 'Barbour at Aberdeen and Richard Rolle de Hampole near Doncaster wrote for their several countrymen in the same identical dialect'; and the East Midland dialect which East Anglia shared was not very different from the northern dialect that covered northern England and the English-speaking parts of Scotland.

In writing this one risks the ire of many Scottish friends because it appears to do them the injustice of hinting that, after all, they are only a kind of northern Englishman. This is the last thing the writer wants to do, but it is necessary to insist that the language of John Barbour, Robert Henryson, and William Dunbar is not very

[1] *English Dialects*, Cambridge, 1911, pp. 33–4.

different from Geoffrey Chaucer's who was addressed by Dunbar as:

> *O reverend Chaucere, rose of rethoris[1] all,*
> *As in oure tong ane flour imperiall*

This similarity has lasted to this day, and there are many words in *Lallans* that would be recognized by an East Anglian dialect speaker.

Again, evidence for the similarity between the arable areas of Scotland and East Anglia can be found in a book on agriculture written during the last century in beautifully measured English by the Scot, Henry Stephens. Although Stephens designed his book, *The Book of the Farm*[2], for use anywhere in Britain, he took most of his examples from Scotland; and it could well be a basis for the history of Scottish farming during the nineteenth century. Yet a reading of the book today shows that it would serve almost equally well for a text-book of East Anglian farming during the same period. There is also another link between the farming of north-east Scotland and East Anglia. These regions were together in the van of the new agriculture that was emerging in the eighteenth century; and it was probably more than an accident that when Pitt established the Board of Agriculture in 1793 its first President was Sir John Sinclair (Statistical Sir John) of Thurso, and its first Secretary Arthur Young of Bradfield Combust in Suffolk.

The third reason for including the Scottish evidence here is the striking similarity between the horse-practices in north-east Scotland and East Anglia. These have undoubtedly grown out of a common historical background, the 'dark period' when the invaders brought their own farming techniques and their beliefs and customs from the Continent; and these practices had their full flowering when the horse was harnessed to the plough and became closely identified with arable farming. But there is also one big difference in this respect between the two regions, and it can be summarized in the question: why have the practices and especially the old organization survived much more completely in north-east Scotland? The reason is largely a historical one. In England by the middle of the

---

[1] Orators.
[2] Third Edition, London, 1877.

sixteenth century the ancient craftsman's guilds or corporations had practically died out, and many handicrafts became open to all who cared to practise them. In Scotland,[1] however, these craftsman's guilds lasted until very much later and remained tight little societies bitterly opposed to the merchant's guilds. This opposition continued until recent times in the *Horsemen's Society* particularly; for no farmer was admitted to the Society, not even a farmer's son despite the fact that he might be working as a ploughman. But other craft societies have also lasted up to the present in north-east Scotland; the Sadlers, for instance, and the Hammermen. And remoteness, too, has probably played a part in the continuance of the old tight organization in Scotland. Although there was a fairly vigorous persecution of witches there during the seventeenth century, it probably did not equal Matthew Hopkins's drive in East Anglia; and from a period well before this the horsemen, by the nature of their practices, by their form of initiation and their secret meetings, must have been firmly identified with witches. The members of the *Horsemen's Society* were always exposed, but they were careful not to take risks and offend the Kirk overtly. They became adept at covert activities and survived; and when the danger of being dubbed witches receded the horsemen seem to have adapted their ancient horse-cult to the purposes of an underground trade union in the modern sense of the word, lampooning an unpopular employer with scurrilous songs. These songs are called Bothy Ballads or Corn Kisters, and were so named because at the horsemen's meeting the men used to sit on the *kists*–chests or bins where the corn was kept for the horses–singing the songs and beating the kists with their feet to keep time.

The initiation ceremony has already been mentioned. The following details will show how suspect the Scottish society must have been during the witch-hunting period and how great was the need for secrecy. The initiate is blindfolded, and he is brought to the altar by two conductors. The altar is usually a bag of corn with an up-turned bushel on it; and upon the altar are laid the sacramental elements–bread and whisky. The man standing behind the altar is

[1] P. Hume Brown, *History of Scotland*, Cambridge, 1909, Vol. III, p. 59.

the one who is conducting the ceremony – the priest, head-horseman, devil (his function and standing are the same by whatever name he is known). He is a man with a great force of personality, who is able to give weight and urgency to his instructions to the initiate. On his way to the altar the blindfolded entrant is taken by devious ways through *crooks and straits*, in any direction but a straight line. A path fraught with difficulties, a symbol of life, but with this difference that while he has his conductors, the sworn brethren he is about to join, he will have nothing to fear as long as he trusts them implicitly. The initiate's path to the altar, moreover, is an analogue of a young horse's progress during the first stages of his training; and if he does not obey instructions correctly he is liable to get slightly hurt or at least be made very uncomfortable. This in itself is proof of the age of the ceremony because it is the mark of primitive ceremonial that it must be carried out to the letter, otherwise the magic does not work, and the participant who causes the lapse is punished. The ritual of initiation contains question and answer, in which the initiate has been previously coached, but also direct instruction. The main part, however, is the taking of the oath. Having taken this he is given the secret Horseman's Word which admits him as a sworn member. The oath itself reads like a piece of ancient poetry which, no doubt, in some part it is. It was found in the effects of an old horseman who lived during the last part of the nineteenth century.

The Horseman's Oath

'I of my own free will and accord do hereby most solomly vow and swear before God and all these witnesses that I will always hele,[1] conceal and never reveal any art or part of this secret of horsemanry, which is to be revealed to me at this time, or any other time hereafter except to a true and faithful brother after finding him to be so after due trial and strict examination. Further more I vow and swear that I will not give it or see it given to a fool nor to a madman nor to a drunkard nor to any one in drink nor to anyone who would abuse or bad use his own or his master's horses. Further

[1] O.E. *helan* — to hide, conceal.

more I vow and swear that I will not give it nor see it given to a tradesman except to a blacksmith or a farrier or to a worker of horses. Further more I vow and swear that I will not give it nor see it given to any one under 18 or above 45 years of age nor without the sum of £1 sterling or anything of the same value being placed on the table as I do at this time before three lawful sworn brethren after trial and examination finding them to be so. Further more I vow and swear that I will not give it nor see it given to anyone after the sun sets on Saturday night nor before he rises on Monday morning nor in a public house. Further more I vow and swear that I will always be at a brother's call within the bounds of three miles except I can give a lawful excuse, such as my wife in childbed or my mares in foaling or myself in bad health or in my master's employment. Further more I vow and swear that I will not give it nor see it given to my Father nor Mother, Sister nor Brother, nor to a woman at all. Further more I vow and swear that I will not write it nor endite it, paint nor print it, carve nor engrave it in the valleys nor on the hillside, on rock nor gravel, sand nor snow, silver nor gold, brass nor copper, iron nor steel, woolen nor silk, nor anything moveable or unmoveable under the great cannopy of heaven; or so much as wave a single letter of it in the air whereby the secrets of horsemanry might be revealed. And if I fail in any of these obligations that I go under at this time or any time hereafter, I ask to my heart's wish and desire that my throat may be cut from ear to ear with a horseman's knife, my body torn to pieces between two wild horses and blown by the four winds of heaven to the uttermost parts of the earth; my heart torn from my left breast and its blood wrong out and buried in the sands of the sea-shore where the tide ebbs and flows thrice every 24 hours that my rememberance may be no more heard among true and faithful brethren. So help me God to keep this solom obligation. AMEN.'

As one of the members of the Horseman's Society has said, this oath was not fabricated but has grown and been distilled over a long period of time. The beginning of the oath is remarkable in itself:[1]

[1] Personal communication from A. A. Dent.

'There is a fine metrical flavour about the opening sentence, full of the echoing cadences so typical of the old Germanic legal formula— parallel and repetition for emphasis—"hele, conceal and never reveal". I've never heard a modern use of O.E. *helan*. I think the last time I saw it was in Barbour who wrote *helit horse* for barded horses.'[1]

The reference in the last sentence to burial on the sea-shore is also a clue to the cultural provenance of the oath. The belief implied here is that unless the body of a man who suffers violent death is laid under running water his ghost is likely to walk. Running water, as in the frog's bone ritual and many other ancient practices, especially Anglo-Saxon, had special qualities.[2] It is also recorded that the precaution of burying on the sea-shore was followed in England in 1797.[3] Richard Parker, leader of the Nore mutineers, is said to have been so buried after his execution. But his widow and three helpers dug up his body and gave him Christian burial in Whitechapel Churchyard.

The revealing of the Horseman's Word is symbolically the most important part of the ceremony. The Word is still secret, but we know fairly conclusively what the Word is not. It is *not* the magical word supposed to have been used by the Whisperers who claimed to stop a horse by the word's inherent mystical force. That is pure blarney as most horsemen knew but would not trouble to deny; just as they would not attempt to uncover or give a glimpse of any mystery that grew up spontaneously about their craft. The idea of a magical word has been mooted by George Borrow's discussion in *Romany Rye* (Chapter 42) and in *Lavengro* (Chapter 14); and there Borrow stated very succinctly the objection to a magic word: 'No words have any particular power over horses or other animals who have never heard them before—how should they?' The old Irish horse-witches encountered by Borrow were using a principle known for centuries to the Gypsies.

The Gypsies wanting to sell an old horse, for instance, one that

---

[1] Horses covered with armour on breast and flanks; alternatively, a horse decked in an ornamental velvet covering.
[2] Grattan and Singer, *op. cit.*, pp. 34, 197.
[3] James Reeves, *The Everlasting Circle*, London, 1960, p. 89; see also *F.L.H.*, p. 30

had been worked almost to a stand-still, would treat him for some time before the date of the sale. After tethering the horse to a post they rattled a pail full of pebbles under his nose incessantly until the horse became almost frantic. After a few days of this treatment it would only be necessary for the horse to see the dreaded pail for him to go into a frenzy of restlessness. At the time of the sale while the seller of the horse approached him with a buyer, an accomplice of the seller would appear carrying the apparently innocuous pail. The horse would react; and the buyer would soon have the illusion that he was about to buy a horse of spirit with a number of years of service in him. The Gypsies used the same principle in training their dancing bears. They tied the animal to a stake, getting him to stand on a heated iron plate; and while the animal lifted alternate feet in an attempt to relieve the pain, someone played a lively tune on a fiddle or a pipe or beat out the rhythm on a drum. After this has been done a sufficient number of times it was only necessary to strike up the tune or the rhythm for the bear to simulate dancing irrespective of where he was standing. But an instance of this principle has already been given in the practice of sweating oatcakes or ginger-bread biscuits and keeping the frog's bone under the horseman's arm-pit to condition the horse to his groom's individual odour. Incidentally, Borrow's horse-witches also used gingerbread buttons as rewards; and the word, or one of the words, they used as a 'magical' one was *deaghlasda* (sweet-tasting, as Borrow translates it); but *cock-robin* would have done just as well, provided the animal had been suitably 'treated' while the word was being spoken. There is no need to point out that this principle is the keystone of the behaviourist school of psychology—Pavlov's conditioned reflex.

But the word given to the initiate to the *Horsemen's Society* must be much more subtle and interesting. The horse himself never hears the word. It is, so it appears, a word of symbolic almost mystic intent which points to the very core of the reason for the Society's existence. It binds the horseman not only to his brother horseman but also to the horse himself. The horse was held to be, in one respect, one of themselves by the horsemen; and this, as one initiate has stated, is the basis for the immense sacred bond between the old Scottish ploughman who was an admitted member of the Society and the horses who were in his charge. He lived with his horses, often sleeping in the loft or bothy above the stables: at midday he brought the horse into the stable for his bait and he himself often lay down half-under the horse with his head resting against one of the hoofs – a position he knew he could assume with impunity. There was no question of a 'training' word in the Scottish society: on the contrary, any admitted horseman who was thought to be ill-treating his horses would stand exposed to immediate correction by one of his fellow-horsemen. To the power of the Word, the initiates claim, to its psychological and almost mystical understanding of the bond between animal and man is due most of the remarkable control the old Scottish ploughman had over his horses. The Word, they say, and its underlying meaning is a positive one: the Word was lived rather than used, and was a symbol of an attitude both towards the animal and to the other members of the group or clan.

This declared aspect of the Word is significant in itself, but of deeper significance still is the evidence it gives of the age of the *Horsemen's Society* and the cultural seed-bed from which the Society grew. For the attitude which assumes a direct kinship between the animal and the man is the basic attitude of totemism: the animal is a full member of the clan and is respected as such. It is, moreover, the pre-requisite of that mysterious control over animals that the primitive shaman regarded as being necessary to his attaining the mystical state:[1] the behaviour of the lions with the Old Testament prophet, Daniel, for example. But David Thomson in his book *The People of the Sea*[2] has shown clearly that the horse was not the only animal so regarded in Britain. Right down from Shetland to south-west Ireland the seal was held to have real kinship with man; and the taboo on killing a seal or eating seal-flesh, the mystical veneration of the animal, and the ambivalent light in which the seal was sometimes regarded – half animal, half man or woman – clearly point to the beliefs' origin in the same cultural stratum as the horse-beliefs as preserved in the Society of the Horseman's Word.

[1] Mircea Eliade, Chapter 3 in *Myth and Mythmaking*, New York, 1960.
[2] London, 1954, and 1965.

In this connection it is relevant to say that it was not regression in the primitive's eyes to be identified with the animal: it was promise of entry into a fuller life, with perhaps, too, some of the nostalgia for *illud tempus*, as Mircea Eliade calls that lost time when man and all nature were one, a state that many Christian saints aspired to attain by establishing rapport with birds and wild animals.

Those who have knowledge of Freemasonry will have noticed many points of resemblance between the ritual of the Society of the Horseman's Word and their own: the blindfolding or hood-winking of the initiate; the correspondences in the formula of the oaths in both societies; the archaic language in both (*hele* in the Horseman's Oath, *mote*[1] (So mote it be) in the Masonic ritual, and the use of the word *cowan*[2] in both rituals). But before the seventeenth century when Freemasonry was in its *operative* stage—that is, when all its members were working masons—the points of resemblance between these two societies or craft guilds must have been great. For both Freemasonry and the *Horsemen's Society* had their origin in pre-Christian times: the ritual of both proclaims this to be so. The merchants' guilds, to which the horsemen and the masons as craft guilds would be opposed, were committed during the Middle Ages to the religion of the kirk. This in itself would have been sufficient reason for both horsemen and masons to keep to their old beliefs. But the horsemen and the Society of the Horseman's Word must have retained many more elements of the pre-Christian religion than the masons; chiefly because this was essentially a fertility religion, and as the horsemen were themselves tied to animals and the soil the chthonic elements in the old cult were more likely to be preserved in their organization. Moreover, since the time when Freemasonry reached its fully *speculative*[3] stage (The Grand Lodge in England was formed in 1717) its origins have been glossed over

[1] O.E., *motan*.
[2] An unqualified or failed mason or craftsman.
[3] The middle of the seventeenth century saw the beginning of a new spirit of scientific and philosophical enquiry in England. The old operative guilds of masons were breaking up and philosophers, or 'intellectuals'—Elias Ashmole, founder of the Ashmolean Museum was one of the first—joined the masonic guilds; and taking over its ancient ritual and formulae sought to make it a framework for their ideas or *speculations* about life in general.

to a certain extent in order, presumably, to qualify for full respect-
ability in a Christian polity. But the Scottish *Horsemen's Society*
still retained its ancient origins and was not self-conscious about
them because it remained purely operative, right up to the last few
years, not admitting anyone who was not a practising farm horseman, and—as already stated—excluding all those who were farmers
or farmers' sons, thus recognizing and retaining the ancient polarity
between craftsmen and merchants.

During the latter part of its existence the *Horsemen's Society* has
become an informal trade union and also a sort of 'fun-and-games
committee' of the countryside preserving the old forms of festivity
wherever it could. But now that nearly all the working horsemen
have left the farms there are hardly any operative members in the
Society at all, and it needs must move into a speculative stage,
admitting—as it is already doing—those who are interested in horse
matters in general and also in preserving the rich oral lore that has
accrued to the Horseman's Word down the centuries: the corn-
kisters or bothy ballads, the ancient formula of its proceedings and
its ancient phraseology. But it is clear that when the *Horsemen's
Society* was fully operative, that is, up to twenty or thirty years ago,
it could also be considered as a kind of operative witchcraft—the
remnant of the old fertility cult one of whose main concerns was for
mair yird, in the formula of the Scottish society, more growth or
more fertility for the land—a purpose that should have assured it
full social sanction down the ages. But the Society of the Horseman's
Word appears always to have been under suspicion. For the Kirk
identified the *Deil* (*The Auld Chiel* or *The Auld Gudeman*), who
presided as vicar of the old god of fertility at the horsemen's ceremonies using many of his ancient trappings (stirk's feet, horn symbol, either actual or in the form of the crescent moon), with 'the
Satan of theology', as one initiate to the Society has put it. And
this has been enough to discredit the Society in some people's eyes.

This functioning of the *Horsemen's Society* as an underground
trade union in Scotland suggests another reason for the absence of
remnants of any tight organization among East Anglian farm
horsemen. In East Anglia the movement to form open trade unions

received a long set-back after the notorious lock-out of 1874.[1] After
this date any form of combination resulted in the threat of immediate loss of job and in many cases of house as well. In the conditions that followed—the succession of disastrous harvests and a
general slump in agriculture—any organization among the men that
had existed up to that time could hardly have escaped fragmentation.
But if the East Anglian horsemen were, in fact, able to meet in
groups formal or informal after this time, their secrecy was so
effective that no evidence of their corporate activities now remains.

But in spite of their isolation, individual horsemen in East Anglia
—the rare but real *master* horsemen—had apparently as great an
amount of lore as their counterparts in Scotland, operative lore,
that is: and this can be demonstrated pretty clearly from a Suffolk
horseman's manuscript note-book[2] compiled towards the end of
the last century. These individual horsemen practised on their own,
and went through the ritual on their own, which shows how deeply
rooted the practices were in the countryside; but undoubtedly the
practices had derived their sustenance from their direct link with
some of the processes and methods of arable farming that up to the
First World War had not changed basically for centuries, animal
power being its chief motive force from very early times. Although
they worked alone, or with the most tenuous links with other, like
horsemen, they believed in the practices absolutely. They were, it is
clear, completely involved in the frog's bone ritual. Whether they
acted as a result of a self-induced trance caused by staring at the
bone in the stream, or whether there is some other explanation
cannot be easily ascertained.[3] But having got or used the frog's bone
they were fully convinced of its power. Here is an account from one
old horseman whose experience with the frog's bone caused him and
his wife great concern:

'You know the frog's bone is a funny thing, and also I must
mention that not one man ever know'd what dragon's blood is—
and they never will. Well this bone is a marvellous thing which when
you have done with it you want to make a fire and burn it away 'fore

---

[1] G. E. Fussell, *From Tolpuddle to T.U.C.*, Slough, 1948, Chapter III.
[2] See next chapter.
[3] Ronald Rose, *op. cit.*, p. 161, for use of hypnosis in the initiation ceremony.

anything happens in your house, 'cos there's nothing only the Devil behind you, I'm sorry to say. I was once at home one night, and I was abed, and my horse come right to my bedside; and in a while in the night, I thought to myself: "I don't know, you are bringing trouble on yourself, and you are going to be crazy with that stuff if you don't mind."

'My missus said: "Well now, you'll soon have to do something. Don't matter what I've got indoors there's nothing that bakes right; and I don't feel right; and you are the same. Of a night," she said, "you are awake and your horse come to the side of your bed. You'll have to do something!"

' "All right," I said, "the only thing to do is to get rid of it."

'So I dug a huge hole down through the clay, put the tin with the bone in it; filled it full of milk and vinegar first. Put it down the hole and covered it up. And I never knew more about it. But I couldn't never get on so well with my hosses after that.'

The horse this man led was a stallion weighing about a ton. It was, of course, impossible for the horse to come to his bedside; and the horseman knew it and was accordingly very frightened by his hallucinations. It is likely that this fear of the results of dealing in the 'black art', or fear of an uninitiated person getting hold of dangerous horse-drugs, is also the explanation of a recent discovery at Shelford, Cambridge. Reginald Lambeth collected from the Shelford blacksmith, Stanley Webb, dozens of jars, bottles and phials, ranging from bellarmines to delft ware. They contained horse-cures, and were undoubtedly connected with the type of practices described here. The bottles were found when the smith was modernizing his shop. He and his assistant had already removed a ton or so of material from an old brick forge when they unearthed the bottles. The presence of the bellarmines is instructive; and if one of the bottles contained the powdered frog's bone as part of its contents, it was probably another instance of someone having second thoughts about his methods of horse-control, and therefore bricking up the 'implements' out of his own and anyone else's reach.

There is also a persistent belief among old country people in East Anglia that a man who had undergone the frog's bone ritual invariably went mad or came to a violent end. This may well have been true and may have been the result of a horseman's going through the ritual on his own. For his feeling of guilt about 'having truck with the Devil' and the assumption that by the very act of the ritual he had put himself outside the community of his fellows on the farm may well have gained more force as he got older and have preyed on his mind after his retirement. In effect, these old horsemen who had continued in the ancient practices alone and against the feeling of the community in which they lived were at the tension point between two antagonistic cultures—the old prehistoric religion of the countryside and the newer dominant culture stamped by the Christian Church. Although they went through the practice in secret and no one was able, therefore, to tax them with it, subjectively they were terribly exposed, lacking the support of a tightly knit group and the mutual assurance of their fellows that were the props of the Scottish horsemen in the Society of the Horseman's Word.

bridle rack

24

The Horseman's Note-book

THE horsemen in East Anglia and in north-east Scotland used the same herbs, oils, and chemicals on their horses either to improve their condition or to cure them in sickness: they also used roughly the same drawing and jading oils and substances. Most of these had been handed down orally, but the curing and conditioning herbs and substances used by the old horsemen were common knowledge in the eighteenth and early nineteenth centuries and were included in the *receipts* of veterinary books printed during that period. But each horseman had his own particular methods and his own lists of herbs and chemicals; and many added to the common store by direct observation of their own horses as did one Suffolk horseman:

'I used to watch my horses when they were in the fields. They whoolly liked to eat some trees. I'd watch 'em going to the hedge and see what trees they'd stop at. Some of my horses used to strip the bark off an oak and some would take to the ellum. Chance times I used to give 'em some of the bark grated up in their bait. It used to make their coats shine like satin.'

But occasionally a horseman wrote down all the lore he knew in a note-book, or to be more exact *most* of the lore he knew. For although he would put down the remedies and the herbs, the drawing oils and the jading substances, he purposely left out much of the mode of administering them. So that a beginner or an outsider who would attempt a mechanical application of the instructions in the note-book would soon meet with disaster after giving a horse one of the *receipts*. The horseman would, for example, not put down in his book that to ensure a particular mixture be administered safely the horse should be allowed no water for a period of twenty-four hours

after the mixture was given. The members of the Society of the Horseman's Word were well aware of these dangers; and the older horsemen instructed the entrant at his initiation not to give a horse any herb, drug, or chemical unless he was under the guidance of one of his experienced brethren. The old horsemen in East Anglia used to give the same kind of warning. Bryony root, or *big-root* as they called it, is an example. It was used for improving a horse's condition and making his coat shine; it was scraped and moistened and added to the horse's bait. But it was a very dangerous herb to use and if too much was given it could have disastrous results. But it had another danger as shown in this mnemonic couplet:[1]

> *Bryony if served too dry*
> *Blinded horses when they blew.*

Another such conditioning or medicinal herb was *saffen* or savin (Thomas Tusser recommended it as a cure for botts in horses). It was a tree or shrub, and the leaves were the part used. One horseman describes how he obtained and used the leaves: 'If I wanted to make my horses' and colts' coat look very smart and to make 'em eat I used to go into my boss's garden and I used to pick out a tree in there. They called it the *he* yew tree (there's a *she* yew tree and a *he* yew tree: the *he* was the man I wanted): I used to take a double handful of these leaves or twigs off this tree. Then I wrapped them up in brown paper, and put it underneath my bed and I laid on that for a year under my mattress. When I took it from there it was all dry: it had crumbled up into a fine powder. Well, I mixed this with other stuff and put it on the horse's bait. It was sometimes a very trying job to get the horse to eat it, because it was rank poison. You could kill a horse in a week if you didn't know how to use the *he* yew tree. But my horses' coats used to shine, my colts they used to eat: they were so fat in the middle they could hardly walk. If you used this stuff right you could make the horse bite the sieve with his food as you carried it up to his manger.'

This same leaf was also used as a contraceptive as a Cambridge-shire farmer describes: 'Oh bless my soul! If a stallion leader went round and he found out that you'd got any of that plant, saffen, in your stable he wouldn't cover your mares; because he'd never get them in foal. I know an old stallion leader once went to . . . House; and he covered several mares there. Later he went to the governor and told him: "Look! I shan't cover any more mares for you. 'Cos I know I shall never get them in foal till you make your horse-keeper

[1] Mrs Phoebe Lockwood, Thorndon, Suffolk.

unlock that corn bin." You can guess what he had in there, mixed with the horse's bait. You see, this horse-keeper didn't want his mares in foal. They were the pride of him, and he didn't want them in foal so that he'd have to lose them for a time. There was no doubt about it, they'd give 'em this stuff and they could stop a mare from conceiving, just as they could stop a stallion from serving a mare or make a stallion serve a mare as fast as you like.' This herb saffen was known as the *threepenny bit* herb in some parts of East Anglia because it was used in a dosage that would no more than cover a silver threepenny piece.

All this is confirmed from other sources; these horse-leaders were extremely well-informed in all matters connected with breeding. One old stallion leader had a device for getting a *ghast* or barren mare to conceive: 'Stand before her with your pocket-knife ready, and just as the stallion is a-seeding thrust the knife into her nostril—not far, about a quarter of an inch. The blood will rush out; but that will do the trick. It will take the mare's attention off the job the stallion's a-doing. I tried it once with a retriever bitch that couldn't have pups. It worked. It's a trick I learned from my father.'

Some of the material from the note-book written by a Suffolk horseman over sixty years ago has already been quoted. It is a small black book with about two hundred pages of close, rather laboured writing and twenty-one pen-and-ink drawings as illustrations—*Plates* the old horseman called them. Most of the first part of the book is concerned with the conduct of the horses, the 'magic' material especially. One additional aspect of this is worth quoting, as it deals with a long-standing belief about the toad referred to by Shakespeare.[1] But the toad is a special one and was prepared in a special way, according to the horseman who wrote in his note-book: 'As for the maginet [magnetic] powers as I gouted [quoted] before I cannot thourly understand of what its qualitys realy consist of. But it is gouted that there is a verey powerful quality of this kind in the different spiceis of toad. I have the history as thus. Take a ground toad and put it in a leather Bag full of holes. Lay it in an

---

[1] *Sweet are the uses of adversity*
Which like the toad, ugly and venomous,
Wears yet a precious jewel in his head.   *As You Like It*, II:1.

ant hill; and they will eat the toad. You will then find a Stone in the Bag. Place the Stone on a greaved [aggrieved] part of man that is outwardly poisoned and it will expel the poison. And if a man is inwardly poisoned let him Breath on the stone and it will Expel it.'

The toadstone was the popular name for bufonite, the fossilized teeth of fish often found in oolite and chalk formations. The stone was once supposed to be a natural growth in the head of the common toad. This was one of the 'Vulgar Errors' which Sir Thomas Browne the Norwich physician exposed in the seventeenth century; and the fact that the belief was still going strong in the same region over two hundred years later shows how far the exposure of error often lies from its subsequent removal.

horse gagging-link

A further passage in the book provides a note to another reference in Shakespeare. One, at least, of the readers of *Hamlet* always assumed that the killing of the king by Claudius's pouring of 'cursed hebenon into the porches of his ears' was more a poetic adumbration of a murder than an exact description. But it appears that drugs and poisons were once administered through the membrane of the middle ear:

To Still the Horse from Kicking by Druging him

Drop 4 or 5 drops of . . . into his ear, or make a nott of tow and drop a few drops of the essence of . . . on it; and put it into his ear. And the oil of rhodium up his nostrils and the oil of asp.

Or put 5 drops of . . . in each ear. Will make him work kindly.

The horseman who forsook the frog's bone because of his doubts about its associations afterwards took to the *cords* which were often used, he reported, in the circus. These were strong but very thin cords which prevented the horse's free movement. One of the most effective of the cords was the one which was passed through the horse's mouth and up at the side of his head. There it was attached to a *gagging iron*, a small—usually blacksmith made—device which enabled the horseman to tighten the cord by pulling on one end of it and loosen it by pulling on the other. This cord was, if possible, the same colour as the horse's coat; and as the gagging iron was concealed under the *dutfin* or bridle the device would pass unnoticed except in the closest inspection. The horseman devoted a large part of his carefully compiled book to the control and training of the horse by cords. He also used what he called *pillows* [pillars] for training young colts. These are two wooden posts set firmly, two or three feet apart, in the ground: the young horse is tied between the posts and conditioned to respond to certain signals. It is likely that the old horseman took some of his material for training horses by means of cords from equestrian manuals of the last century; for the methods he used and the diagrams he drew to illustrate them indicate that he had been influenced by the training of the *Lipizzaners*, the horses of the Spanish Riding School in Vienna.

One section of the horseman's note-book draws attention to a very old sport in which Suffolk horses excelled. This was the *drawing match*,[1] a contest of a horse's strength in drawing or pulling heavy loads. The following advertisement is in the *Ipswich Journal* of 22nd May, 1742:

Notice is Hereby given

That on Friday the 28th of this Instant May, at the sign of the Lion and Castle at Theberton, alias East Bridge, in the county of Suffolk will be given gratis:

FIVE DUTFINS of Forty Shillings Value to be drawn for by any five Horses, Mares or Geldings harness'd together to draw Twenty Pulls upon the Rein; and they that make the fewest Blanks and carry out the biggest weight to win the Prize; to enter their

[1] *A.F.C.H.*, pp. 123–6.

names by Ten of the clock in the Forenoon at the Place and Day aforesaid.

This sport was in its hey-day in the eighteenth century but the following entry shows that it lasted well into the following century. The horsemen taught the Suffolk Punch specially to go down onto his knees to exert his full strength in a *dead pull*; that is, in pulling a loaded tumbril or wagon that had its wheel blocked by an obstacle to make the pull more difficult.

Sam Friend

To Learn Young Horses Game of Drawing

First learn him to go down on his knees. Then put him into a long pair of traice. Chain him to a tree. Take the traice off the shoulder hook. Tie a peice of cord on each side of the bit and tie it to the traice. Touch his flank and his knees till he go down. Then whip him over the *wallows* till he draw kindly. Give him comfort and coax him on the neck with the whip. And give him a little corn and leave him with a feed of corn.

In the section of the book dealing with control the horseman shows that he used all methods – drawing oils, cords and psychology or *horse-sense* to discipline a particularly vicious horse. He advises: 'Avoid throwing them if you can: avoid all harsh punishment as much as you can. Use judgement, justtice and mercey, and teatch them to fear, love and obey. When the horse is travling, mind you do not lead him with a Bit to long that he don't like. Change his Bits, and when you find he goes Comfortable lead him with that Bit as often as you can. Never pinch his mouth aney more than you can help. If you do he will take a dislike to you, and he will never go Comfortable with you aney more.

'To make him fond and to know you aney where, take half a pound of Lunarce and a half pound of oat flour mixed with treacle or honey. Make them into Cakes and Slack bake them. Sweat them well under your arm. Let him get hungrey. Then give him the Cakes with a few drops of this mixture: oil of Rhodium, Cumin, otto of rose, Essences of new mown hay, and the Essence of Helletropium. Give a few drops on the Cakes. Let him eat them. He will never leave you; and if he is a little upset at aney time when he is travling, as often is the case, give him a ginger Bread Cake with a few drops of the oils, or on a peice of loaf sugar.'

And at the bottom of this page which marked the end of his section on control of horses he wrote:

'It is no use of writeing aney more on this subject, as you have erithmitic of horses Enough to master all the horses in the world with practice, patience and gennarl study: these are the three things most wantin.'

plate 14

plate 5

To do with whip and reare
Or heard Robin and free
him

a for training horses
the Bits

Self turner for
Vicious horses or
wild Colts

Plate 12

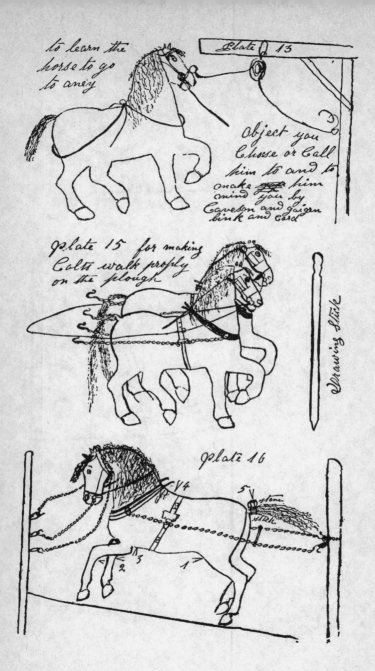

to learn the
horse to go
to aney

Plate 13

Object you
Choose or Call
him to and to
make him
mind you by
Caveston and gaigen
bink and card

Plate 15 for making
Colts walk profsly
on the plough

Drawing Stick

Plate 16

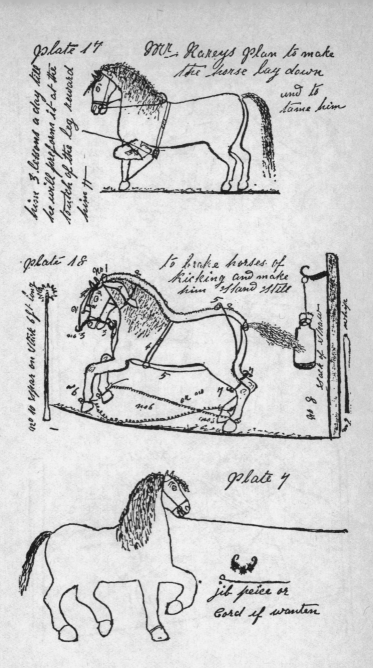

plate 17

Mr. Rareys plan to make
the horse lay down
and to
tame him

have 3 lessons a day till
he will perform it at the
touch of the leg reward
him —

plate 18

to broke horses of
kicking and make
him stand still

no 10 letter on stik 6ft long

no 8 load of straw

plate 7

jib peice or
cord if wanten

Conclusion

First of all I should like to re-affirm my conviction – arrived at after six years' work in collecting and attempting to order material for the present book – that the folk-life approach to the old rural society in Britain is the most fruitful one at the present time. If the separate disciplines continue to investigate the past of rural Britain each in its own way, much will be lost irrecoverably. I hold this view chiefly for two reasons: first, according to the evidence in the preceding pages, the old rural community was essentially the true remnant of a primitive society that has lasted since prehistoric times. And in writing *primitive* I am not making a value-judgment and using the word as a synonym for backward; for it is undeniable that in certain aspects of living some primitive societies were very much forward compared with modern western civilization. The word as used here implies that it was a different society from the modern one, characterized by an essentially different mode of production whose supplanting also meant the end of the social structure that it supported. The antecedents of the old rural economy in its material aspects have been exhaustively studied, but all that the anthropologist implies in his objective use of the word *primitive* has been almost entirely ignored by the historian in Britain. This is a great hiatus in the study of rural history. Marc Bloch recognized this need in France and pointed out:[1] 'The study of popular rites and beliefs is barely sketching its first outlines.' Yet it is not simply a question of the historian's acquiring the technique to incorporate a new field into his study but the more difficult one of his coming to recognize that a problem exists at all, and of admitting that here is

[1] *The Historian's Craft*, p. 58.

material that should be embraced by his discipline, and that by leaving it out he is exposing himself to the charge of giving a totally incomplete view of the historical rural scene. But in my experience most rural historians are not concerned with giving a true picture of their field of study but merely a safely accurate one. And if I am challenged to explain the difference between truth and accuracy I have politely to disclaim any qualification to engage in semantic or philosophical dispute and instead to offer a crude tale which has been told before but nevertheless bears telling again as it points the difference between truth and accuracy reasonably well enough.

The captain of an east coast trading vessel put into Lowestoft and told his mate he could go ashore. The mate went; and later the captain recorded in his log-book: *Mate drunk all day*. About a week later the vessel docked at Hull. This time it was the captain's turn to have a day off, and the mate's turn at the log-book. In this, as soon as opportunity offered itself, he wrote in a bold, uncompromising hand: *Captain sober all day*. Now we can consider the first statement, Mate drunk all day, *true* because he went ashore presumably to enjoy himself, and out of boredom or definite purpose got himself drunk. But as it stands the statement is not quite accurate, for apart from the sober intervals he experienced while attaining his purpose he must have been sober to start with or else the captain would not have allowed him ashore. But the second statement, Captain sober all day, was dead *accurate* but quite untrue because it was so obviously false in its implications. It was in fact a specialized statement carried to extreme. For what is specialization but the making of finely accurate statements out of a context; statements that need constant re-examination against this context not simply for accuracy but for a concinnity—the truth if you like—that accuracy of itself does not possess? This, however, is not to be obscurantist and to attack specialization in historical studies or elsewhere; we have to specialize, and specialization is patently the most effective means of pushing forward exploration in any discipline. But it will only remain so, especially in the social studies, as long as we do not deceive ourselves into assuming that the divisions or separations we create for our convenience have any real validity beyond our own making. This needs to be said particularly about rural history because so much of it has been written within the last twenty years. Tracts of it have been surveyed and charted over and over again, especially the Middle Ages; and yet it is difficult to recognize the countryside and country people in much of these writings. This, I suppose, is because the present-day historian on the whole tends to leave men out of the picture, and historical studies have been so reified that there is now little life in them; and, what is more serious, no life is really expected of them. Theses and scholarly monographs lie about the landscape like accurately cut and beautifully trimmed blocks of stone—ashlars that will be built into no tower, details that will never be lifted off the ground and included in any design, knowledge that has never aspired to nor ever will attain that collective wisdom which is knowledge's only justification.

It seems to me that if the rural historian will only concede that what he is faced with in the countryside today is the valuable remnant of the old primitive society (the evidence is inescapable); if he casts aside his inborn 'Fifty-year Rule'[1] inhibitions to study the old society that is precariously about him now, he will be doing much more to promote the subject of history as a corporate discipline than he is doing at the moment which is too often a repetitive harrowing of old ground without gaining any harvest worthy of the name. He will, moreover, be likely to get direct information and enlightenment about, say, the open field and the manorial system, and an insight into the beliefs and the preoccupations of the men who actually worked these medieval fields. It is suggested that the folk-life approach, which is basically that of social anthropology, will yield a tremendous amount of valuable historical information in the rural areas at this period. For the temper and atmosphere of the old rural society that lasted for so long is still recoverable to a certain extent from its survivors. Yet the historian will get little unless he supplements his orthodox techniques with those of the anthropologist and the sociologist—the technique, chiefly, of observation, patient questioning, empathy, and a systematic recording of the living survivors. And if he objects that this is not, after all,

[1] But even this is likely to be relaxed: *The Times*, 11th July, 1964.

history and therefore none of his concern, it can be pointed out that the sociology of today is the history of tomorrow and the anthropology of his own field of study is at this particular and special time a true historic present. The historian, moreover, is admirably equipped to record the material he will find in the countryside at this time; he will be able to place it in a reasoned and a balanced context and to relate it to the material he has found in another period or in another setting. The historian, too, with his training will also be able to avoid the mistakes which have given the study of some of the matter written down in this book such a bad name—the holding up of a strange fact, belief or custom for general wonderment; and instead of the asking of considered questions of the material the making of mere exclamations over it: 'How curious!' 'How odd!' or 'How wonderful!' or, worse still, the making of a superior judgment: 'What fools people were (or are) to believe in such nonsense as this!'

The second reason why the folk-life approach is so relevant to the present is this. In Britain the anthropologists themselves do not appear to be aware that they have the remains of a primitive society on their own doorstep. They have been so captivated by the exotic and have so taken for granted the composition of their own society that they have always gone abroad, in spite of the fact that—as Margaret Murray so aptly pointed out—there is just as rich a harvest to be gathered in the so-called civilized countries of the west as in parts of Asia, Africa or the South Seas which are still the anthropologist's natural habitat. This is truer today when some of the under-developed countries are being changed so quickly that their old cultures are in danger of being swept away in a bare generation.[1] But in a slow, gradual change such as Britain has experienced during the last three centuries since the growth of the modern scientific method[2] much of the old culture and its archaic way of thought has been preserved, sinking—as it were—into society's unconscious in the old rural community. And, as we have seen, the material environment was sympathetic to its survival until the early years of

[1] Dilim Okafor-Omali, *op. cit.*, p. 159.
[2] Christopher Hill, *op. cit.*, *passim*.

this century. The same apparent contradiction is to be seen in the material relics of the old culture. Ffransis Payne has observed that often there is a greater wealth of the tools and furniture of the old rural community in Wales to be discovered near the industrial conurbations of the south than in the remoter areas where change, albeit late, was swifter and more uncompromising. Experience in East Anglia bears this out: I have noticed that more of the old farm tools and the domestic equipment associated with the former culture have been kept and adapted to secondary uses in those areas border-ing the towns than in the isolated districts where change was delayed even to as late as the Second World War, but having arrived was quicker and more complete.

In the anthropologist's default the rural historian is therefore called upon to bridge the gap between his own subject and anthropo-logy, making a direct study of the living remnant of an old society in order to supplement his study of it through documents, books and archaeological evidence. He has rightly been urged in recent years to get out of the library and the records office and to walk round his parish, or whatever is his area of study; to examine the fields, the shape of the land, to look for evidence of change in the ancient boundaries and the ancient buildings he sees and to collate this change with the material he has uncovered in the documents. No doubt the rural historian is tired of being urged, and impatient of busy-bodies pointing out which path he ought to take for his best profit. But at the risk of further provoking him to exasperated comment, it should be brought to his notice that the old farmer or farm worker he meets on his perambulations is worth more than a nod or a polite giving of 'the sele of the day'. He is likely to be worth talking to for his own sake, and he may well give the historian valuable information about the land he is walking over.

I have suggested that the old rural society was society's un-conscious, possessing two more-or-less distinct levels like the unconscious of the individual: the preconscious into which sink out-dated customs, half-forgotten science, outmoded fashions, and words and phrases once the coin of polite conversation but gradually demoted into the rural dialect; and beneath this at a level more rarely

exposed the true phylogenetic unconscious where the most archaic
beliefs and modes of thinking have lasted until recent years. This
level is a rich repository of much of the rural history of these
islands. Yet historians whose stance appears to have anchylosed
in the correct atmosphere emanating from nineteenth-century
'scientific' history have rarely attempted to bring this evidence of
irrationality within their purview. Instead, the average historian
calls it *folklore*, thereby hoping that in giving it an opprobrious
name he will thus excuse himself from having anything to do with
it. And even if he has misgivings about this treatment of material
which at first glance has certain relevance to his study, he shies away
from it either through fear of losing face among his colleagues or
through the prevailing rigidity of mind that sees our civilization as
so superior to the primitive, so rational and self-sufficient that he
can afford to ignore primitive evidence as having nothing to teach
him about the task he himself has in hand: 'We are the people.
Wisdom was born with us. Chaos was before us; but wisdom will
come after us.'

Yet events do not wait on the historian's conception of what his
study should embrace nor on his estimate of his own achievements.
Even Sir James Frazer who had a greater knowledge than most of
the play of the irrational in human society could make the unspoken
comment on his researches: 'We should be thankful that we have
put all this stuff behind us.' If he had survived the Second World
War he could hardly have continued in this conviction. For the
last thirty years has seen the biggest outbreak of irrationality the
world has experienced—the Nazi phenomenon in Germany. And
only one historian seems to have sensed what was coming, Jacob
Burckhardt[1] who in his day was hardly considered an historian at
all but just an art-historian. It was left to others—to D. H. Lawrence
in his well-known 'Dark Gods' essay and C. G. Jung in his essay
'Wotan'[2] on the spiritual state of Germany during the early 'thirties
—to give the warning. But it will be objected that it is not the historian's duty to warn. That may or may not be true, but at least he

[1] Jacob Burckhardt, *Judgements on History and Historians* (with an introduction by
H. Trevor-Roper), London, 1959, p. 15.
[2] *Essays on Contemporary Events*, 1947.

should know what is going on, for no one—least of all a historian—should be ignorant of his own times. The attitude of historians and thinkers in Britain to the rise of the Nazis is typified by H. G. Wells's observations[1] while it was happening: he thought that there was nothing in Hitler's doctrine of race (founded on a tentative and quite 'unscientific' remark of Tacitus[2] and built upon during the nineteenth century[3]) that a well-informed sixth former could not easily refute. The irrational, that is, should not be taken seriously. But the greatest illusion of all was to believe that by explaining the irrational we are by this very act explaining it away. The Nazi theory of race, although noisome nonsense, was actual; that is, it could be acted upon. And this is what the Nazis did, and the consequences were more real and disastrous than the worst pessimist could have imagined.

It is not suggested, however, that the outbreak of irrationality in Germany is of the same order as the material to be found in the countryside. The German outbreak was a mass-psychosis of a very complex nature, and we are probably still too near it to assess it in all its aspects. But there are similarities between this and the rural magico-religious tradition, which we have touched on continually in this book, in that both were using elements that have common roots in the pre-Christian and prehistoric times. Much of it is associated with witchcraft which has become an umbrella title for all the elements of the archaic tradition; and it is necessary to clarify the different meanings of the word. First, it is loosely identified with the kind of mass-psychosis just mentioned. But an analysis of the mechanics of this, even if it were possible, has fallen outside the terms of reference of the present study, and nothing further needs to be said about it here except to add that both in mass-psychosis and what is commonly known as witchcraft archaic and therefore unconscious material is activated and appears to arrogate to itself a dynamism of its own; a phenomenon, it is emphasized again, that should fall well within the historian's purview.

[1] *Experiment in Autobiography*, London, 1934, pp. 100–2.
[2] *Germania*, II: *Ipsos Germanos indigenas crediderim minimeque aliarum gentium adventu et hospitiis mistos.*
[3] Henry Hatfield, *The Myth of Nazism. Myth and Mythmaking*, New York, 1960.

But the kind of witchcraft we meet in the countryside has two distinct trends. The first is what can be called real witchcraft, the authentic remnant of the old fertility religion associated with the 'Horseman's Word' in Scotland and some of the old horsemen's practices in East Anglia and elsewhere. This, in my view, is the true witchcraft which was embedded in a definite cultural setting. It was, in fact, functional or *operative* in the old rural community in Britain; and if the old culture were still at this moment more-or-less intact as it was in most parts of Britain up to 1914—still dependent largely on animal power for tilling the land and with farming still essentially the same as it had been for an era—this tradition would still be uncovered, still secret and deeply imbedded underground in the old rural community as it had remained for centuries. This tradition or witchcraft had *use* and was therefore tied to the soil and reality as part of the whole cultural complex. It was, in a word, practical, concerned with the fertility of the soil and the increase and control of animals; and it was not isolated but used alongside a large corpus of practical lore. The *magic* side of this witchcraft, as already suggested, was directed at those parts of the process that could not be reached by the ordinary physical measures the operator took to gain his ends; and one of these parts, as the primitive instinctively recognized, was that area of his own psyche that was ordinarily inaccessible but which could be aligned by the help of magic to promote his best endeavours in the project he had in hand. Thus the magic was primarily addressed to his hope, his desire, or his conviction that his ends could ultimately be attained.

The other aspect of witchcraft is best described as *speculative*, although this terminology is bound to invite invidious comparisons. But *speculative* is a good description of it because it cut loose from any direct or operative connection with the original purpose of the magic-religious cult—the fertility of the soil and the increase of men and animals—and like Freemasonry sought to make the old cult a vehicle for other aspirations. This aspect of witchcraft became a shell of the ancient cult which had been removed from its context in the old rural society, and in the hands of *speculators* became inflated into pure magic or illusion, a vehicle for all their unattached desires and imaginings. These, it seems, were largely the need to experiment with new sensations, to make new explorations, and to console themselves with the superior comfort of being part of an *imperium in imperio*, an 'in-group' that was all the more exciting in that it worked in secret wearing the trappings and under the specious standard of an ancient tradition. The eighteenth-century 'Hell-Fire Club' and the modern outbreaks of Satanism seem to have everything in common except their scale; and they should be sharply distinguished from the true thread of operative magic which has been an identifiable part of the rural tradition from earliest times right up to the recent past.

It has been assumed throughout the present book that there has been a real break in the countryside: the old social order has changed, the temper of mind has altered and most of the old irrational beliefs have been jettisoned. This I believe to be a true account of the position, though many of the beliefs will undoubtedly be transmitted and will continue in a thinner, more abstract form for many years to come. But what we must beware of assuming is that, having got rid of these irrational beliefs, we have therefore basically altered our own cast of mind. Hope and desire are still stronger than reason, and although we have successfully thrown off many of the old 'superstitions' there is a real danger of acquiring others that are infinitely more disastrous. The irrational belief about race has already been mentioned; and there are many more which, like the old beliefs we have been concerned with, are the direct resultants of existence in a certain type of culture: for instance, the uncritical belief that anything in print is canonical, that the 'magic' of science has no limitations, or that what is advertised and what everybody wants is necessarily indispensable. But these are much more difficult for us to detect as they are part of our own cultural situation. If, therefore, we are tempted to feel superior to the old countryman who still looks for light where we should expect to find none, we would do well to remember that he could be equally and as reasonably critical of many of what we value as our newest and most enlightened assumptions.

SELECTED PRINTED SOURCES

Selected Printed Sources

Addy, S. O., *The Evolution of the English House*, London, 1938.

Armstrong, E. A., *The Folklore of Birds*, London, 1958.

Ashby, W. R. C., *The Modern Craftsman* (Masonic Light on Modern Doubts), London, 1962.

Azzi, Girolamo, *Agricultural Ecology*, London, 1956.

Barley, M. W., *The English Farmhouse and Cottage*, London, 1961.

Bloch, Marc, *The Historian's Craft*, Manchester, 1954.

Feudal Society, London, 1961.

Braun, Hugh, *The Old English House*, London, 1962.

Briggs, K. M., *The Anatomy of Puck*, London, 1959.

Pale Hecate's Team, London, 1962.

Burckhardt, Jacob, *The Civilization of the Renaissance in Italy*, London, 1944.

Clebert, J. P., *The Gypsies*, London, 1963.

Coulton, G. G., *Five Centuries of Religion*, Cambridge, 1923–50.

Davidson, H. R. Ellis, *Gods and Myths of Northern Europe*, London, 1964.

Dent, A. A. and Goodall, D. M., *The Foals of Epona*, London, 1962.

Eliade, Mircea, *Myths Dreams and Mysteries*, London, 1960.

Images and Symbols, London, 1961.

Elsworthy, F. T., *The Evil Eye*, London, 1895; New York, 1958.

Evans, E. Estyn, *Irish Folk Ways*, London, 1957.

Evans, George Ewart, *Ask the Fellows Who Cut the Hay* (Second Edition), London, 1962.

The Horse in the Furrow, London, 1960.

Evans-Pritchard, E. E., *Witchcraft, Oracles, and Magic Among the Azande*, London, 1937.

Social Anthropology, London, 1962.

Anthropology and History, Manchester, 1963.

The Position of Women in Primitive Societies, London, 1965.

Evans-Wentz, W. Y., *The Tibetan Book of the Dead* (Third Edition), London, 1957.

Frazer, Sir J. G., *The Golden Bough* (Third Edition), London, 1932–5.

Aftermath, London, 1936.

Graves, Robert, *The White Goddess*, London, 1961.

Grattan and Singer, *Anglo-Saxon Medicine and Magic*, London, 1952.

Hays, H. R., *From Ape to Angel*, London, 1959.

Hill, Christopher, *Intellectual Origins of the English Revolution*, London, 1965.

Hole, Christina, *English Folklore*, London, 1940.

Innocent, C. F., *The Development of English Building Construction*, Cambridge, 1916.

Jenkins, J. G. (Editor), *Folk Life*, Journal of the Society for Folk Life Studies, St Fagans Castle, Cardiff.

Jung, C. G., *The Integration of the Personality*, London, 1940.

Essays on Contemporary Events, London, 1947.

Symbols of Transformation, London, 1956.

The Practice of Psychotherapy, London, 1954.

Jung and Kerenyi, *Essays on a Science of Mythology*, New York, 1963.

Kerenyi, C., *Prometheus*, London, 1963.

Leather, E. M., *The Folklore of Herefordshire*, London, 1912.

Lethbridge, T. C., *Witches: Investigating an Ancient Religion*, London, 1964.

Levy-Bruhl, L., *How Natives Think*, London, 1926.

Madge, Charles, *Society in the Mind: Elements of Social Eidos*, London, 1964.

Malinowski, B., *Magic, Science, and Religion*, London, 1925.

The Argonauts of the Pacific, London, 1953.

Mellor, Alec, *Our Separated Brethren the Freemasons* (Translated by B. R. Feinson), London, 1964.

Murray, A. H. (Editor), *Myth and Mythmaking*, New York, 1960.

Murray, M. A., *The Witch-Cult in Western Europe*, London, 1963.
   The God of the Witches, London, 1933.
   The Divine King in England, London, 1954.

Owen, Trefor, M., *Welsh Folk Customs*, Cardiff, 1959.

Peate, Iorwerth C., *The Welsh House*, Liverpool, 1946.
   (Editor), *Gwerin*, St Fagans Castle, Cardiff, 1956–62.

Radford, E. and M. A., *Encyclopaedia of Superstitions* (Revised and Edited by Christina Hole), London, 1961.

Sewell, Elizabeth, *The Orphic Voice*, London, 1961.

Spence, Lewis, *An Encyclopaedia of Occultism*, London, 1920.

Turville-Petre, E. O. G., *Myth and Religion of the North*, London, 1964.

Vansina, Jan, *Oral Tradition*, (Translated from the French by H. M. Wright), Chicago, 1965.

Weber, Max, *Essays in Sociology*, London, 1961.

Wilhelm, Richard (Translator), *The Secret of the Golden Flower*. London, 1957, with a commentary by C. G. Jung.

Whistler, Lawrence, *The English Festivals*, London, 1947.

White, Lyn, Jr., *Medieval Technology and Social Change*, London, 1962.

Index